We know u...

There were no signs that any... ...
citadel. A chill ran up Adeenya's spine.

She climbed the short steps to one of the barracks. Ten
cots lined each wall, with space for many more. A bedroll
was neatly folded at the foot of each and twenty chests sat on
the floor. Two Maquar were examining the contents.

"What have you found, durir?" she asked.

"Just these things, sir," Taennen answered. He held up
a cheap brass symbol of the Adama. "It's as if they never
left."

"No bodies? No discarded weapons?"

Taennen shook his head. "I wish I could say there was
any clue at all, sir, but so far we've seen nothing. The food
stores are intact, the citadel's log shows a final entry that
describes no problems at all. The gate locks still function,
and from what we've seen, the personal belongings of the
lost company are still here."

Adeenya shook her head. "This is damned strange."

When we are free, we will tell you.

*Honorable soldiers face off against greed and treachery in
the Shining South. In the formians, Ed Gentry achieves a
genuine sense of "otherness." If you're tired of monsters that are
nothing but humans with scales, feathers, or carapaces, you'll
love these guys.*

—Elaine Cunningham,
author of the Songs and Swords series

THE CITADELS

Neversfall
Ed Gentry

Obsidian Ridge
Jess Lebow
April 2008

The Shield of Weeping Ghosts
James P. Davis
May 2008

Sentinelspire
Mark Sehestedt
July 2008

THE CITADELS

Neversfall

✠

ED GENTRY

The Citadels
Neversfall

Cover art by David Seidman
Map by Rob Lazzaretti
First Printing: December 2007

9 8 7 6 5 4 3 2 1

ISBN: 978-0-7869-4782-9
620-21625740-001-EN

U.S., CANADA,	EUROPEAN HEADQUARTERS
ASIA, PACIFIC, & LATIN AMERICA	Hasbro UK Ltd
Wizards of the Coast, Inc.	Caswell Way
P.O. Box 707	Newport, Gwent NP9 0YH
Renton, WA 98057-0707	GREAT BRITAIN
+1-800-324-6496	Save this address for your records.

Visit our web site at www.wizards.com

dedication

To my wife, Lara, who makes everything I am and do better with her love, warmth, intelligence, and humor.

acknowledgements

I would like to give special thanks to my editor, Erin Evans, whose wonderful ideas, insights, and never-surrender attitude made this book better at every turn. Also I would like to thank Susan Morris for her help in shaping the story. I would like to thank Phil Athans for giving me my first break and for his continuing support. Also, thanks go to Ed Greenwood for giving me notes on his brainchild that is the Forgotten Realms.

I have been fortunate enough to be embraced by a community of other writers and friends without whom this process would have been much more difficult. Thanks for incredible ongoing support go to: Elaine, Erik, Harley, Jaleigh, James, Jeff, Kameron, Paul, and Richard."

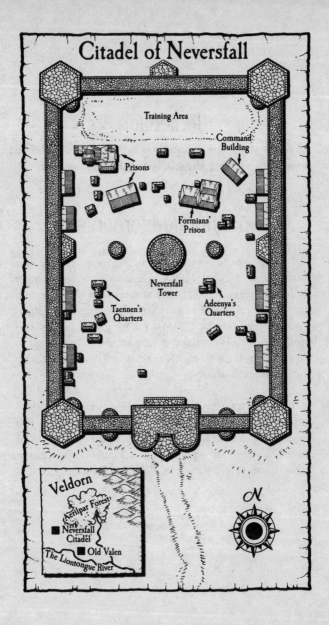

Citadel of Neversfall

Training Area

Command Building

Prisons

Formians' Prison

Neversfall Tower

Taennen's Quarters

Adeenya's Quarters

Veldorn

Aeilpar Forest

Neversfall Citadel

Old Valen

The Liontongue River

N

chapter one

They approach, sir," the dwarf said, handing the spyglass to Adeenya.

She took no notice of Marlke's calloused hands as they brushed against hers, her own skin toughened from years of swordplay and training. She brought the glass to her eye to see the bright colors of the Maquar silks waving in the wind as the troops approached.

"Not much for subtlety, are they?" she said, scanning their ranks.

"They've little need for stealth, sir," the dwarf replied.

It was true the Maquar, the elite warriors of Estagund's rajah, might be as subtle as a blow to the head, but they were also as deadly. Their battle prowess was legendary, as was their discipline.

The marching lines of the Maquar were nothing short of perfect. No soldier marched faster than another, not one stood too close or too far from his neighbor in the lines. Their formations were arranged by height with the taller troops at the ends of each line. Marlke was right; they cut an impressive swath across the grassy land as they came. Though only a few score soldiers, each Maquar's chest, shoulders, and head were held high as though the entire army of Estagund rode behind them in deference and support.

Adeenya handed the spyglass back to Markle with a nod. She had heard stories of the Maquar's prowess her entire life, and the spectacle that moved toward her sent a shiver up her back. Most of her childhood she had been enamored of the stories her father told of the peerless, loyal Maquar with their pageantry and glorious battles.

When she was still a young girl, Adeenya had begun training behind her father's back, in preparation for join the Maquar. Under the guise of learning responsibility, she worked hard in her father's shops to earn coin to pay for sword lessons. Paying the tutors to remain quiet had cost as much as the training itself. Her skill in fighting was as undeniable as her love of the art.

Her lessons continued until she learned that the Maquar never accepted foreigners in their ranks, not even those willing to expatriate. The Maquar took only natives of Estagund, as though the land somehow lived in their blood. Without Estagundian blood, Adeenya's place in the mercenary ranks of the Durpari was clear. As soon as she became of legal age, she'd joined the Durpari mercenary forces. She'd had nowhere else to go, after all.

Adeenya turned to study her own soldiers. They had broken camp and were packing away gear to be ready to march anew if the Maquar commander so ordered. The Durpari uniform of dark brown and gray stood in stark contrast to the bright, vivid blues and greens of the Maquar. The Durpari soldiers maintained most any hairstyle they wanted, while the Maquar were all neatly cropped. Adeenya watched as one of her troops tripped another, prompting a bout of laughter from many others standing around. She shook her head and turned back to the approaching force. Her soldiers were different, that was for certain. She glanced back over her shoulder and saw the tripped man come to his feet, mirth clear on his face. Different was all right.

"Sir, what's our move?" the dwarf asked.

"We have no move, Marlke. We wait for them. The Maquar commander is in charge, be he genius, fool, or lout," she said with a shrug. "There's nothing to be done for it now."

"And if he's a fool or a lout, sir?"

"He wouldn't be the first soldier with those afflictions that I've met," she replied. "We'll work around it."

The Maquar were two bowshots away, still locked in their battle-ready arrow formation. Adeenya swallowed and smoothed her short, ruddy hair slick with sweat and nodded to Marlke to prepare the troops to meet the Maquar. The soldiers fell in behind her like dead leaves following a gust of wind and Adeenya strode forward to meet the Maquar, a weak smile on her face. Maquar or no, Adeenya was used to being in charge of herself and her own people. She often thought it was for the best she had never been able to join the Maquar. Subordination was not a talent she'd grown into.

"Orir Adeenya Jamaluddat," she said with a salute to a dark-skinned man at the front of the Maquar lines. She stood nearly a head taller than him but was half his width. His broad shoulders were straight and strong without seeming rigid or tense. His broad nose hovered over full lips that showed no smile or frown.

"Greetings," the man said. "I am Urir Jhoqo Valshu. This is Taennen Tamoor, my durir, and Loraica Hazshad, my terir," he said, indicating a tall, thin, much younger man to his right and an enormous woman to his left.

Taennen stood with his shoulders rolled back tight,

his chin straight, and his hands folded behind his back. Cropped black hair covered his head but his clean, smooth face, which had never seen a razor, showed his youth. His armor and clothing were cleaner than even his commander's, no small feat while on the road.

The woman beside him, Loraica, was the largest Adeenya had ever seen. Most men did not compare in stature with the towering, muscled figure. Tight, dark curls crowned Loraica's head, forming a loose braid that drifted to her shoulder. Her square jaw gave her face an unfeminine but not unattractive visage. The two Maquar stood close together as only those who are completely comfortable with one another can.

Jhoqo's eyes scanned her troops, though Adeenya never felt them leave their scrutiny of her. She inwardly scowled. She had heard the Estagundian dialect before and the pronunciation differences it caused. Be he in charge or not, she was Orir Jamaluddat, not Urir.

The Maquar leader nudged his chin toward the dwarf. "And this?"

"My dorir, Marlke Stoutgut," she said. The dwarf stared straight ahead, his eyes focused on nothing, the same attitude as the durir and terir across from him. Proper subordinates, all. Adeenya was pleased.

Jhoqo nodded again, and a long silence passed between the five of them. "And your third?" he asked.

"None, sir," Adeenya said.

Jhoqo eyed her for a moment. "I'd heard the Durpari didn't have extensive command successions. How do you find that works for you, Orir?" the man said, his tongue catching hard on the final word.

"Fine, sir," Adeenya replied, her forehead wrinkled.

"Well, that's what matters, isn't it?" Jhoqo said, waving a

4

dismissive hand for everyone to stand at ease.

"This is Khatib, our resident intellect," Jhoqo said, indicating a stocky man in a peacock blue robe who approached from within the ranks. He wore no armor and carried no shield.

"With your permission, Khatib will quickly examine your men," Jhoqo said. "Just as a precaution."

Adeenya nodded, keeping her mouth tightly shut. Caution was always merited, but the line between prudence and insult was a thin one, she knew. If her superiors hadn't advised her to keep her forces small and leave the spellcasters behind, she would have been sorely tempted to send one over to examine the Maquar.

The wizard bowed again. "If you could simply ask them to form a line, single-file?"

Adeenya nodded to Marlke, adding a significant glance for her second alone. The dwarf saluted with a curt, short snap of his hand and began barking orders. The soldiers from Durpar fell quickly into line and submitted as one to the wizard's examination. Adeenya knew Marlke would understand her implicit order to watch the wizard carefully.

"They seem to be good soldiers, Orir. You are to be commended," Jhoqo said to Adeenya. He motioned for her to join him as he began to walk.

"Thank you, sir. I have found them loyal, brave, and resourceful in my time as their commander," Adeenya replied.

"How long has that been?" Taennen asked from his position behind them.

"Durir," Jhoqo said without looking at the younger man.

Taennen flinched but continued to walk. His dark eyes

were locked on his commander, his lips were pursed and his stance rigid. The breeze had mussed his cropped black hair.

"My apologies for my second's manners," Jhoqo said to Adeenya.

"No need, sir," she said. "I have led most of these men for nearly two years. A few, my dorir included, have been with us for a little over six months."

"Your previous second died?" Jhoqo asked. His gaze lingered on the distant Curna Mountains as he spoke.

"No, sir. She was transferred. Promoted, actually. She now leads her own regiment," Adeenya said. She wondered at the life of conflict the man must have led to assume her second had died. In that moment, the glorious shine of the Maquar seemed a little scuffed to her.

"Ahh . . . I see the pride you feel for her," Jhoqo said. "It is a wonderful feeling, isn't it? And it speaks highly of your skills in teaching her how to lead, daughter."

She nodded. "Yes, sir. May I ask a question, sir?"

"Of course. Everything begins with a question," he replied.

"When will I learn why my troops and I have been called here, sir?"

Jhoqo stopped and turned to face her. "Straight to the point. A fine quality, I suppose, Orir."

"Yes, sir," Adeenya said. She could hardly imagine what urgent need demanded that she lead her forty soldiers to the middle of the wilds at the northern end of the Curna Mountains.

"A reconnaissance mission," her superiors had said. "Nothing to worry about."

Which did not explain why they had met the Maquar— or, more importantly, why they were expected to be subordinate to the almost equal force.

"Have you spent any time in Veldorn, Orir?" Jhoqo asked, resuming his stroll once again.

"I've passed through a few times, sir. Never very deep into those lands, though," Adeenya said.

"Why is that, do you think?" Jhoqo asked.

Adeenya chose her words carefully and said, "Between business interests and the Durpari government, many campaigns have been launched with the intention of clearing Veldorn of the monster tribes. They've all failed. It is not our custom to throw good money after bad. The few civilized folks who do choose to live there are on their own. "

Jhoqo nodded. "I appreciate your honesty, Orir."

"Sir—we're to go to Veldorn, then?" she asked.

Jhoqo seemed to gauge her carefully. "We travel to the one place that might eventually solve many of the problems we in the South have in Veldorn," Jhoqo said. "To Neversfall."

Adeenya did not speak for several moments. "For what purpose, sir?"

"You've heard of Neversfall?" Jhoqo said, watching her.

"Aye, sir. My father mentioned it a few times," she said. She remembered how casually her father had talked of his interest in the citadel when the proposal had first come to him. She knew then that he was interested. Her father only responded so coolly when he was excited about a proposition.

The urir raised his eyebrows. "He is Yaviz Jamaluddat," she added reluctantly.

"Ah! Of course," Jhoqo said. "Such a wealthy merchant would certainly know of it. No doubt he invested in it."

His tone made it clear that his last words were not a question so Adeenya did not address it as such and forged ahead. "What is the mission at Neversfall, sir?"

Jhoqo stopped walking and faced Adeenya and both of his subordinates. "To secure it."

"Sir?" Taennen asked.

"The conditions at the citadel of Neversfall are currently unknown," Jhoqo said. "The last report from the commander assigned to Neversfall is three days overdue."

"Three days? By the One," Taennen said.

"Yes, the councils are quite concerned," Jhoqo said. "Estagund and Durpar have invested too much time, coin, and mutual respect into this endeavor for anything to go wrong."

Adeenya puzzled at the man's notion of respect as an investment. Though, she supposed, respect often yielded the finest returns. "Yes, sir. Do we have any theories as to what might have happened to the troops stationed there?"

"Yes, sir, how many were there?" Taennen added.

"The citadel was held by nearly forty combined Maquar and Durpari troops," Jhoqo said.

Adeenya reeled at the number. What could possibly overcome forty well-trained soldiers with a strong fortress as their line of defense?

"Sir, are there more reinforcements on the way?" she asked.

Jhoqo shook his head. "Not yet. We're to scout the situation and call in more if needed."

Adeenya quelled her immediate reaction and offered a measured response. "Sir, we could be dealing with a huge enemy force here if they overwhelmed that many troops. We aren't prepared for anything larger than a clean-up effort. We need battlemages, clerics—the safety of our two nations could be at stake."

Jhoqo nodded. "Or perhaps it's nothing serious at all," he said. "That's what we're going to find out. No need for expensive magic-users then. It's best not to jump to conclusions, Orir. Try to remember that."

Adeenya restrained herself. "Yes, sir."

"Our first goal is to make sure the men and women at the citadel are safe."

"Of course, sir," Adeenya said. "I'm just trying to keep the bigger issues in mind."

"I believe in the Adama, Orir. Do you?" Jhoqo said.

"I'm not sure I see the relevance, sir," Adeenya said.

"If all is one, if everyone and everything are connected as that thinking would have us believe, then we should treat one another with great care, don't you think?"

Adeenya nodded, though the relevance still eluded her. "The wholeness of the All is a fine and good concept, sir."

Jhoqo nodded. "The Adama is a wise formula that benefits us all. Too often, we hurry through life without thinking about the small connections and opportunities we pass up every day. Those small things cannot be sacrificed for the bigger issues. Details, Orir."

Adeenya said nothing but nodded again. The Maquar were known for their devotion to the ways of the Adama, the belief system of most inhabitants of the Shining South. Never one to give the matter much thought, Adeenya usually just smiled and nodded when the topic was broached in conversation—especially when the person doing the broaching was also her commander.

"When do we move out, sir?" Adeenya asked, hoping to leave the previous conversation behind. She had used the word 'sir' more times in the few moments she'd known the Maquar commander than she had in the previous two weeks. It didn't fit well in her mouth.

"I want to address the troops before we go, but we will move out immediately after," Jhoqo said.

"Yes, sir. My people will have our camp broken down in two bells," Adeenya replied.

Jhoqo gave her a hard look and said, "No, Orir. You'll be ready to move before next bell." With that the man offered a nod and moved toward the rest of the Maquar soldiers who still stood in perfect formation, awaiting their next command. Adeenya held back a sigh, hoping she had never come across to her subordinates as Jhoqo just had to her.

✚
chapter two

Taennen fell into step behind his commander. He felt the anticipation in the air among his fellow Maquar. Jhoqo was a true orator, his many speeches worth the waits between and good for morale. Taennen glanced over his shoulder to the Durpari commander. She nodded tightly.

Taennen wondered at the woman's inattentive expression. He needed no mirror to see the enthusiasm on his own face. He saw it reflected on the faces of his brothers. The Maquar stood rigid—disciplined but excited to hear their commander speak. His words led to their deeds and their deeds were great. Yet Adeenya and her troops stood quiet in body and spirit, their eyes seeming attentive but dull and lacking illumination. Was there a better moment in the life of a soldier than the one just before a mission?

He basked for a moment in the pride of knowing that when the troops heard their new mission, they would cheer. They would celebrate the opportunity to bring the rule of the Rajah to new places and people. They would revel in simply being soldiers, doing their duty and helping one another along the way. Taennen cast an eye back to Adeenya and wondered if she ever felt such joy. Probably not—she was still a mercenary. Soldiering was all about money to mercenaries.

Jhoqo paced before the soliders as the last few Durpari fell into their places. Next to one another, the differences between the two forces came into sharp focus. The bright, bold colors of the Maquar arranged next to the subdued appearances of the Durpari provided an extreme contrast. The Maquar looked ready to take the battlefield while the Durpari looked ready to skulk through city streets at night. The pride and joy of Estagund beside the best Durpar could offer.

Jhoqo stopped his pacing and raised his arms. "Brothers, sisters, sons, and daughters, let us take this moment to share in our joy of being given this awesome task. The One, the All, has come together and presented us with an opportunity to add our balance to the world. We will do just that!"

The Maquar slapped their gloves on the boiled leather of their bracers in response, though their demeanor never changed, their disciplined stance never wavered. Startled by the sound, several of the Durpari moved their hands instinctively to the hilts of their weapons, only to release them when they realized the source of the sounds. Taennen offered a reassuring smile to Adeenya, who had also started at the ritual applause.

Jhoqo continued. "We are in the most dangerous of the southern lands, my friends. It doesn't take much of a fool to make a mistake in Veldorn that costs someone's life."

The Maquar again pounded their appreciative rhythm but stopped short when the sound of further pounding came from the Durpari ranks. Each Durpari soldier was slapping the shoulder of the nearest comrade. A moment of silence passed when the pounding stopped, and Jhoqo walked to stand before the Durpari, looking Adeenya in the eyes.

"You honor us, our Durpari brethren," Jhoqo said, clapping Adeenya on the shoulder.

Adeenya bowed her head in thanks to the man.

"And you, my loyal Maquar. I would enter battle beside no one else!" Jhoqo said, turning from her.

The Maquar roared in return, a brief, violent burst chorus. Taennen felt a burr in his throat, but that only made him shout all the more.

Jhoqo continued, "We all know what awaits us in Veldorn. We will be in the land of beasts, my friends. We must defend ourselves. We may even have to kill!"

The pounding of fists and chests rattled in Taennen's ears, the syncopation of solidarity. He hit himself harder, adding his own effort to the clatter. The troops of both countries seemed to pound all the harder, attempting to outdo one another in friendly competition. Taennen was proud to see the Maquar allowing the Durpari mercenaries to stand with them as though they were equals in a sign of solidarity.

"Let us do so together, as family, as a whole within the Adama," Jhoqo said. "Let us defend one another against the monstrous hordes should they be fool enough to come against us!"

The reactionary noise hit a new level, and a few affirmative shouts joined the chorus. Jhoqo beamed as he paced before the gathering, his colors fluttering and chin held high.

"Come!" Jhoqo said. "We begin our journey together!"

Taennen saluted and turned to give orders for his troops to form up just as a loud horn sounded in the distance. The durir drew his weapon at the sound. Adeenya's eyes widened and the Durpari leaped to their feet. Adeenya shouted a string of commands to her people.

Taennen's eyes found his commander, who nodded once in permission of Taennen's unspoken request. He scanned the area and spotted what he needed—all twelve hundred pounds of it. Taennen sprinted toward an unburdened brown and white pack horse and vaulted atop the creature with a shout. His heels dug into his mount's side, and the horse dashed away. Usually loaded down with goods, the horse rarely had the opportunity to sprint, but unburdened now, the horse covered the ground quickly.

From the east, a Durpari soldier waving an unfamiliar signal flag sped toward him at an arrow's pace. Though the man's face was indistinguishable, Taennen felt the terror pouring off the runner, even from so far away. He looked over his shoulder, shouting.

"Threat to the east!" Another Maquar took up the call, carrying the news further into the ranks until all present had received the information.

Taennen kicked the horse into a gallop toward the fleeing soldier.

The thundering hooves became a war drum to his ears. No anger, hate, or violence bubbled in his mind, but rather adventure and opportunity. His father had always said that young men should fight every so often just to remind themselves that they could. Jhoqo disapproved of such philosophy. Taennen grinned a little and kicked ahead, his pulse pounding.

Fifteen paces from the fleeing soldier, Taennen could clearly see wounds on the man's arms and neck, thin oozing cuts. The horn-blower rasped and wheezed, his lungs strained from running, but one word was clear: "Monsters."

Taennen reined his mount to a stop next to the young soldier. The runner sucked hard for breath, collapsing against Taennen's horse. Taennen looked back to see the rest of the Maquar and Durpari. They marched toward him but were still several long bowshots away.

"What's the danger, soldier?" Taennen said.

The soldier tried to speak, but still Taennen could only make out that one word. Taennen reached down and turned the man's face toward him. His eyes were glossy and distant, his pallid face streaked with blood. Taennen released him. Whatever had stricken so much fear into this man would not drive Taennen to the same state. He was Maquar.

The Durpari man pushed away from the horse and ran to the rest of the troops. The Durpari mercenaries had fallen in with the Maquar, both forces approaching but still some distance away. Taennen pulled his steed's reins and turned the horse to take his place among his men. He froze in place when his ears began to vibrate with an unfamiliar sound. It felt like dozens of flies buzzed in unison inside his head. There was no pain, but the sound was discomfiting.

He stared toward the east, still unable to see what might be causing the sound. Taennen slid off the horse. Something was close. He jogged forward, coming to the top of a small hillock, and looked over its edge into the valley below. He nearly cried out. Behind him he heard the horse scream and take off towards the Maquar and Durpari. He shook his head to clear it, and glanced back at the fast approaching army.

"Sirs," he said as Jhoqo and Adeenya reached him. "We have a problem."

Below the gathered troops, at the bottom of the gently sloping hill and charging toward them, was an army of creatures. Taennen's practiced eyes scanned the mobbing beasts. "Approximately fifty individuals," he reported. "Maybe ten bugbears, another dozen goblins, a score of kobolds, more than a dozen humans and . . . by the One! A pair of girallons and a half-giant." Jhoqo nodded, his brow furrowed, his mind already working on a strategy, Taennen was certain.

Goblins, bugbears and kobolds together, Taennen could accept, but never had he seen so many humans alongside the black-hearted creatures.

But that was not their greatest concern. What Taennen, and no doubt the others near him, found so amazing were the creatures behind that gathered mass.

Ranging in sizes that matched everything from a dog to a horse stood another twenty or so creatures, looking like twisted and mutilated centaurs crossed with insects. Taennen was reminded of desert ants, only these creatures were less graceful in appearance and many thousands of times larger. Their reddish brown flesh shimmered in the midday sun. They stood on four legs that bent at multiple joints. Two arms attached to shoulders topped by wicked, bony protrusions. Bulbous sacks erupted where their legs and backs met and carried short barbs on some of the creatures. There could be no doubt that they were pressing the other creatures, human and goblinoid alike, up the hill toward the waiting soldiers.

"What in all the order of the Adama are those?" someone from the ranks exclaimed.

Taennen had seen a wemic once, a leonine creature similar to the centaur-like ants below. The wemic had been beautiful and frightening at the same time, elegant death in motion. The same could not be said of these creatures. They moved with twitches and jerks, their gait uneven. Thin to the point of emaciation with hairs covering their legs, they clattered along with their stomping cohorts. They could not be creatures of this world. Where they came from was a mystery, but they did not belong in Veldorn, that much he knew.

"Something is terribly wrong," Adeenya said.

"We should continue to the citadel," Khatib advised. There was no fear in his voice, only practicality.

"I doubt they'll let us just stroll by, wizard," Marlke said.

"Soldiers!" Jhoqo shouted, drawing his broad falchion from its scabbard with a scrape. It shone bright with magic in the midday sun, a bright star against the dull plains of Veldorn.

"We are brothers and sisters in battle! Surely together there is no force to stop us on the face of Faerûn!" Jhoqo shouted. Maquar and Durpari alike shouted in response.

"For the Rajah!" Jhoqo shouted and turned to face Taennen and Adeenya. Through the cheering and scrapes of steel being pulled from sheath and scabbard, Jhoqo shouted to be heard. "Taennen, take half our men as yours to flank the left. Orir, take your men and circle around to flank them from the right. Terir, you're with me." He turned again and faced the gathered forces. "For the South! Clean every last beast from our path! None of my soldiers die today! Is that clear?"

Cheers erupted again. Taennen's ears ached with the sound, but his heart raced with anticipation. He drew his khopesh.

"No prisoners, sir?" Adeenya asked.

Jhoqo turned from her and strode away without answering. Whether or not he had heard her question was unclear. For her part, Adeenya clenched her jaw, but she rallied her soldiers and drove them to the right.

She had a point, Taennen realized. Prisoners might be useful in gaining information. Perhaps this ragged army

17

of creatures was somehow involved in the trouble—if there was any—at Neversfall. An army of beasts this organized could have taken the regiment by surprise.

Taennen threw his hands high, signaling for two of the four Maquar squads to follow him. He pushed his way left to approach the enemy from a flanking position. Once away from the other units, Taennen shouted to the men gathered about him. "Kill if you must, but if you can incapacitate an opponent to claim a captive, do so."

The soldiers saluted. Seeing Jhoqo's troops setting off down the hill to meet the charge, Taennen thrust his khopesh high and loosed an ululating war cry. His troops returned his cry as they charged down the hill, falling into position as they ran.

As they descended the hill, Taennen's troops came into a wedge formation to punch through the enemy ranks and prevent the beasts from flanking Jhoqo's men as they attacked the center. Taennen stayed behind the forward line of that wedge by several strides, out of the heaviest fighting, in order to better command his forces. Leading troops meant living long enough to make sure that you lost as few soldiers as possible. His secure position gave an advantage in this.

He watched the forward soldiers pouring down the hill and felt nostalgic. It wasn't long ago that his place was in the action. Taennen held his shield and khopesh ready, looking for openings and opportunities to assist his soldiers.

With shouts of "For the rajah," Taennen's troops plunged into the fracas, scattering a group of goblins. The clatter of steel on steel made Taennen's blood race, and his eyes devoured the battle scene before him. He watched for gaps in the lines of the wedge formation, shouting out directions to fill them as the fighting force plowed through the battle.

He stepped over the corpse of a goblin as a line of blood sprayed across his chest from a nearby kill made by one of his soldiers.

A bugbear dodged through the formation of soldiers, its bulky body surprisingly nimble, and charged Taennen. The Maquar durir met the attack by launching his khopesh at the creature's neck. The bugbear parried the blow with a strong upward sweep of its club. The blade carved into the club with a thunk. Taennen pivoted on his left foot, brought the blade around, and drove it into the bugbear's groin.

The beast didn't make a sound. It stumbled and fell forward as Taennen snarled and plunged his sword into the bugbear's side.

"Right side! Disabling blows!" Taennen shouted. "Form up and get in there!" Two of his soldiers tightened their formation in response, without so much as a hesitation between swings.

A pair of goblins harried a soldier in the rear of the wedge. She plunged forward with her blade, aiming low for one's legs instead of delivering a more deadly blow to the head or chest, and nicked one of her attacker's knees. The little goblin leaped backward and its companion took advantage of the woman's extension, driving a spear through her neck. Her mouth opened in a silent cry and blood spilled down her chest and arm.

Taennen dashed forward but had made only half the distance when another of the Maquar broke formation to come to her aid. The goblins met the newcomer with low slashes. The soldier parried them and launched one of the goblins several paces with a quick kick. The other creature latched onto the man's leg and began climbing the soldier like a tree. The Maquar shifted his sword to his off hand and throttled the goblin, tossing it away. Before he could regain his defenses, the first goblin scrabbled toward him and drove a small axe into his gut. The Maquar shouted for help, but his fellows were engaged with enemies of their own.

Taennen reached the Maquar's side and severed the goblin's head with his blade while loosing a scream. The head fell to the ground, lips curved in a grim smile. Taennen took a step and continued the stroke into the other goblin, obliterating its abdomen. The Maquar wedge formation continued to gain ground, pushing through the gathered monsters and leaving Taennen and the two injured soldiers behind.

Taennen bent over the fallen woman to look for signs of life, but her chest did not move. The lake of blood spreading beneath her face left no doubt of her demise. Taennen choked back his anger at her death and turned his attention to the man who clutched his stomach and cursed the dead goblin. Taennen pried the man's hands away to check the gushing wound. Reds and pinks of many shades greeted him, squirming organs like so many worms, leaking their precious fluids. Taennen pressed hard on the gaping hole causing the man to moan in pain.

"Cleric!" Taennen shouted before he turned back to see the Maquar's face. "Hang on, soldier. We'll get this taken care of. Hold that wound like it was a gift from the rajah himself!"

The soldier grimaced but mouthed his affirmation. Unable to help the man further, Taennen stood from the fallen soldier. He ran toward the rest of his troops to prevent the same fate from befalling them. Let the cleric get to him, Taennen prayed. The Maquar did not pay for resurrections.

The durir scanned the scene and watched in horror as, in the back of the formation, a half-giant nearly twice his height took the arm from one of his Maquar with a single stroke of her axe. Taennen roared a challenge to the creature, who trudged toward him instead of chasing the still-charging wedge. Taennen rolled to his left as the half-giant swung her huge axe at him. Her hulking muscles and dark brown skin seemed to soak up the sunlight. Her bald pate glistened with the fruit of her efforts and she swung the weapon slowly but with alacrity enough to do the job.

Taennen hopped to his feet and sprinted, circling behind the beastly woman. Teeth the size of Taennen's fingers gnashed together as she spun her axe low behind him. Taennen stopped his run and jumped straight up, pulling his legs up tight to his body. The huge axe whirred by just as he pulled his feet from the ground, grain plucked before it could be cut by the scythe. He gained his feet and drove right with his khopesh, slashing the blade at the half-giant's left side. The blow glanced off her hardened skin. Taennen grunted with frustration and shook off the pain in his wrist from the impact.

She turned to face him again without a sound. Taennen took two large steps back to escape the range of her terrible weapon. Her eyes were glassy and devoid of the battle rage he expected. She fought without anger or passion. She hefted the weapon above her head and drove down hard and straight, a blow easily dodged. Dirt sprayed as the axe head bit into the earth.

Before she could tug the heavy axe from the ground, Taennen was beside her, jabbing his khopesh at her. Twice his blade bit her before she wrenched her huge weapon from the soil, and twice it barely penetrated her rock-hard flesh. She pulled her weapon from the ground and straightened herself to stand tall again.

Taennen dashed behind her and jumped as high as he could, swinging his weapon like a pickaxe. He sank the curved end of the khopesh into her broad back and held tight to the hilt. His own weight on the blade tore at her flesh as he fell back to the ground. His blade slid down several inches, cutting a trail of pain, and the gash splashed blood. Still, his opponent made no scream of pain or any sound at all.

Taennen's heart sank. An opponent who felt no pain could fight forever. What drove these monsters so inexorably through the battle that they would not scream?

The enormous woman turned to him with her freed weapon, her face going slowly pale from blood loss. Her eyes were vacant and hollow. It was not just as though she felt no pain, but as though she felt nothing at all.

She drove her axe in hard on Taennen's right, and he prepared for the feint, assuming she would pull the weapon short and sweep it up toward him. The attack was no feint, though, and Taennen dodged the blow by leaning back. His opponent's lack of tactics only furthered his befuddlement. He pushed forward, shoving her arm hard against her stomach with his shield as he sent the khopesh at her chest with a mighty swing. The blow sank deep, dropping the half-giant to her knees. As she fell forward, Taennen jumped out of the way. Her face hit the dirt, her life over—and she had never once made a sound.

On the other side of the battle, Adeenya drove her spear into her opponent's throat, finishing off the little goblin before she brought the blunt end of her weapon up in an arc to smash into the jaw of a nearby hulking girallon.

The apelike creature turned from its opponent and its four arms grabbed for her. She brought the sharp end of her spear around and thrust it into the creature's chest. As the spear sank deep into the beast, the wild thing tried to drive on. The force of its ferocity lifted Adeenya from her feet and drove her back, legs flailing in the air. She released her grip on her spear and rolled to her right. The creature continued a few steps and then turned to charge again, Adeenya's spear still protruding from its chest. Blood poured from the wound, but the girallon did not stop, tear the weapon out, or even howl in pain.

She let the creature come at her, grabbing her spear and yanking it out as it ran by. She pivoted on one foot, spinning around to crack the pole of the spear across the beast's back. The girallon stumbled forward but did not fall. Adeenya charged but pulled up short when a yell to her right caught her attention. She turned to see one of her men being pressed by four spindly goblins. Her lines were falling apart. She left off the wounded girallon and raced toward her soldiers.

With a few well-placed thrusts, she helped the soldier make quick work of the goblins and turned to find her girallon opponent again. Her heart sank when her eyes fell upon it. The hairy beast had gotten its second wind. Its upper arms wrapped around one of her soldiers, crushing the air from the man's lungs, while the claws on its lower arms tore viciously into his stomach and sides causing a shower of blood. His entrails raced down his dangling legs and fell to the ground, sending up clouds of dust.

Adeenya sprinted to the scene, using her momentum to thrust her spear into the girallon's side. The spear pierced through organs and erupted out the far side of the beast. Still, the creature lurched around to face her without a

23

sound. Nothing in nature she had ever seen or heard of could hold its tongue against such a strike.

Adeenya yanked the spear out and drew the bloodied weapon over her head as far as she could before leaping into the air and plunging its pointed tip downward. It sank through the creature's shoulder, into its torso. The beast convulsed, dropping its shredded victim to the ground. The girallon managed a weak swipe of its paws at her to no avail. Adeenya left the spear in the creature until it hit the ground and stopped moving. She spared a glance to the dead Durpari at her feet, his death—as most all their deaths could be—a tally in Durpar's books. She said a quiet apology that she could not give his death more reason or purpose. She wrenched the weapon free and shouted for her troops to continue their push through the back ranks of the beastly army. The Maquar were cutting through the lines on the opposite side. The Southern forces had the creatures in a pincer movement and would meet in the bloody middle soon.

At the rear of the monstrous army, just ahead of Taennen's beleagured forces, the ant creatures were calmly watching the battle. The largest one on the field was the size of a horse and its skin was darker in color than that of the rest of its kin. It had fingered hands, unlike its clawed cohorts. The creature wore a bronze helmet on its head, and its antennae twitched endlessly. Taennen's stomach lurched. He broke formation and ran toward the monsters without a spare thought.

The creature's spear met his sword almost as soon as it was raised. The beast turned slowly from the battle to regard Taennen with cold, alien eyes. Taennen roared and swung the khopesh into its legs, but again the spear met the blow.

No matter what attack Taennen attempted, the alien beast seemed to know what he was going to do. He dived over an incoming blow and rolled to come behind the beast. He almost cackled with glee as he thrust forward immediately, sure he had the creature by surprise. But somehow it twisted and contorted its torso so that it met his attack with a counter that sent his weapon hand high and found his own torso shying away from a spear point it could not avoid. The wooden weapon sank into his shoulder and Taennen screamed.

He leaped back, the weapon making a wet sucking noise as it exited his flesh. He fought the pain, focusing on what he had learned about his opponents in the course of the battle. Where the other opponents he had faced that day had seemed unskilled to unusual levels with their slow, lumbering ways, this ant-thing seemed far above his aptitude. It was as if the creature had eyes all over, watching everything Taennen did even when it was not facing him.

Taennen glanced around the battlefield hoping to find some advantage and noticed that most of the beasts— including many of the enemy humans—were dead or dying. Yet many of the ant creatures still stood. Maquar and Durpari alike were now engaging the ants, giving the combined army the tactical advantage of outnumbering their enemies. Taennen's troops had split their wedge formation and spread themselves out to cover one portion of the field. Their battles had drawn them apart, and he cursed himself for not having watched over them more closely, keeping them together.

He locked eyes with the alien foe and nearly felt his heart stop.

He saw himself working hand in hand with the ants to bring about order and sense to a chaotic world. He was the key, the instrument that could finally stop the terrible randomness and furious meaninglessness of the world. Faerûn would be a better, more ordered place if only he went with them. Together they could make the world lawful and productive, a goal he had long dreamed of making a reality.

Taennen stumbled over a jagged rock the size of his fist. The pain jarred him, drawing his attention away from these new thoughts. He looked with awe at the creature before him. It had been in his head. The images of working with the foul things kept rising in his thoughts and he howled with anger. He drove forward with another attack. The ant matched him, blow for blow.

The clattering din ebbed. Taennen could hear only his own weapon clashing with his opponent's. Several Maquar surrounded the monster. It warded them off with a quick slash before continuing to try to penetrate Taennen's defenses.

"Surrender!" Adeenya shouted, approaching the fight.

Taennen saw a flash of movement from his opponent before several of the Maquar leaped to action, tackling the large beast. Taennen felt pain in his stomach and looked down. He watched blood dribble out and splash to the dirt below, the crimson turning black as it mixed with the brown earth. He heard shouts for help but they were muted, as if underwater. Taennen could no longer feel his legs. He lost his breath as his body crashed to the ground.

Taennen saw the glint of Jhoqo's magical falchion swinging for the ant's neck as several other soldiers restrained the beast. The blade missed as Adeenya barreled into Jhoqo,

26

making his swing impossible. The two leaders crashed into the ground together. Jhoqo hurled Adeenya from atop him and jumped to his feet, weapon in hand.

"Urir! It's over," Adeenya said, placing her spear before her.

Jhoqo snarled and stepped toward her, his arm drawing back for a blow. Adeenya swung the spear between them.

"It's over," Adeenya said, motioning to the large ant-creature. The beast had ceased struggling and was being bound by a pair of the Maquar as she spoke. "It might have information we need, sir," Adeenya said, her weapon still ready.

Khatib stepped next to Jhoqo and spoke. His voice was soft but carried nonetheless. "She speaks truly, sir. It helps us alive and does us no good dead. It is well in hand."

Jhoqo stared at the woman for a long moment before turning his gaze to his durir. Taennen nodded, his head spinning out of control with each motion. Vengeance was not as important as useful information. Jhoqo would realize that, once his fear for Taennen had settled in his mind. The commander of the Maquar withdrew his weapon and turned to survey the battlefield. As Adeenya bent to help Taennen, he looked at the creature he had been fighting. Its face was alien and strange, sculpted of what seemed like impossible angles. His head swam and he could ponder no more as the voices around him became echoes and his eyes closed beyond his control.

+ chapter three

The evening light pried Taennen's eyes open. His head screamed. He squinted, trying to focus his eyes in the low light, and scanned the dim room, shying from the beams of light seeping into the tent directly over him. He spoke a soft word of greeting and, when he received no response, tried to pull himself up from his prone position. His stomach and shoulder ached and burned, and his head pounded. Propped on his elbows, he pulled back the blanket to find bandages. He pulled the cotton back and saw the source of his ache. The spear wound was small now, no doubt thanks to the healing of one of his paladin brothers.

Taennen grunted against the stiffness and pain and rolled from the cot to his feet, but he immediately fell to his knees. He paused, taking several deep breaths, then stood and stumbled out of the tent into the dwindling evening light. The joint troops were camped, preparing dinner fires and finishing setting up their tents. Before he could speak to any of them, he heard a whistle and turned to see Loraica shaking her head. Her curly hair danced from side to side, sliding past a few scrapes and bruises that dotted her face and neck.

"I doubt you're supposed to be moving around yet," she said.

"When did that ever stop me?" he asked. "How long was I down?"

"Not long, just a few bells," she said.

It even hurt to smile but he could not help himself. Since they met so many years ago, just laying eyes on his friend always made him smile. No one fought harder, listened more closely, or backed her comrades as fiercely as Loraica did. Even when they were only sparring, she gave her all. Taennen's smile grew when he realized that Loraica was probably the main reason he was able to move even in so much pain at that moment. Her fierce competitive nature had taught him how to deal with pain. He had given his fair share of lumps as well. Every one seemed only to draw them closer together.

"The healers managed some progress on the wound but they say there's some sort of poison in your body."

"Poison?" he asked.

"Yes, from the formian's weapon," Loraica said.

"Formian?" he said, laying his arm around her shoulder for support.

"That's what the ants call themselves," Loraica said, taking his weight upon her as if it were nothing. "We've been questioning the one you were fighting. He . . . " she paused and then started again. "It's their leader."

"Show me this formian," he said.

On the Durpari side of the camp, Adeenya nodded to her men, who closed the circle behind her, hiding her from the sight of the Maquar. She crouched, the smell of hot grasses tickling her nose. She pulled a pendant from a pocket on her belt. Solid bronze but otherwise quite plain, the piece was round and etched with simple designs of clashing weapons. She concentrated hard and touched the piece to her forehead, whispering the word her commanders had given her to activate the item.

Report, she heard in her mind. The sound was both one voice and many at the same time. One part boomed, others whispered, some sang.

Sirs, we were engaged and took heavy losses, she replied without speaking. The sound of her own mental voice reverberated in her head, and she wondered if her own voice sounded as cold and empty to those receiving her message as theirs did to her.

What enemy, Orir? You've reached Neversfall?

It surprised Adeenya that her superiors had known the nature of the mission where she had not. *No, sirs. We encountered a large force of monsters and humans led by a type of creature we've never seen before, sir. They call themselves formians,* she said, her mental tongue stumbling at the last word.

A long pause followed, and Adeenya nearly severed the connection, believing there was a problem with the medallion's sending, when the voices returned.

We'll expect a full report on these creatures.

Of course, sirs, but what about the present situation?

Proceed as ordered, Orir, came the response.

Adeenya could not hide her surprise. Though she articulated no words in her mind, the response was rapid.

Is there a problem, soldier?

We lost troops on both sides, sirs, she sent. *Two of our clerics are dead. We will be less capable in our mission at the citadel. We should wait for reinforcements.*

You will succeed, Orir.

Adeenya knew not to say more on the subject. She

had long thought that part of the process of becoming a high-ranking officer must have been losing your memory of what it's like to be in a bad situation with few troops at your disposal.

Adeenya felt a snap in her mind, like a twig breaking, as her superiors severed the mental connection. The response of the command council went against her own thoughts on the matter, but that was nothing new for her. She stood, clapping her soldiers on the backs in thanks for providing her privacy for the sending as she pocketed the device once again, but still held it in her closed hand. She found it soothing to run her thumb across the smooth metal surface of the device while she thought.

"Sir?" Marlke asked as Adeenya strode to her tent.

"We're to proceed," she replied.

"Anything else, sir?" the dwarf asked.

"No, Marlke," she said.

The dwarf saluted and turned tightly on his heel. He began barking orders at the Durpari soldiers who were already working hard on setting up their camp and low fires. Adeenya watched the Maquar side of the camp and noticed Taennen, leaning on Loraica, moving toward the prisoners. She was relieved to see the durir standing, even if not under his own power. The ant leader's spear had nearly rent the young man in half. When she had seen so much blood gushing from his stomach, she had been certain he was already dead.

Adeenya spotted Jhoqo near the prisoners and squinted to make out any details on the man's face. He was writing on a parchment as he watched the prisoners. Cataloging them, perhaps? Even from her present distance, Adeenya felt the tension on the man and she could not blame him. The mission he led was of dire importance, and their first engagement had gone poorly.

"Odd species, aren't they?" came Khatib's voice from behind her.

Adeenya cursed herself for not paying more attention and turned to face the man. She had not noticed his thin moustache when they met earlier. It lent his face a feline quality she found bothersome. He focused his gaze on the prisoners and Jhoqo just as she had done a few moments before.

"The Maquar or the formians?" Adeenya said.

Khatib laughed. "Before I joined them, I often wondered if the Maquar were human!"

"They aren't, at least according to some of the stories I grew up with," Adeenya said.

"Indeed, I've seen them perform some amazing feats. Especially him," Khatib said, nodding toward Jhoqo.

"That does not surprise me," Adeenya said. "What brings you to my side of the camp?"

"I did notice it was a bit segregated," Khatib said.

Adeenya chuckled. "Why wouldn't it be? To the Maquar we're just mercenaries, aren't we? Hired blades who will do anything for coin?"

"Oh, I don't know about that. I think the Maquar respect anyone who fights as well as your people did back there. But, to answer your question, I was here to see if I could assist you, but it seems you have things well in hand, as it were," Khatib said, looking toward her pocketed hand that caressed her amulet.

Adeenya did her best to hide her surprise. "Yes, I think so. Is that all, then?"

Khatib smiled wide, his thin lips a mockery of the effort. "Yes, commander. I'll take my leave, now," the wizard said. He walked past her, giving a slight bow, and moved to the Maquar side of the camp.

32

Adeenya watched him go, wondering if he had come on his own or if the Maquar commanders had sent him to spy. She pulled the amulet from her pocket and looked at her distorted reflection in the polished metal. Either way, it didn't matter. She had no doubt they possessed a similar device to remain in contact with their people. She placed it once again in her pocket and moved to help her people finish setting their camp. She wanted half a bell to sit and think, to absorb everything going on around her, but there was never time for such a thing. She grinned to herself. She had grown so accustomed to living at a fast pace, she would probably fall apart if she ever had to slow down and think too hard about anything.

Taennen navigated the uneven terrain of the camp, having shaken loose Loraica's supportive arm. He passed the sand-colored tents, the cooking pots, and the supply corral on his way to the holding pens. The Maquar set up their camps the same way every time, leaving no need to learn a new layout.

Stumbling as much as walking, he crossed the last several paces of the camp to the holding pens, which were nothing more than rope strung between thin poles sunk into the ground. The field did not lend itself well to keeping prisoners locked up. Taennen's vision, still blurry from blood loss, picked Jhoqo out of the figures standing near the prisoners, and he approached his commanding officer.

"Sir, Durir Tamoor reporting for duty," he said. Taennen saluted, wavering unsteadily.

Jhoqo turned and grabbed for Taennen, steadying the younger man. "You ought not be up and about yet, son."

Taennen turned and looked to the pen. Seated on the ground were a few goblins, kobolds, humans, and a half-ling. In another pen nearby, the formians were bound at the wrists and there were strips of black cloth across their mouths and eyes. There were a few of the smallest, a hand-ful of the pony-sized ant creatures—the guards eyed one of these as it had no mouth to gag—and the large one who had given Taennen the wound that now ached and pained him so.

"What have they said, sir?" Taennen asked, never taking his eyes from the large creature.

"This one's been quite open, actually," Jhoqo said, indi-cating the large one. "The formians have one goal and one goal only."

Taennen looked to the man steadying him and saw con-cern on Jhoqo's face. "What is it, sir?"

"To bring order to the world." Jhoqo said. "And as best I can tell, they plan to do it by making slaves of us all."

Taennen stumbled, but Jhoqo did not let him fall. "Slaves? All of us?" Taennen asked and turned his eyes back to the creatures. "What of the other prisoners, sir? The humans and the halfling?"

Jhoqo turned from the holding area and walked away slowly. Taennen followed him as best he could, the world still wobbling a little under his feet.

"They say that they were slaves, put to work as manual laborers. They say the formians had some sort of control over them," Jhoqo said quietly. "Hence, the blindfolds and gags. No telling what kind of magic they used to manage it."

Taennen nodded, the itching of the invasions into his own mind coming back to him. "I'd sooner die than be a slave to those things," he spat.

Jhoqo stopped and turned Taennen to face him. "It's not that easy, boy. If they're telling the truth, they had no choice."

Taennen nodded, remembering his own experience on the battlefield but not wishing to share it with his commander. A Maquar should not be so weak. But he had a duty to report all he knew. He took a deep breath. "Sir?"

"Son?"

"Sir, during the battle . . . that large formian . . . it did something. Or it tried to anyway."

Jhoqo stepped in close to Taennen. "Go on."

"I could feel it trying to convince me to help it, but it wasn't speaking. In my mind, it just all seemed like such a good idea for a moment. It made sense to work with them instead of fighting them," Taennen said. "But I fought it off, sir. I shoved it out of my mind. I wouldn't have followed them."

Jhoqo nodded and stepped away, watching Taennen closely. Jhoqo had been the one consistent, solid influence in his life since Taennen had left his old life, and his father, behind. To see that immovable force waver with an uncertain look made Taennen shiver. Did the man think less of him? What could he do to ensure Jhoqo's continued trust?

"Sir, I thought you should know so we could be watchful," Taennen said.

Jhoqo nodded and said, "Well, let's hope that the bindings we have on them make it impossible for them to try that again. I wouldn't mention your experience to anyone else."

Taennen said nothing but wanted to know more about the formians. It had all seemed so sensible and logical, if even for those few moments.

"I've not told the others about the domination plans of

the formians yet. Only you, Loraica, and I know," Jhoqo said.

"And the Durpari commander, sir?"

"I'm just not sure yet. For now, we keep it between us."

Taennen nodded but said nothing.

"You take issue with that, son?"

"No, sir," Taennen said.

Jhoqo sighed. "I know they are our partners in this. Partners are well and good when there is danger to be faced and blood to be spilled, but I will not compromise the safety of Estagund until I know more about these Durpari mercenaries."

"Yes, sir," Taennen said, lifting his gaze again. Jhoqo was right, of course. The Durpari had acquitted themselves well in the fight but they were an unknown element. They had no code or rules. They were not like the Maquar.

"Very good," Jhoqo said.

"What do we do next, sir? What of Neversfall?"

Jhoqo was looking to the ground but raised his eyes to meet Taennen's. "What if it was these beasts that took it?"

Taennen nodded. "We should be on our way, sir."

"Before we go," Jhoqo said, turning a soft eye to Taennen, "I need you to tell me what happened out there."

"Sir?" Taennen said.

"Son, you lost nearly a quarter of your men in that fight. Those are not acceptable losses and you know it."

"What?" Taennen's legs went out from under him, and he fell to the ground. He watched in silence as the dust settled back around and on him, covering his shins in a light powder. Jhoqo offered his arm to help Taennen stand.

"Who?" Taennen asked.

"The terir has the list for you," Jhoqo said. "I asked her not to inform you before we had a chance to speak."

Taennen accepted the man's assistance and paid no mind to the dizziness as he stood. His eyes scanned the camp, looking for those he had led into the battle. The fight played out in his mind. He watched the deaths of the first two soldiers. Every commander had lost men under him—nothing could be done for that. But what if his idea of taking captives had cost his fellows their lives? He thought of the low strike the first woman had used. A few inches higher and the goblin would have been too dead to kill her.

His thoughts were interrupted as Jhoqo leaned in close to him. The man's face was grim and tight. "What happened?" Jhoqo repeated.

Taennen focused on his commander and said, "Sir . . . I . . . I told my people to try to take prisoners if they could. I thought we could get some useful information out of them about Veldorn and maybe even Neversfall."

Jhoqo shook his head and said, "Durir, I've never been in a battle where every member of either side was killed. I knew we would have a few prisoners, that's why I didn't specifically request that any be taken. It's a given in any battle and soldiers fight harder if they're fighting to kill."

Taennen tried to pay attention but found his eyes wandering the camp for those who had fought under him. Who hadn't made it?

Jhoqo grabbed the younger man by the shoulders and looked him hard in the eyes. "This sort of thing is why we must adhere to the chain of command so strictly, son. I'm disappointed in you. I had hoped for better from you in that fight. I lost men, too, son, but . . . by all the One," Jhoqo said.

"Sir . . ." Taennen said, his mind back on his situation. He winced away from the look of disappointment on his commander's face and wondered if he had looked the same to his father all those years before.

"Rest now, son. Just . . . leave me for a while," Jhoqo said.

Taennen saluted and limped toward his tent, Jhoqo's words stinging in his ears. The man he loved as a father was disappointed with him, much like Taennen had been with his own father. Taennen stopped his wobbling walk as the setting sun caught his eye. He wanted to wallow, to drown in the lament of his mistakes and the sorrow of the soldiers he lost. But he knew he could not.

His father had told him to attach his hopes and dreams to the rising sun and let the setting sun take away his pain, fear, and sadness. That way, he had said, every day was new. Taennen stared at the orange and red hues of the horizon and did just that. Ironic, he thought, that something his father had taught him long ago would come to him when he needed it most.

"Let me help you," Loraica said beside him, drawing him from his memories.

He accepted her arm, and together they walked to his tent. The Maquar they passed whispered to one another as they continued their work. The air was filled with the scent of mucjara soup, a staple among the Maquar. The citrus scent itched at his nose and his stomach growled despite the pain from his wound.

"You should have told me before I talked to him," Taennen said.

"I know. I'm sorry. I just couldn't," Loraica said. After a moment she continued. "What did he do?"

"Nothing," Taennen said.

"Nothing? What do you mean?"

"I mean nothing. He told me what I needed to know, and that was all."

"What did he say?"

"That I acted foolishly and that I need to be a better soldier if I don't want more lives on my head, Terir."

Loraica stiffened at her title but said nothing.

"I'll take the list now."

"You should rest tonight," she said.

"I have letters to write to the families of our fallen, Terir. I'll have the list now," he said.

Loraica paused in her steps to look him in the eyes. "Aye, sir." She pulled a parchment from her belt and offered it to him.

Taennen took the list and released his grip on Loraica. "Thank you, Loraica. I can manage it from here."

Loraica studied him a moment longer. "Yes, sir. Rest well."

"And you, Terir."

Being so stern with Loraica felt like lying. Even through rigid military training they had always been close and had been a source of support, a stable rock of sanity for one another their entire careers. But as he stumbled into his tent and read the names from the list by the low light of a candle, Taennen knew Jhoqo was right. Soldiers followed the chain of command so strictly for a reason, and Taennen had failed to follow his orders. He had taken it upon himself to win information and, he admitted to himself, Jhoqo's admiration by trying to take prisoners. It had cost him the lives of his men and the trust of his commander. It would not happen again.

The sound of gravel grinding under booted feet woke Taennen from his restless sleep. He could only guess the time, but the sun was nowhere near relieving Lucha of her nightly travels. Taennen took in a slow breath and held it to better hear. The grinding sound repeated. Someone was pacing outside his tent. Taennen released his breath and rolled from his cot. His stomach jarred him more fully awake with a jolt of pain. He covered himself with a light brown tunic and grabbed his khopesh. The pacing continued outside, but there were no other sounds, no indication of an invasion of the campsite. If hostile, the person outside his tent was either slow or foolhardy. Few enemies were ever gracious enough to be both.

Taennen stepped beyond the flap of his tent. A tall, thick man stood a few strides away, his pacing stopped. Haddar had been with the Maquar for a very long time, longer than Taennen. His rank of muzahar was well earned. He was known by all for his skill with the scimitar, and his drinking prowess was equally legendary. He stood with his arms crossed and his brows furrowed. He was fully dressed, including his leather armor and his blade hung at his belt.

"Muzahar," Taennen said.

"They are dishonored," Haddar said. "Wajde is dishonored."

Wajde, one of the men lost under Taennen's command that day, had been Haddar's cousin and closest friend. Taennen felt his loss more than any other, as Wajde had been a guide and aide to Taennen since his youth. As much as Jhoqo had been like a father, Wajde had been an uncle. Where Haddar was gruff and firm, Wajde was warm and patient.

"I would gladly give my life for his honor, Haddar, if I could," Taennen said. "It is a dangerous life we lead, and my actions did not help matters."

"Wajde knew he could die in battle. We all know that!" Haddar said.

"I led them and it is——" Taennen started.

"I do not question your ability!" Haddar said.

Taennen frowned. "What, then?"

"Your mistake went unpunished!" Haddar said. "The honor of the dead demands a price be exacted. The urir should have done that, but no! You are like his own blood, his child of favor! He could never punish you. If any other man had led your troops into that fight with such a disastrous result, what would have happened? What would Jhoqo have done to him?"

"Do you believe, even for a moment, that I asked to be absolved?" Taennen said.

Haddar stared at him, his chest heaving and his hands clenched. From nearby tents, heads peered out at the commotion, and whispers filled the tense air. Another muzahar approached the two men from behind Haddar, motioning to Taennen that she could subdue him, but Taennen waved her away and motioned for everyone watching to return to their tents.

After a few moments, Haddar stepped in close to Taennen and grabbed the younger man by the shoulders. His grip was like iron and his breath was hot on Taennen's face. Haddar snatched the back of Taennen's neck and squeezed hard drawing him closer to his face.

Taennen looked at Haddar's curled fist and nodded. "Exact the toll for them," he said.

Haddar's face twisted, but his grip relaxed. "No. I will not. Because Wajde loved you like his own and because you wish for me to do it," Haddar said. "Better for you to live without the absolution."

"What in all the . . .?" came Loraica's voice from nearby. "Muzahar!"

"Terir," Haddar said, releasing his hold on Taennen as he stepped back.

"Taennen, are you all right?" she asked.

Taennen nodded and turned his eyes to the ground. The weight of Haddar's words pressed down upon him, and he forgot the pain in his stomach and the new ones in his shoulders.

"Explain yourself, Muzahar," Loraica said to Haddar.

"No," Taennen said. "It's fine, Terir. Everything's fine."

"Sir, I just saw him—"

"He did nothing. Let him be," Taennen said as he turned back toward his tent.

Loraica sighed but nodded to Haddar who narrowed his eyes and screwed up his face tightly. "I have wronged a commanding officer, Terir. What is my punishment?"

"You heard the durir, soldier. Back to bunk," Loraica said.

"Sir, I assaulted an officer. I am to be reprimanded, at the least," Haddar said. The warble in his voice could not be mistaken. Without punishment, he had no discipline, no honor.

"Back to bunk," Loraica repeated.

"Wait," Taennen said, facing the man again.

Haddar stood at attention, unmoving, his gaze distant. Taennen watched the man for several moments before moving to stand before him. Haddar's jaw clenched with tension, but he did not flinch.

Taennen stepped back from the muscular man and drew his right arm high over his left shoulder. He sent the back of his hand searing across Haddar's cheek. The blow sounded with a snap, but still Haddar did not react.

"You are dismissed, Muzahar," Taennen said.

"Yes, sir," Haddar said. He nodded, his eyes thankful, and marched away toward his tent.

"Do you want to tell me what that was about?" Loraica

asked. "I thought you said he didn't do anything. So why did you punish him?"

"Because I care for him as we care for all of our soldiers, Terir," Taennen said. "Good night, Loraica."

Without waiting for a reply, Taennen passed into his tent and lowered himself onto his cot. He cradled his right hand, still stinging from the impact with Haddar's face, and wished Jhoqo had done the same for him. He thought of Wajde and of the mistakes he would never make again.

✛
chapter four

Adeenya spotted Taennen in the marching lines. He looked better in the morning light, though it was obvious his wounds still pained him. She fell into step next to him. He gave her a small smile and saluted.

"Durir, it pleases me to see you're well. Be at ease," she said, returning the salute.

Taennen dropped his arm to his side. "Thank you. What can I do for you, Orir?"

"I wanted to see how you were recovering," she said.

Taennen nodded. "Fine, thank you. I hope the battle went well for you and yours, sir," he said.

Adeenya nodded. "As well as any fight can," she said, her lips forming a tight smile.

Taennen raised an eyebrow and tilted his head.

"No fight is a good fight, Durir Tamoor." Her goal had not been to remind him of his losses, but by the look on his face, she clearly had. Regrettable but she had no time to worry about such things.

"That seems a strange attitude for a mercenary," Taennen said, "if I may so, Orir."

"Does it?"

"I meant no offense," he said with a bow and a gesture

44

of apology, wiping three fingers down his chin.

"It's quite all right, Taennen. May we talk frankly?" she said. If she was going to try to get answers, she might as well go straight to the heart of the matter. "Taennen, I have been unable to speak with the prisoners yet. Urir Valshu said it was unsafe and that with more time to examine them, he could allow me to interrogate them myself."

"They are very dangerous, Orir," Taennen said.

"I know that, but I hope you can understand my position. I need to know what's going on. I'd be a poor leader if I led my soldiers blindly without gathering all the intelligence I possibly could," Adeenya said.

Taennen nodded, looking vaguely uncomfortable. She was getting to him.

"I'll be blunt, Taennen. I need your help," she said.

"I would be pleased to help if I can, Orir," he said.

Adeenya smiled. "Excellent. Tell me about the prisoners."

"I know very little, sir. I haven't even been able to interview them myself," he said.

"What you do know would be helpful," Adeenya said.

"Orir, if I had any answers for you, I would share them," the Maquar said. His stiffened posture told her what she needed to know. She was being excluded. The urir obviously didn't think much of her command. He'd rather share information she needed with his skittish second.

Adeenya frowned and nodded. "Very well. If you do learn anything or find you can share something you might feel unable to share now, please let me know."

"Good morning," Jhoqo said as he fell into step beside Adeenya.

"Good morning, sir," Taennen said.

"Good morning, commander," Adeenya said, with a smile she didn't feel. "You've trained a tough one here."

"I certainly have. How are you, son?" Jhoqo said to Taennen.

"Well, sir, thank you."

"Actually, sir, " Adeenya said. "I was just asking Taennen what he knew about the prisoners as I've not yet had the opportunity to interview them."

"We've spoken about this, Orir," Jhoqo said. "No one has been allowed to interact with them yet. It's much too dangerous."

"Very well, sir, can you at least tell me what you've learned?" Adeenya said. "Clearly that information is not too dangerous as you know it and stand before me unharmed."

Taennen started at the woman's bold words. "Orir, I don't think—"

Jhoqo chuckled and waved a hand casually. "No, son, it's fine. If I were in her position, I'd be asking too. So, what have you learned from my durir so far, daughter?"

"Nothing, I'm afraid," she said.

Jhoqo nodded at the woman and turned a smile on Taennen. Pride shone in his eyes. Adeenya bit back her anger. She needed to know more about the creatures, and their secrets were in her way.

"Commander, I am already disadvantaged with a company appropriate only for the simple task I was advised of." she said. "I cannot do my job here if I don't have all the information available."

Jhoqo cocked his head and looked at her. "You have all the information you need, Orir," he said. "Unless perhaps we're of differing opinions as to what your job here is."

"Sir?" she asked.

"Your job, Orir, is to follow my orders and support the Maquar in this endeavor," Jhoqo replied.

Adeenya took a deep breath and said, "Sir, this is a joint mission. We are here to support one another."

"But you must agree that I am in charge?" Jhoqo said.

"Yes, sir. Of course, sir," she said.

"Very well. Then, why are we still discussing this?" he said with a small smile.

"Sir, the safety of this mission is part of my duty. Important information necessary to honoring that duty is being kept from me, sir," she said.

Jhoqo squinted at her for a moment and said, "Are you accusing me of something, Orir?"

"No, sir," she said. Adeenya did not fear the man before her, but his rising ire did not bode well for her career. Accusing an officer of negligence was a serious offense. Add it to that the fact that she had already tackled the man, and Adeenya saw her life as a soldier falling away.

"You need to be sure of what you are saying, Orir," Jhoqo said, stepping toward her.

"Sir," Taennen said. "I believe the orir is just trying to do her job. I would be just as persistent as she were our roles reversed."

Adeenya did not know who was more surprised by Taennen's statement, she or Jhoqo. The Maquar commander spun and faced his second. "Durir?" Jhoqo said.

"Sorry, sir," Taennen said, lowering his head.

Adeenya could almost see the younger man's spine melting away and thought it a pity. Her hopes for him had been raised when he had stood up for his principles.

She spoke again before she lost her momentum. "Urir, we've never seen anything like these creatures. Before she died of her injuries, one of my people told a comrade that the ant-creatures had done something to her . . . had tried to do something to her mind but had failed," Adeenya said.

"I need to investigate that. It could be disastrous for this mission."

Taennen's head snapped up and his eyes met Jhoqo's.

"Gods damn it. You knew!" Adeenya said.

"Orir, keep your voice down," Jhoqo said, glancing around.

Adeenya seethed and wished to say more, but after several breaths nodded. "Yes, sir," she said.

Jhoqo sighed. "You may as well tell her now," he said to Taennen.

"Yes, sir. I . . . experienced something similar," Taennen said.

"What is it? What are these ant-things doing?" Adeenya asked.

"They call themselves formians, Orir," Jhoqo said.

"Formians . . . where are they from? What are they doing here?"

"We don't know," Jhoqo said.

"Urir, I need—" Adeenya began.

Taennen stepped nearer her and shook his head. "We really don't, sir."

Adeenya was skeptical but decided she didn't have much choice. She had achieved more progress than she had expected to. "May I speak with them now that I know?" she asked.

"I suppose it couldn't hurt," Jhoqo said. "Once we've halted for meals. But I'll have your word that even your second-in-command doesn't learn of this. I want this no further than it's already gone."

"Agreed," she said.

Under the baking southern sun, the army stopped briefly to eat and rest. Adeenya followed Jhoqo and Taennen through the marching lines to where the prisoners were being guarded in a single-file line. A thin but strong rope bound their arms and formed a chain between each prisoner as they gnawed at waybread. The dozen or so humans and the halfling were at the front of the line, kept separate from the goblins and kobolds.

Behind them were the formians. Their flesh was dark but shone faintly iridescent in the bright sunlight. The formians were bound with double ropes—extra caution seemed prudent given their mysterious nature. The largest creature, the one who had felled Taennen, stood at the center of the others. The smaller formians seemed to surround the largest, as if protecting it. The cloths over their eyes did not seem to diminish their ability to be aware of one another as they flicked their antennae over the offered waybread. The Maquar guards kept several paces away from the formians, their crossbows trained on the creatures. Jhoqo signaled one of the guards to remove the gag from the largest creature's mouth.

"Go ahead, ask your questions. Anything you learn will be for your ears only," Jhoqo said. "And keep your voice down."

Adeenya moved close to the largest creature. "Who are you?" she asked.

The creature turned its head toward her, and Adeenya felt as though dozens of eyes were watching her even though she was looking only at the dark cloth encircling its head. After a long moment, the beast spoke in a voice that sounded like twenty voices speaking through a hollow log, all jumbled together and with gravel in their throats. It proceeded to say a word so long, so incomprehensibly full of syllables, that Adeenya was reminded of a magic spell she had heard before.

She fought off a shiver and picked the only syllable from

the garbled mess that could be made out. "Would it be all right to call you Guk?"

The formian twitched for a moment, the tiny append-ages on either side of its maw clacking as it said, "Yes."

Adeenya straightened herself and asked, "Are you . . . male or female?"

What Adeenya could only assume was a laugh, the sound of bird cries turned inside out and piled atop one another, burst from the creature and set her gooseflesh tingling.

"Male," Guk said.

"Why did you attack us?" she asked, wishing now she'd never demanded to interrogate the strange creature.

"For work, for the hive," Guk said.

"The hive?"

"My people."

"What does attacking us get your people?" she asked.

"Workers," Guk said.

"Slaves," Taennen interjected, stepping closer to Guk.

"The other creatures with you were workers?" she asked, glancing at Jhoqo. The commander's face was unreadable.

"All creatures should work for the hive," the formian said. "All creatures will."

"No one should be your slaves," Taennen said.

"Why?" Adeenya asked the formian. "Why should everyone work for your hive?"

"There is work," Guk replied. "There is always work. The work needs to be done."

"But what if we do not want to work for the hive?" she said.

"The work must be done. You will work. Every creature will work. No work is chaos. Chaos cannot be allowed. You will work."

Adeenya stepped away from the prisoners and took in a

deep breath. The formian's sort of devoted thought was dangerous. The world had experienced such zealous devotion before, and the results were never positive or pleasant.

"Do you see, now?" Jhoqo said, joining her.

"Aye, sir. We'll keep this from the troops," she said. She did not enjoy admitting the man was right, but the formian's dedication had certainly put her on guard.

A melodious but melancholy voice called out ahead of them. "Let me go!"

Adeenya turned to see a grim-faced halfling covered from head to toe in leather and furs waving his bound arms as best he could. He was standing at the back of the line of humans just in front of the goblins.

"My name's Corbrinn Tartevarr, miss. A little help?" he said.

Adeenya looked to Jhoqo who nodded for her to respond. The three officers moved closer to the human prisoners. Adeenya was relieved to leave the presence of the formians.

"I am Adeenya Jamaluddat, commander of the Durpari troops on this expedition. How do you find yourself fallen in with these creatures?" she asked, nodding toward Guk.

"He was a worker and will be again. Like you will become," Guk said from farther back in the line, his voice grating, like thrown ice shattering against a wall. Adeenya wondered if the blindfold inhibited the creature at all.

"Get that gag back on him," she shouted to the guards.

Corbrinn sighed. "What he said, I'm afraid. Well, at least that I was," the halfling said with a sneer toward the formian. "I'm from Thruldar in Luiren. I remember being with a caravan of folks from Var the Golden. I'm a woodsman and often act as a scout in these parts. I was guiding the caravan back from a successful trading trip to

Mulhorand. After that, everything gets a little fuzzy, but I know I was working for these things."

The sun glinted off the halfling's reddish blond curls. Adeenya boggled at how the halfling was not sweating himself dry in his many layers of clothing and furs.

"Why did you work for them?" she asked.

The halfling's eyes went to the ground for a moment before turning to rest upon her again. "It wasn't really like that. The reason didn't seem to matter . . . just the work." The halfling shrugged. "I can't explain it. It was like my body just did what they needed to be done, and I couldn't really stop it or even ask why I was doing it. But, I think the strangest part was that it was . . . somehow satisfying."

"Sir," she said, turning to Jhoqo, "we should let the humans and the halfling go, at least. They shouldn't be bound so close to those things. They might try to reassert their control over them again."

Taennen stiffened. "Sir, we can't allow that. No one should. . . ." he said, unable to finish his thought.

Jhoqo did not speak as he moved away, waving for the two to follow him. Adeenya followed, already knowing the man would say no. She did not know Jhoqo well, but he was not difficult to read at that moment. He wore his displeasure like a heavy cloak.

"Urir, these people did nothing wrong of their own will," she said. "Surely we must—"

Jhoqo stopped her with a raised hand. To her relief his scowl turned to a look of exhaustion, and he seemed to deflate with a long sigh. "Surely you see why I can't let them go yet? You worry about them falling back under the control of the formians? What if they are still under the control of those . . ."—his face curled in distaste—"things? How do we know how far that manipulation extends? We could set them loose only for them to come back and attack us to free their masters."

Adeenya sighed. Jhoqo was right.

"And even if they're not being controlled, even if they are the freest of spirits, look where we are," Jhoqo said, extending his arm in a wide arc. "This is the wilds, my children. Aerilpar. There's none worse."

Adeenya followed the man's gesture to the distant tree line. While small compared to the Lluirwood to the west, the Aerilpar Forest was home to dozens of clans of foul beasts that fought each other for power nearly as often as they fought the humans who tried to cleanse the woods of them.

Huge, ancient trees with twisted, gnarled limbs rose tall from the sparse grass all around them. Green and brown foliage dotted the edge of the woods, a sign of the heat. A branch of the Liontongue River far to the east fed the trees and allowed the forest to exist at all.

Taennen nodded. "Anyone we freed would be killed instantly."

"Or recruited," Jhoqo said.

"You're right," Adeenya said reluctantly. "We'll figure out how to deal with the humans once we arrive at Neversfall."

Jhoqo smiled. "Good. I'll leave it in your hands. Both of you," he said. "Now, I think it's time we got moving."

The Maquar commander offered a salute that Adeenya returned before he turned and walked away. The horns were blown to signal the soldiers' rest was done, and the trek to Neversfall would begin again.

Taennen walked beside her, stealing glances back at the big formian. His face revealed neither anger nor fear. He was curious. Adeenya recalled his earlier outburst and wondered what really had happened to Taennen on the battlefield.

"Thank you for backing my play, Durir," she said. "I appreciate the information."

"It seemed like the right thing to do, sir," he said. "Not that we learned anything."

"You're trying. It's more than some would do."

Taennen nodded. "My father always said—" he started but stopped when shouts erupted from behind them.

Adeenya spun to see a goblin's arm hit the ground. The creature shrieked in pain as its life's fluid pumped from the stump at its shoulder to splash into the dirt.

"Stand down!" Taennen shouted to a Maquar soldier with a bloody falchion in his hand. The man stood at attention, and the entire squad of guards and prisoners came to a halt. One of the small formians showed a trickle of blood on its abdomen, and another of the Maquar guards had his sword drawn and bloodied.

"What in all the One happened?" Taennen yelled, looking to the guard nearest the oozing beast.

"Sir! This one," he said, pointing to the bleeding formian, "suddenly moved and pushed the goblin out of marching file."

"And the goblin died for that?" Adeenya asked. When Taennen looked at her askance, she nodded and stepped back. These were his troops; this would go smoother if she did not interfere. Trying to command someone else's troops was like wearing a stranger's boots. The fit just wasn't there and never would be.

The Maquar with the sword answered, "I thought it was trying to flee, sir. I didn't see that thing push it."

Taennen sighed. "Get the prisoners ready to move again and be sure to secure the bindings. Remember, stay with a comrade when dealing with them. Watch your partner closely, make sure they're acting like . . . themselves," he said. He turned to the soldier wiping blood off his sword. "Take someone with you and bury that body, anhal," he added, pointing to the goblin's corpse. "Be quick about it and catch up to the line."

The man nodded and scooped the creature's remains into his arms.

"And someone get some attention for the wounded one," Adeenya said, motioning to the small formian.

"Go!" Taennen said when the soldiers did not move. One of them ran for a cleric.

Adeenya began to turn away, but Guk caught her eye. The formian's face was impossible to read, so new and strange were its features, but there was something in the way it turned blindly towards her that seemed full of intent. To do what, she could not guess, but it was there. Guk turned away, facing forward as the army began to march again. The guards unwound new rope and set about securing the creatures even more carefully.

Adeenya motioned for Taennen to walk with her. "The large one . . ."

He nodded. "I saw it, too, Orir."

They continued walking beside the ranks. After a few moments she spoke again. "You were saying something about your father, Durir?"

Taennen gave her a puzzled look and then nodded. "Yes. My father always said a man's intentions don't make him good—acting on them does."

Adeenya nodded, finding wisdom in the adage. "Sounds like a wise man."

Taennen sighed. "A fool and a criminal, I'm afraid, but everyone is due their moments of wisdom, I suppose."

"A criminal? Sounds like my father," she said with a

laugh which she cut short when she saw the look on her companion's face. "Really . . . a criminal?"

The man nodded, and she regretted her comment. "My apologies," she said.

"Mine's just a merchant like everyone else's."

Taennen chuckled. "Your family is one of the major chakas of Durpar. Everyone knows what they do."

Adeenya nodded and shrugged. Everyone knew of her family, but few actually *knew* them. Those who did rarely showed the kind of admiration she could see on Taennen's face.

"How did you end up working as a mercenary with a family legacy like yours?" Taennen said. "If I may ask, Orir."

She smiled. "I'm trading services instead of goods. What's the difference? At least this way I had to rely on myself and no one else to get where I am," she said. "I prefer it that way."

Taennen looked at her and tilted his head to one side. "Truly?"

"When your father is a famous—infamous, really—merchant, you don't see much of him. When you do, there's a lot . . ."

"To live up to?" Taennen asked.

She nodded and gave a half-smile. "And to live down."

"Still . . . I'd love that life," he said.

"Maybe," she said. They were approaching the front of the lines. Jhoqo would need to be informed of the goblin's death.

"I meant no offense, Orir. I've just always dreamed of having an honest man as my father. Someone who held the Adama close to his heart and lived his life with it every day," Taennen said.

She nodded. "I understand."

Taennen smiled and said, "My father always said that phrase meant only one of two things: either the person didn't understand, or they didn't want to talk about it anymore."

"He was quotable, wasn't he?" Adeenya said with a smile.

"Yes, sir."

"You speak of him as a wise man, yet condemn him as a criminal," she said.

Taennen shrugged. "Wisdom does not equal prudence. That's another of his."

"I'm sorry, Durir. That was much too personal of me," she said.

"No harm done, sir," Taennen said. His pace slowed, and she matched him. She lifted her waterskin to her lips and took a long drink. She offered the skin to Taennen, who declined.

"He was a tinkerer, I guess you could say. He made magical items for folks, mostly things to make life a little easier," Taennen said.

"Sounds like an honest living," Adeenya said.

"Aye, sir. It is, so long as you don't use your talents to provide aid to criminals," he said.

Adeenya waited a moment before leaning in toward him to prompt more details. She didn't need to.

"There was this woman from Var," he continued. "I remember she smelled of sage and lemons, and her clothing was spotless. Even her servant dressed better than I have in my entire life—silks and brocades and exotic fur trim. She came in to pick up her order—a pair of ruby earrings that my father had enchanted to help the wearer hear better. The woman tested the pieces and offered my father her praise and a bonus for the excellent work. I was always heartbright of him, but seeing this regal woman compliment him . . . I nearly swelled to bursting for him."

"That must have been a wonderful feeling," Adeenya said.

Taennen smiled wryly. "Yes, it was. Father asked the woman if her elderly mother, for whom the earrings had been made, could come by his shop sometime as he would like to make sure they were working well for her," Taennen said. "I remember her laugh. It was like . . . like that twitching sound a hare makes when it eats, only louder. She said she would be sure to stop by her mother's grave and ask the woman to come to his store. When father asked what she meant, the woman laughed harder and asked if he had really believed that story. When he said he had, the woman called him stupid, and even her servant sneered. She said a fool had never helped her beat her rivals in trade negotiations before, and she hoped he was honored to be the first."

"Eavesdropping? She wanted the earrings to help her eavesdrop on trade competitors?" Adeenya asked. "What did he do?"

"He asked for them back, to reverse the sale, but she refused and left. He didn't even try to stop her. Didn't even go after her," Taennen said.

"And the authorities?" Adeenya said.

"He never informed them," Taennen said, shifting his gaze to the distant tree line.

"Why? They would have believed him. There are trade dispute panels convened for situations like this," she said.

"I asked him to report her. Begged him, actually," Taennen said. "But he said we were too poor to lose the coin she had paid him. So he kept it. I knew it bothered him. It really showed. He aged several years in the few days after that incident."

"He felt guilty."

Taennen nodded. "But not enough to do the right thing."

"That must have been hard, growing up with a father you knew had done something illegal."

Taennen turned to look at her and she saw a buried anger there. "I didn't. I was raised by the Maquar after that. By not reporting the crime, he committed one."

"I don't understand."

"I reported him a tenday after it happened," Taennen said.

"You had him arrested?"

"One day I realized I couldn't live that way, and so I went to the local magistrate. A Maquar there on other business took my father into custody and offered me a place in the Maquar ranks," Taennen said.

Adeenya studied the young man. She'd had disputes with her father frequently, but betraying him, even if he had done something wrong . . . such extreme adherence to the law, such pragmatism, was unnatural. Taennen watched her. She schooled her face against her thoughts. "The Maquar was Jhoqo," she said.

"Yes. I left with him that day to train as a Maquar. Over the years we became close and he watched my progress. When I was ready for assignment, he made sure I wound up in his unit," Taennen said with a smile. He seemed lighter and brighter when talking about his surrogate father than he had when talking about his birth father.

"What happened to your father?"

Taennen's smile fell, and he turned away from her. "He was sentenced to hard labor for a year. I hear he lives in Kolapur now."

They walked in silence for a long time. The sun was well past its zenith, and they would camp soon.

Adeenya could think of nothing to say to Taennen, her mind reeling from his revelation. Betraying his father seemed such a cold thing to do, but the man walking beside her was warm and kind. She knew him very little, but she saw that much for certain.

She wondered how a such a simple incident had left him so single-minded in his dedication to truth. What had that cost him throughout his life? Certainly he had missed out on having his real father around, but it also must have made the rest of his life difficult. Life was full of situations that were best handled with restraint, flexibility, and openness. Had he developed those traits since his youth? Zealotry was dangerous, and Adeenya could not afford to take any chances. The question she needed to ask would cost her the bond she was forming with the man, but she was unwilling to risk not asking it.

"Durir, do you think the prisoners are safe?" she said.

Taennen stopped and turned to face her. "Sir?"

The rest of the troops continued their march. When she was not moving with them, they looked like a parade. "Well, Durir, I'm sure your troops are well trained, but they've already killed one prisoner and injured another."

"With all due respect, sir, my troops said the prisoner was trying to escape," he said. His tone was sharp and left no room to press.

"Very well. I will trust your faith in them," Adeenya said.

Taennen nodded. He sped his pace and grabbed one of the soldiers near him by the shoulder. "Go to the Durpari dorir. The dwarf. Tell him to send four soldiers, himself if he likes, to stand watch with our men over the prisoners."

The young man nodded and cast a glance to Adeenya before darting away.

"That wasn't necessary, Durir, but thank you," she said.

"A gesture of good will," Taennen said. He offered a small smile, but his shoulders and arms were stiff and he kept his strident pace. Though her words had stung him, Adeenya knew her concern had been valid, and she was never one to back away from a gut instinct. The sparkling image from her youth of the Maquar faded a little more.

✠
chapter five

Taennen walked between Jhoqo and Adeenya at the head of the marching lines, the thinning grass and hills ahead of them and the forest to their right. Taennen tried not to look at the Durpari woman.

Taennen was responsible for his soldiers. Questioning their ability or behavior was the same as questioning his. He glanced at Adeenya and then at Jhoqo. His commander would tell him to ignore the orir's doubt and to do his job as well as he always had. Taennen put aside the insult that itched at the edge of his pride and decided to do just that.

"Durir, a moment," Jhoqo said, his step slowing.

Taennen matched his pace, and they fell back from the front of the line. Adeenya watched them for a moment before turning back to the front of the march.

"Yes, sir," Taennen said.

Jhoqo said nothing for several moments before speaking. "Son, why are there mercenaries near my prisoners?"

"Sir, the orir was concerned about their safety. There was an incident, sir. One of the goblin prisoners is dead."

"Explain, soldier," Jhoqo said.

"Sir, our people thought it was trying to escape. We think the formians were involved," Taennen said.

62

"That is unfortunate, but that does not explain why our duties are being performed by Durpari," Jhoqo said. "Were my earlier misgivings about sharing information and responsibilities with the Durpari unclear, Durir?"

"No, sir. Maquar still guard the prisoners, sir," Taennen said.

"I did not ask if they did. I can see they still do."

"Yes, sir."

Jhoqo clapped him on the shoulder and said, "Son, we need to stay in control of this situation. Now our control is . . . less than total."

"I am sorry, sir," Taennen said. His decision had been a rash one, like that which had cost the lives of his men. At this rate, he'd be demoted back to anhal by the time they reached Neversfall.

"Son, you know that sometimes you have to trust what I say even if you don't see the reason for it, don't you?"

"Sir, of course, sir."

"Taennen, do you trust me on this?"

Taennen looked the man in the eyes. "Yes. You know I do."

"Good. Thank you for that."

"I'll rescind the order, sir," Taennen said.

"No, no. That will put the orir on edge. I would rather have the Durpari settled, not wary," Jhoqo said. "I simply don't understand why you are second-guessing my commands. Have I done something to diminish your faith in me?"

Taennen felt as though he had been hit in the gut with a club and said, "No, sir! Not at all, sir!"

Jhoqo's face hardened again as he said, "Then in the future, Durir, you will respect my wishes and not give orders which countermand mine, understood?"

Taennen snapped to attention and said, "Yes, sir!"

Taennen followed his commander and fell into step next to Adeenya. The woman gave a friendly nod, which Taennen returned. Had her doubt of him forced his hand? Had he given in to her only to prove her wrong, or did he believe it fair that her soldiers join in on guarding the prisoners? Taennen wasn't sure and decided it didn't matter since the time for doubt was past. He settled his mind into the march, an unconscious rhythm beating out in his mind as his feet made contact with the ground over and over.

Jhoqo's wisdom and helpful nature made the constant marching easier. Taennen listened as Jhoqo pointed to the trees looming in the distance at the edge of the Aerilpar. They were marching parallel to the woods, perhaps a dozen long bowshots from the treeline.

Jhoqo spoke to all nearby, but seemed to focus his attention on Adeenya. "Do you see that darker patch of trees there to the left? The ones near the slight mound?" Jhoqo asked.

Adeenya's eyes followed the Maquar's hand and she nodded.

"Do you know why they are like that?" Jhoqo asked.

Adeenya shook her head. She did not seem to think about it for even a moment. Taennen saw the annoyance on Jhoqo's face, but the man said nothing ill of her lack of an attempt.

Taennen stepped forward and said, "Is it because of heavy passage in that spot, sir?"

Jhoqo smiled and nodded. "That's it exactly, son. Well done," he said.

Taennen returned the smile and fell back into his spot in the pacing order. He glanced at Adeenya, who had turned her eyes back to the horizon ahead, away from the treeline.

"You see, the trees have been somewhat damaged by the constant passing of the foul beasts of the forest that they spend their resources repairing themselves rather than growing stronger, bigger and brighter," Jhoqo said.

Taennen had assumed as much but it was good to hear his commander affirm his conclusions. "Fascinating, sir."

Jhoqo pointed to a crumbling hump of dirt near the passage. "Ah, further evidence of the beasts—that mound there . . . That's probably their attempt at burying a kill or their own feces. Maybe others use it and it grows all the time, covering their filth," Jhoqo said.

Taennen's nose wrinkled, but he nodded. That made sense. Taennen glanced toward Adeenya again. She had moved several paces ahead, probably out of earshot. Her loss, he thought.

The mage Khatib stepped up next to Jhoqo, his hands cradling a parchment. "Sir, I do not wish to interrupt, but I have checked the maps. We should reach the citadel inside of two bells," he said.

"Excellent," Taennen said with a smile.

Next to him, having fallen back from her lead, Adeenya said, "Yes . . . excellent."

Jhoqo called for a stop after another half-league and took advantage of the break to move himself a little closer to the woods. Taennen gave the man his privacy and moved to check on the prisoners. Jhoqo clearly had a personal interest in the woods, and Taennen left him to it. He watched as his commander stood several hundred paces away and stared at the forest, his back to his troops. The soldiers took the time to rest, their feet no doubt pounding like Taennen's from the long walk.

After a short time, Jhoqo returned to them, and they resumed their march. The air was dry, and Taennen sipped from his waterskin frequently as the dust of the plains coated his tongue.

The Maquar and Durpari, though not disdainful of one another, marched in separate groups with several paces between them. Adolescents at coming-of-age ceremonies could have learned much from the divisiveness the soldiers exhibited. Trust was difficult, he supposed. Their mission promised no shortage of danger, and the two forces would need to find some cohesion soon.

"Orir," Taennen said, stepping closer to Adeenya. "We must find a way for our people to bond. Their lives may well depend on it soon."

"I agree, Durir. Suggestions?"

Jhoqo's voice broke in as they crested a hill. "I think it may be moot for the moment. If this does not bring them together, I am uncertain what would."

Taennen followed Jhoqo's gaze to where a form took shape in the distance. Tall and thin, it stood out dark and solid against the bright blue sky. It was farther off than his naked eye could distinguish, so he pulled a spyglass from his belt and held it to his eye. In the small circle of his view, Taennen saw it for the first time: Neversfall.

Through the lens it appeared like some child's construct of blocks. High walls on each side held what was likely a large courtyard. Two lean towers stood on each side of a third, larger tower that rose into the sky to at least twice the height of the others. What could only be windows showed as dark spots at a distance. The wood came from the Aerilpar, no doubt, but the stone? Taennen had always heard that magic was involved in the making of the tower, and now, seeing the sheer size of the thing, he believed it.

He handed the lens to Jhoqo who stared through it for

a long time before returning it. Murmurs wove their way through the marching troops as the structure came into sight.

"Very impressive," Jhoqo said.

Taennen offered the spyglass to Adeenya who studied the citadel through the lens for several breaths before handing the spyglass back to him.

"It makes you ponder how they craft such wonders, doesn't it?" she asked.

Taennen nodded.

"Well, no time like the present to find out—right Durir?" Adeenya said, before turning to Jhoqo and saying loudly, "What's our approach, sir?"

Jhoqo called the troops to a halt with a wave of his arms and shouted orders that followed down the lines. "Take twenty people, half Maquar and half Durpari, and scout outside the citadel, around its perimeter."

Adeenya affirmed the order and saluted.

Jhoqo looked to Taennen before he continued. "You will take ten more people, again from both parties, and secure the entrance. Once the perimeter is secure, scout the inside. The rest of us will stay here and guard the prisoners until you confirm the area is safe."

Taennen accepted the order and motioned for Adeenya to lead the way through the lines to choose their squads. Jhoqo barked orders for troops to form up and to secure the prisoners in a holding position.

"Bright and true, Orir," Taennen said as he walked beside the Durpari commander.

"Thank you, Durir. Splitting our units into combined commands should yield some results as well," she said.

The two leaders chose twenty of their own soldiers and, after brief summations of special skills that existed among the troops, split them evenly. Adeenya rallied her new unit and began a wide circle to the west that would take them around the distant citadel. Taennen asked each of the Durpari soldiers in his command to state their names as a means of introduction. He repeated each name, hoping to commit it to memory. Impersonal commanders often led troops that did not care about their leader. Taennen never wanted to be that leader.

He offered a final salute to Jhoqo before moving toward the citadel at a jog, his troops behind him. Neversfall came into clearer focus with each step. Taennen felt the itch of mystery and intrigue but had learned that curiosity could kill even more easily than a sword. He called for sharp eyes from his soldiers and took pleasure in his vocation and the opportunities for discovery it offered.

After a considerable jog, Taennen called a stop and put his spyglass to his eye again. He scanned the area around the citadel, hoping the proximity might yield more results. He expected some sort of scarring on the walls, bodies on the ground, or some sign of disturbance. He found nothing but dirt, grass, and stone walls. He continued his scan to find the edge of the woods and was lowering his spyglass when a splash of color caught his eye, something that seemed out of place. He tried to focus in on where he had seen it but saw only green, leafy plants and brown tree trunks. Everything appeared normal until he realized that some of the plants were bouncing as though they had been disturbed. Taennen watched the area for several more moments, seeing nothing. He tucked his spyglass away once again and resumed his march to the citadel. If something had been in the woods, it was gone. Their mission could not wait. Taennen's excitement turned to caution as he approached the gates of Neversfall.

Rectangular blocks of stone as long as a man were carved smooth and fit together tightly to form the outer wall of Neversfall, with each block reaching a height near six men high. Clay and mud lined the cracks between the stones to seal out the gusts of wind common to plains, though the craftsmanship was extraordinary and the lines were thin and hard to find. Crenellated walks topped the wall, and narrow slabs of stone taller than a man stood every sixty or so paces atop the walkway. Each slab had an opening carved in the middle, arrow slits for archers. Two men could stand behind the slab atop the wall, totally protected. They could alternate their shots through the slit while still remaining well covered—a clever design.

The force that had come to Neversfall previously had also been comprised of both Maquar and Durpari troops. Adeenya wondered if those two forces had similar difficulties meshing together. Moreover, she wondered if her expedition would find that company and in what condition. She kept a fast pace, ordering her troops to spread wide and look for anything out of place as they circled the citadel west to east.

Behind the walls she could see the towers of the citadel, three giant fingers stroking the sky. The two smaller towers rose to twice the height of the wall, and the central tower was half that tall again. The high but sparse grass of the plains had been burned away from the citadel for several hundred paces. Adeenya ordered a contingent of her troops to the grassline to ensure no surprises waited there. She hoped to find clues to the location of the former force sent to the citadel. She feared the worst. The squads should have seen someone by then.

The area around Neversfall was quiet, with a soft breeze rustling the grass in light gusts. Adeenya continued around the citadel to the north side. To her east was the Aerilpar, to her west open plains. Though stories abounded about the Aerilpar, Adeenya found the plains more foreboding. Forests hid their secrets in their dark depths and that was understood. One walked through a forest on guard. Plains, though, had their secrets hidden in the open, where they were least expected.

All the walls of the citadel looked identical. She saw no damage and that bothered her even more. If the previous force of Durpari and Maquar soldiers were dead, what had killed them? She saw no scorch marks, no stains from hot oil being poured through the machicolations onto attackers. Not even a single errant arrow in the ground.

Adeenya could see the disquiet on the faces of her troops. She picked up her pace to reach the gate of Neversfall. The mystery ate at her, and she wanted it resolved, regardless of the outcome. As she rounded the corner, she saw the large, dark doors of the citadel. They stood open, four of Taennen's force guarding them. They saluted as Adeenya approached.

"Orir, the durir awaits you inside," one of the guards said as she reached the gate. The doors were three men high and two wide. They were easily as thick as Adeenya's upper arm, as were the iron bars that stood nearby to hold the doors against attackers.

She walked through the opening into the courtyard of Neversfall. Adeenya split her troops into four squads, commanding each to examine the inside of one outer wall, looking for signs of struggle and checking the walls for weaknesses.

Adeenya continued toward the center of the courtyard. Like the walls of the citadel, the three towers were made of smooth, dark stone. In addition to the towers, small one- and two-story buildings were spread around the courtyard, most of them built on short, sturdy stone pilings. Between the stilts were ditches about knee deep.

"Fire," Taennen said beside her.

"What?" she asked.

"The trenches. If an attacker were to lob fire over the walls, it could spread along the ground, but without a strong wind to force it along, it wouldn't make it past the trenches," he said. "It protects the buildings and gives the citadel forces a place to escape the fire."

"Arrows too," she said. "You could shelter yourself from arrows under each building."

Taennen nodded. "Yes, sir, you could. Good eyes, Orir."

The courtyard itself was large and well kept. Each wall looked to be twice as long as the tallest tower was high, giving the interior courtyard a spaciousness that the other buildings did not fill up. No buildings at all stood along the northern wall, likely intended to be used as training grounds and an assembly area. There were also no signs that anyone had ever occupied the citadel. A chill ran up Adeenya's spine.

She climbed the short steps to one of the barracks. Ten cots lined each wall, with space for many more. A bedroll was neatly folded at the foot of each and twenty chests sat on the floor. Two Maquar were examining the contents.

"What have you found, durir?" she asked.

"Just these things, sir," Taennen answered. He held up a cheap brass symbol of the Adama. "It's as if they never left."

"No bodies? No discarded weapons?"

Taennen shook his head. "I wish I could say there was any clue at all, sir, but so far we've seen nothing. The food

71

stores are intact, the citadel's log shows a final entry that describes no problems at all. The gate locks still function, and from what we've seen, the personal belongings of the lost company are still here."

Adeenya shook her head. "This is damned strange."

"No doubt about that. I'll call in the commander," he said. "Unless you object, Orir?"

"Go ahead," she said.

Taennen nodded and shouted to one of his men, instructing the soldier to inform Jhoqo to bring in the rest of the troops.

"The towers have been checked?" Adeenya asked, facing the monoliths.

"Yes, sir."

Adeenya moved toward the tallest of the three towers. Though the citadel itself was named Neversfall, it was named for the tall central tower. The stones comprising the tower were smaller and more rounded than those that made up the outer wall. Though they were the same color, the tower stood out against the backdrop of the wall as separate, different in a profound way. Impossible and distant, Neversfall tower seemed to be watching them.

"I've never seen anything that tall. I never would have thought I might in my life," Taennen said beside her.

" 'Every day we are told what we cannot do, what can never be done. I dream of a day when the nevers will all fall away and leave only what we can do,' " Adeenya said, staring at the rising spire.

"Sir?" Taennen said.

She smiled. "A quote from Jeradeem himself, Durir. It's where this place gets its name."

Taennen said nothing, but Adeenya could see he liked the idea of the prophet's words. Jeradeem was quoted a thousand times every day in the Shining South, and that one had always been Adeenya's favorite. Its hope-filled message about putting aside limitations had inspired her from an early age. She might not revere adherence to the Adama, Jeradeem's creation, like others she knew, but she appreciated the wisdom the man had left behind.

"Commander coming in," boomed a voice from behind them. Adeenya spun to see Jhoqo leading the rest of the expedition through the gates.

"You'll need to update him," Adeenya said.

Taennen nodded but then hesitated. "Orir, perhaps to continue setting a good example for our troops, you could advise him?"

Adeenya smiled. "A fine idea, Durir. I appreciate the opportunity. Thank you."

"I'll give the central tower a closer look," he said with a salute, then began moving in that direction. The anticipation on his face was clear, and she envied him his exploration.

Adeenya moved to meet Jhoqo, reminding herself that, although she was his equal in rank, he was in command and consolidating the two forces ensured a higher chance of safety for her people. Soldiers shouted back and forth to share their findings as they searched more buildings, the courtyard echoing with their voices. Adeenya heard every word and intended to make sure Jhoqo did as well.

"Sir, the citadel has been secured," she said to Jhoqo as his eyes scanned the courtyard. Behind him, soldiers set about unloading the few horses that accompanied them, and lieutenants divided men into smaller units to continue sweeping the fortress.

"Good, commander. Where is the holding area? I want these prisoners secured."

"Aye, sir." Adeenya shouted to Marlke who was just stepping out of the door to one of the smaller buildings in the courtyard. "Dorir, work with the Maquar terir, and secure the prisoners," she said.

"Yes, sir," Marlke replied before jogging off toward the enormous Loraica. The two standing near one another was like something out of a bard's comic tale.

Adeenya faced Jhoqo again. The man stood in the center of the organized chaos with shouts and shuffling boxes all around him, but he never seemed shaken. He was a military man, and whether securing a fortress or taking over a village, the satisfaction at claiming something was rooted deep within him, as it was in any military leader.

"Sir, I recommend we bunk most of the troops in the buildings in the northern two quadrants. They're closer to the open grounds should we need space in a hurry, and they're farther from the front gate if we need time to prepare," she said.

"Let's have a look at one of these, Orir," Jhoqo said.

Adeenya opened the door to one of the many smaller structures inside the courtyard and stepped inside. Inside was another simple arrangement with narrow beds and storage chests for forty soldiers. At her best estimate, Adeenya guessed Neversfall could sleep more than four hundred souls in these buildings alone, and the courtyard was spacious with plenty of room for expansion. Beyond that, there was only the forest hemming in Neversfall's growth to the east.

It was a true citadel, a small city, there in the monster-filled wastes. It was a magnificent and frightening prospect at the same time. Neversfall was positioned perfectly to hold out against the beast scourge in Aerilpar, but the merchant bureaucrats of Durpar and Estagund would be anxious to fill it with stands from which merchants would sell their goods to civilians living in and around the fortress. It would not take long for talk of colonization to come after that. Years, maybe decades, would be needed to clear the area of the monster tribes, if that were possible at all. Commerce couldn't wait that long, so the bureaucrats would attempt to civilize this land before they tamed it. They always did. Adeenya wondered if it would even be a full year before the first traders came to the citadel with their silks and exotic spices to trade with merchants from the north.

"They are all similar to this one?" Jhoqo asked.

"Some less suited for soldiers, sir" she said, kicking one of the storage lockers.

Jhoqo grinned and gave a nod. "Civilians must sleep, too, or so they tell me, daughter."

"Even snakes sleep, sir," she said.

Jhoqo raised an eyebrow and watched her for a long moment. Adeenya chided herself for giving in to the desire to peck at the man, but she did not look away. To her relief, Jhoqo walked out into the courtyard, motioning for her to join him. They walked in silence for a few moments, passing another small building on their way to the towers.

"You found nothing on your sweep of the exterior?" he asked.

"Nothing, sir," she said.

He held her gaze a bit longer before speaking, "I need to know that you and your people are with me," he said without looking at her.

"Of course, Urir. We are with you."

He nodded. "Together we can make this work. You know that, right?"

Adeenya gave her assent and smiled. While his eyes were

upon her, she saw in them warmth, but something else hid in his gaze. Something she had seen often in her father.

"Neversfall will be a bastion of mercantile wonders, Orir. We will usher into this wild land a new age of trade and success," he said, his smile widening.

"Prosperity would be excellent, sir. The local people are having a rough time right now."

"Exactly why this place, this citadel, is needed."

"Yes, sir," she said.

He stopped and looked hard at her. "Do you not see it? The daughter of the greatest of Durpari sellers does not see it?"

She arched an eyebrow and pursed her lips. "See what?"

"This will be the finest Southern achievement of the century. Look over there." He pointed to an empty spot in the courtyard. "That's where we'll put a meeting hall for all the chakas represented in Neversfall." He pointed to another vacant spot. "And there will be the best faukri you've ever tasted, served by some overlooked chef in Assur who will find his second chance here."

The man's enthusiasm was hard to resist. He practically shone with excitement as he described his vision of the place. However, her reservations were strong, and she doubted the transformation would be as easy as the man beside her made it sound.

"Then there is much work to do," she said with a slight smile. "Many monsters to slay, if all of these people are to be safe."

The smile slid from Jhoqo's face, but he nodded. "Yes. To work, then. Please work with Loraica to sort out sleeping arrangements. Let's mix the troops so they can come to know and rely upon one another even more."

"I will use that building," Jhoqo said, pointing to a

small structure near the center of the northern half of the housing area, "as my command office. Find me there when things are more settled."

Adeenya saluted and took her leave of Jhoqo. She cast her gaze around the courtyard looking for Loraica. She was not surprised to see the massive woman already making use of the training yard at the back of the citadel. A handful of Maquar and Durpari gathered to watch the woman spar with two men.

Loraica held a wooden falchion in her right hand and a medium, square shield in her left. The Maquar she faced off against was a large man with a wooden practice halberd, while the Durpari man wielded two long wooden swords which he twirled in a showy display before moving to his left to attempt to flank the Maquar terir. Loraica did not move. Her arms were taut with preparedness and her face serene.

The Maquar soldier pitted against her nodded to his Durpari counterpart and, with a guttural bark, swung the halberd from his hip driving toward Loraica's left side. The large woman moved her shield to intercept the blow as though it were coming at her from a league away. The head of the halberd rang off the metal of her shield with a loud thud, but Loraica did not flinch. She stepped toward the man while all the while keeping her eyes on her other opponent.

The Durpari launched a feint with one sword and a low stab with the other. Loraica knocked the lower attack away with her own blade while side-stepping the feint. The Maquar man pulled the haft of his weapon in close, adjusting his grip. He thrust the weapon toward Loraica as he took a small leap forward. With speed unimaginable for her size, Loraica deflected the stab with her shield and spun her body to face him. She brought the blade edge of the falchion down across the wooden pole of his weapon with a thunderous crash. The man tugged hard, pulling back a stump of a weapon in time to watch the wooden bladed head fall to the ground in a puff of dust.

With her back to the Durpari, Adeenya thought Loraica doomed. Breaking the man's halberd had been impressive, but that would be of little use if Loraica's other opponent could simply step in and finish her off. The Durpari saw the same opportunity and darted in toward Loraica's back.

An experienced fighter and no fool, the mercenary stabbed with one blade while keeping the other in a defensive posture. It was well he did, for Loraica spun fast, sending her opponent's thrust out wide with a stroke of her shield. Her falchion dived for the Durpari, but to no avail as his sword deflected the blow.

The Durpari was far from safe, though. Though he held against the monstrous swipe, he stumbled back from the raw force of the blow. That instant gave Loraica enough time to spin again and send the man flying with a smack of her shield into her opponent's torso.

Loraica dropped her weapons and helped the man to his feet. She turned to face her Maquar opponent who laughed and held his hands up in surrender after dropping the remnants of his broken weapon. The small gathered crowd gave a cheer and Loraica smiled.

Adeenya thought perhaps she could come to like the Maquar third in command.

✠

chapter six

Curving stairs built into the walls wound upward into the darkness of Neversfall Tower. Taennen felt a surge of excited energy and sprinted up the steps two at a time like a child curious to explore a new hidden place. The lack of decorative flourishes inside the tower spoke to its utility. Taennen had peered into one of the smaller towers and noticed a few paintings hung on the wall and plain draperies adorned the windows. The smaller towers must have been intended for visiting dignitaries or honored travelers. Neversfall stood in the middle of nowhere, but it could be used as a resting point on long journeys to destinations north and west of the South.

At the top of the stairs, Taennen discovered a small door. He stopped and stared at the portal. It was like every other door he had seen in his life, but something at the back of his mind stayed his hand as he reached for the handle. He looked closely, seeing no inscriptions or obvious traps.

"You are wise to leave it," came a voice from beside him.

Taennen spun to find the wizard Khatib hovering in midair next to him. Tight robes in shimmering shades of blue adorned the husky man. His narrow mustache and scraggly beard belied his age, but his dark, lined face showed the strain of many years of hard study. A missing finger and burn-scarred arms indicated years of wielding his art in the field of war for the glory of the rajah. Unlike many practitioners, Khatib had always enjoyed being in the field, commanding magic instead of just studying it.

"I've finished my examination of the citadel," the wizard said. "I detected no traces of magic, except for within this tower. And it's heavily enchanted."

"Surely we can get inside," Taennen said.

Khatib chuckled and drifted forward to alight on the stone floor, calling his hovering spell to an end. "Of course, sir. You simply need to know the means of entry."

Khatib closed his eyes and his fingers began a dance, weaving all about but never touching the door. He spoke soft words that Taennen could not understand. The wizard opened his eyes and examined the door for a few moments, his smile growing wider and wider. "If only you could see what I'm seeing, Taennen."

Taennen remembered his father telling him that there were ways of seeing magical spells in places that normal people could not see them. He often spoke of the incredible light thrown off by waiting magic in the devices he crafted.

"The marvel of this is that it can be dismissed," Khatib said.

"Dismissed?"

"Whoever built this door knew that not everyone who would need to use this tower would be a master of the art," he said, turning a pedagogical eye on Taennen. "I can lock or unlock it with the proper words. That will allow you poor souls unschooled in the Art to pass when you have need to do so."

"Your spell revealed the words to you?"

"No, no. My spell showed me what is there. I was given the words before we left."

"When Jhoqo received the order to secure Neversfall?" Taennen asked. Khatib nodded.

Which meant Jhoqo hadn't trusted Taennen with the passphrase. With his performance on the mission, Taennen wasn't sure he could blame his commander. He wanted to share in everything with Jhoqo, all of the responsibilities. But Jhoqo had judged him unfit in this case, and he was right.

"Unlock it, wizard," Taennen said.

Khatib uttered a string of words in some arcane tongue. To Taennen's eyes there was no change, but Khatib stepped aside and waved an arm toward the portal, inviting Taennen to enter. Taennen trusted the wizard and reached for the handle, pushing the door inward. His heart pounded against his chest. He had no idea what to expect beyond the door, but he was unable to contain his excitement at seeing it firsthand.

As the door swung open, the brightness of the circular room shocked his eyes. Taennen blinked several times, dancing afterimages in whites and pinks filling his vision. In sharp contrast to the dim stairwell, the room atop the tower was open, airy, and filled with sunlight. Instead of solid walls, it had only corner supports, holding up the roof, leaving the space between empty. Taennen stepped toward one of the window openings and looked out. The vast expanse of land opened before him, and he could see across the top of the Aerilpar, or at least part of it, to the east.

Taennen was put in mind of his training from his youth. One of his instructors had used tiny wooden models of soldiers, siege engines, even flora and fauna the size of garnishes to demonstrate mock battles. The world below him, the real world, was little more than that from his vantage point. He moved to the west window of the tower and looked down to see his fellow soldiers moving about the courtyard. He could barely make out details, their faces blurred by the distance to the ground. He moved back to the eastern window. The treetops of the Aerilpar became an ocean of green. He felt as though he were floating, lost amidst their waves.

Behind him, Khatib gasped. Taennen turned to see the man squinting as he stared at a stone table in front of one of the windows, identical to three other tables in front of the other windows. Taennen examined the table in front of him. Crystals, evenly spaced, seemed to grow from the stone tabletop. Some crystals were clusters of a dozen or more, others stood tall by themselves in a variety of shapes.

"They glow even to my eyes," Taennen said. "What are they?" The crystals ranged in color from amber to red, green to chartreuse, blue to the dark of midnight.

"They control Neversfall," Khatib said, kneeling before one of the tables. He ran his fingers along one of the crystals and giggled giddily. "Fascinating."

"What do you mean?" Taennen asked.

The wizard moved to the table on the southern side and studied the crystals there for a few moments before grasping two of them and tracing patterns across their surfaces with his fingers.

"Would you like to see the Curnas?" Khatib asked, pointing toward the southern window.

"How do you mean?" Taennen said, turning to face where the man had indicated.

Taennen stepped backward when an image began to form before him where the southern window had been a moment before. The northern peaks of the Curna Mountains shone before his eyes, like a reflection on water but clearer and more distinct. The rocks and trees waved in pulsing rhythm, like an image on a sheet blown by the wind.

"How?" Taennen asked.

The view changed, moving even closer to the mountains. Taennen could see a bear scratching its flabby body on the trunk of a tree.

"That's . . ." he said. "That's over a hundred leagues away."

Khatib nodded. "What better gift to grant a watch tower?"

"You can do that in every direction?" he asked, spinning his gaze around the room.

"Yes."

"Jhoqo will want to see this," Taennen said.

"I'm sure he will," Khatib said. "He was quite interested when they told us about it."

Taennen eyed the man. "You knew of this too?"

Khatib shrugged but affirmed. "Just Jhoqo and myself. They felt we needed to know about the tools that would be at our disposal."

Taennen thanked the man and started past him toward the stairs.

"Wait," Khatib said. "It does so much more."

Taennen turned to face the man. The wizard's smile was contagious. His lined face shone with the merriment usually expressed by children showing off new toys.

"Like what?" Taennen asked.

Khatib waved him over to the northern window. The wizard's hands darted among the crystals on the table, twisting some, pushing others. A low hum tickled Taennen's ears as the crystals began to glow even more brightly.

The view through the northern window shifted, drawing in close and tight on a section of ground. Taennen blinked again, surprised by the closeness of the view. He could see individual rocks and flowering plants that dotted the plains.

"There—that large, light-colored rock," Khatib said, pointing to the image in the window.

"Yes?"

"That rock lies approximately half a league away. Please use that spyglass of yours to locate it," Khatib said.

Taennen drew out his spyglass and stepped toward the window. Khatib waved a hand and the closeup image shrank to consume half the window. Taennen stood next to the hovering image and looked out the unhindered portion of the window. He scanned the ground until he found the rock.

"I have it," he said.

"Excellent. You have seen me use a spell before that emits small missiles of light?"

"Yes," Taennen said.

"Watch the stone carefully," Khatib said.

Taennen held his gaze on the rock. Behind him, Khatib murmured arcane words for a moment. A low buzzing sound vibrated in his ears but he held his gaze on the rock. A few heartbeats later, darts of light plowed into the rock, tossing it on its side, and left a blackened hole in the ground where the rock had been. Taennen jerked back a step withdrawing the spyglass from his eye.

"By all the One," he said.

Khatib chuckled. "Fantastic, isn't it?"

"The tower did that?"

"Oh no. I cast the spell as you have seen me do. The tower allowed me to do it from this distance with that level of accuracy," Khatib said.

"You could kill a man that far away," Taennen said.

"Oh, most definitely."

Taennen turned to face the man. "What else?"

Khatib pointed to a cluster of crystals on the right side of the table. "I can open, close and lock the gate from here. And," he said, pointing to another crystal, "sound an alarm here." He shifted to another set of the crystals, "This one is how we report to command in Estagund."

"This is amazing," Taennen said. "Does each table contain the same controls?"

Khatib nodded. "It was designed so that four masters of the Art," he said with a slight bow, "could each defend one direction from the citadel. With these, I and three others could hold off an army trying to assault Neversfall without risking any of our soldiers in combat. Lucky me, I get it to myself for the nonce."

Taennen gazed out the eastern window. "This is amazing. I would not trust it to be true had I not seen it for myself."

"It is a powerful tool."

"It provokes a frightening question," Taennen said.

"Anyone can abuse power, Taennen, but I should hope you trust me," the wizard said.

"Not that, Khatib. I mean, with all of this power at their disposal, what in the name of all the One could have possibly come to take the lost regiment?" Taennen said.

Khatib thought for a moment before saying, "Perhaps they too felt the price of hiring proper defenders was too high. Let's hope we do a better job with what we've been allotted."

Taennen gazed out over the Aerilpar, the dark space between the trees drawing his attention. He pointed to where he had seen the splash of color upon his arrival and said, "Show me the forest."

The duty and sleeping assignments had been an easy matter. Adeenya was glad to know her guess about Loraica had been correct. The Maquar woman was not only a fine warrior but a well-organized and thoughtful planner as well. The two women had parted ways when Jhoqo had tasked Loraica with staffing the walls with guards and archers. At the same time, he'd asked Adeenya to check on the prisoners.

All around her the courtyard was alive with activity. Soldiers unloaded supplies and moved furniture from building to building to suit their purposes. Adeenya had left it to Marlke to spread the word about sleeping assignments. She strode toward the building that housed the strange formians and changed her mind, deciding first to visit the other prisoners.

The formians and goblins had been placed in Neversfall's cells, while the humans resided in separate barracks under guard but not in cells as they had offered nothing but cooperation. Between the cell houses, Adeenya nodded to a pair of guards who manned a small patrol station. A small, round wall, looking like nothing so much as the top of a well, stood between each of the cell buildings. Guards could be stationed there to keep close eyes on the prisoners. Their presence, in spite of the intense security of the cell houses themselves, spoke volumes about the perceived dangers of the formians.

Adeenya accepted the salutes of the guards outside the small structure housing the humans and went inside. She paused a few moments to let her eyes adjust to the darkness, as the room's tiny windows provided very little light. The place already smelled of sweat and felt twice as warm as outside from the lack of airflow and the number of bodies occupying the small space. The handful of humans milled about, talking in small groups or sleeping, presumably exhausted after what must have been a grueling march for most of them.

"Good day!" came the high voice of the halfling Corbrinn. He bounded up from a bed and came to greet her.

"Hello. Are they treating you well enough?" she asked, having no idea what to say.

The halfling laughed but nodded his head. "Well enough for a prisoner who ought not be one, I suppose."

Adeenya began to apologize but stopped short when a high-pitched, repetitive screech issued from outside. She dashed out the door to see a crowd of men scrambling away from the northeast corner of the courtyard. The guards near her could offer no explanation, but she needed none as she caught sight of a man plummeting from the top of the wall to the inner grounds, an arrow in his neck. Adeenya started off toward the center of the courtyard to find out what was happening.

"Let me fight!" Corbrinn shouted, staying back from the guards outside the door but looking eager to leave the confines of the prison.

A few of the humans behind him shouted their agreement and offered to fight as well. Adeenya offered the halfling an apologetic look and ordered the guards to stay their post and defend the prisoners should it come to that.

She put them from her mind and dashed toward the towers. Who could be attacking? How could they know there was anyone in the fortress for them to attack so soon? Not for the first time since they'd arrived, Adeenya wondered what had happened to the forces that had occupied

Neversfall. She hoped she'd stay alive long enough to ponder the question further.

The courtyard erupted with activity as soldiers poured out of the small buildings and piled into the center of the citadel. A Durpari soldier, whom she couldn't see clearly enough to identify, fell from the eastern wall near her as she ran. His body tumbled through the air to land face-down, an arrow protruding from his side. Adeenya sprinted toward the staircase that joined the eastern and southern walls. She shouted for soldiers to follow her as she ran. A handful, Maquar and Durpari, fell in behind her as she took the stairs two at a time. As she neared the top, Adeenya looked into the courtyard to see that the invaders had already penetrated its area. They wore dark clothing with fabric masks covering their faces. She scanned the courtyard and discovered the gates had been closed.

Adeenya set the thought aside as she drew her sword, reached the top of the stairs, and found herself standing face to face with a man covered in animal skins. She muscled hard to her left against her opponent, pushing the man back, and feigned a high strike with her sword. She longed for her spear, but she hadn't been carrying it as she explored the citadel.

The mustached attacker swung a slender sword up high to block, hopping backward. Adeenya twisted her wrist, changing her blade's direction and sending it into the meat of the man's thigh. His scream rattled in her ear but she ignored it. She stabbed the blade into his stomach as he screamed again and doubled over. She pulled the sword free and turned to find a new foe before the man had even collapsed.

She caught a Durpari soldier out of the corner of her eye. The man stood over one body and was driving hard toward another enemy. Adeenya tried to size them up. All of the attackers wore animal hides, but they fought with obvious training and finesse.

An arrow flew past her head. She ducked low and saw the source of the shot. An archer was nocking another arrow some fifty paces away on the adjacent wall. Adeenya charged the man, knowing that he would get at least one more shot off before she reached him and that she could not let him loose another. She pumped her long legs hard and could feel the sweat trickling down her neck and back.

Running as hard as she could, she'd crossed only half the distance to the archer as he took aim, and she doubted the man would miss again. She pulled her arm back and threw her sword as hard as she could. It spun sideways through the air, a nimble hawk diving toward its prey, emitting a keening cry as it sailed. The blade bit into the man's shoulder, knocking him to the ground, and she wasted no time. She ran for him, pulled her sword from his body, and slashed it across his throat.

More soldiers joined her on the wall, and all the barbarians there were soon occupied in battle. She scanned the courtyard to see it filling with more invaders. They simply appeared, not seeming to arrive from anywhere. A half-dozen invaders ran up the stairs. They ran in formation, using complex tactics to cover one another, reloading their bows in rotation while one in the front and one in the back of their line wielded melee weapons to defend the archers. For the barbarians they dressed as, they used masterful tactics.

Adeenya lunged forward and sank the tip of her reclaimed sword into the side of a man at the front of the line. The stab elicited a growl of pain from the attacker, and he turned his attention to her, bringing his mace to bear.

She pulled her sword from him and sent the hilt of the weapon flying upward to smack her opponent's chin. The man stopped his swing, looking stunned. Adeenya balled the fist of her off hand and punched first his jaw and then his throat, causing the man to step back and swat at her weapon as he gasped. Angered and unfocused, the man charged toward her. His momentum did her work for her and he impaled himself on her sword.

The orir pulled her weapon from his chest and slammed the hilt into the head of the next man in the formation, an archer who was dropping his bow and drawing a sword. Adeenya shook her stinging hand and blocked his attack after missing her first strike against him. The man pushed her sword away and landed a kick to her stomach. The air blasted from her lungs, Adeenya stepped back into the arms of another attacker. Heavy, muscular arms wrapped around her tightly as her previous opponent spun into a kick that crashed into her hip. She held her cry of pain, turning it into a growl as the man punched her.

She felt hands jabbing and prodding around her waist and into her pockets for a moment. Adeenya's adrenaline surged at the probing hands, surprised they would attempt to take advantage of her during a battle. She struggled harder, determined to make their efforts costly. Adeenya would not be the willing victim they wanted her to be. The probing stopped but she was still bound in the arms of her captor. The attacker before her drew back his weapon to strike. She threw an elbow into the man holding her and stepped back on his foot. His binding grip holding her loosened just enough, and she broke free. The swordsman came at her, blade low. He darted in to strike Adeenya with his sword.

She sidestepped the main force of his strike, but before

she could counterstrike, her opponent fell before her, a shortsword sticking out of his back. Behind him, Corbrinn threw a triumphant fist into the air and tossed Adeenya a wink. The halfling ran over the the fallen man and plucked his sword from the man's back.

"Now, don't go blaming those lads guarding us. I can be persuasive in dire situations," he said, winking again.

Corbrinn shouted for her to move, and she did so, turning to her left. Her torso stretched over the edge of the wall over the courtyard. The halfling launched a whip around the neck of a man who had been coming to attack her from behind. Corbrinn yanked hard on the whip. His slight weight did not allow him to pull the man toward him, but instead the halfling crashed into the larger invader. Corbrinn looked as though he were scaling a mountain when he came to a stop with his feet on the startled man's chest. The halfling plunged his shortsword deep into the man's abdomen and pushed off with his short legs, releasing the whip at the same time and dropping to his feet on the walkway.

Two of the invaders remained on the wall while four times that many Maquar and Durpari continued to fight. In the courtyard, the fight was not going so well. The barbarians and citadel defenders looked to be evenly matched in numbers.

"Don't stand there. Let's go!" Corbrinn said, darting down the stairs.

Adeenya charged after him, glad for the assistance. In the back of her mind, she wondered what Jhoqo would say when he saw the halfling free. Adeenya stopped at the top of the stairs, her eyes insisting that something was not right. It took her a moment, but she realized that none of the bodies of the invaders she had slain remained where they had fallen. Adeenya looked down to see several dead barbarians on the courtyard grounds, beside the wall. Somehow, they had been pushed off the walkway to land there. Adeenya continued after the halfling and bounded down the stairs. There was no time to worry about dead bodies when there were so many more to produce.

At the sound of the signal horns, Taennen drew his weapon and made for the door. "Khatib, secure this position! Lock this door, sound the alarm and make sure the gate stays closed and locked!" Taennen shouted.

"Yes, Durir," Khatib said, his hands already in motion over the crystals at one of the stations.

Taennen paused at the door and said to the man, "Do what you can from here—just try not to kill any of us."

Taennen caught a flash of Khatib's smile before the door slammed shut behind him. A low hum emitted from the door and the portal flashed momentarily, indicating it was locked. Taennen vaulted down the stairs. He imagined the formians escaping or the lost Maquar and Durpari company being found in some secret grave. His feet couldn't keep up with his anxious curiosity. Taennen made the bottom of the tower and burst into the courtyard to find unfamiliar figures there. Men covered in hides were engaging the Maquar and Durpari.

Taennen loosened the grip on his khopesh and turned its blade up. He brought his shield close to his chest. There were three of the attackers coming at the tower entrance, their swords low and ready. They dressed like barbarians and wild men, but Taennen knew better. Berserking warriors held their swords high for powerful blows. These men were at the ready with weapons dancing lightly in their hands.

Taennen charged, knowing his only chance was a desperate maneuver, the kind Jhoqo would disapprove of. Taennen grinned a little at that thought but quickly brought his mind back to the moment.

His opponents stood still as he charged them down. He threw his weight backward and to his left as he drew within two sword-lengths of the lead foe, falling to the ground in a forward slide aimed between the two foremost men. Taennen snapped his shield into the knee of the opponent on his left. The man howled as Taennen continued on and sliced his khopesh along the thigh and hip of the man on his right.

He came to a stop on the ground in front of the third man, who brought his sword down in a heavy swipe. Taennen rolled onto his feet. He danced to his right to avoid another blow. One of the first attackers held his injured knee, but was recovering quickly. The other lay on the ground screaming, blood pooling around him.

The man ahead of him came forward in a thrust that Taennen easily parried. He feigned a shield block and thrust out at the bald man with his dangerous curved blade. His enemy was no fool and swung low at Taennen's legs. The Maquar durir hopped over the sword and drove his khopesh forward while still in the air. Again, the man was too clever and stopped his swing short, bending his body backward to avoid the stab. The man drew a dagger from his boot with his free hand and threw it hard. Taennen tilted his head and felt the dagger brush past his ear.

Taennen feigned a straight thrust. His opponent sliced across low and to the right. Taennen jumped again, letting the sword go under his feet, but this time he kicked out toward the man's wrist.

He felt his foot connect and knew that with thinner soles on his boots, he would have felt the bones in the man's wrist break. The man howled in pain, and Taennen brought the blade of his khopesh across the back of the man's neck in an easy, fluid movement that cut between his vertabrae, killing him quickly.

Taennen crouched, only to see the man whose knee he had damaged moving on the offensive and holding two swords, one long and one short. The long sword sailed toward Taennen from his right, and he knew he would have no chance to parry it.

Before death found him, he expected that his life would flash before his eyes or he would come to some grand understanding of the world around him, but nothing happened. He merely watched, as if everything were slowed by some arcane spell, as the blade that would be his end cut through the air toward him. He pulled his neck low with what little time he had left, hoping beyond hope that the blow might miss his head.

His nose found the dirt and several heartbeats passed. Confused, he rolled to his left to stay low as his would-be killer fell to the ground, an arrow shaft protruding from the middle of his back. Taennen followed the line of the shot to see Loraica standing across the courtyard, bow in hand. Not for the first time, Taennen thanked the Adama for linking his life to hers.

Taennen saw a group of his own men cornered by a larger number of the barbarians, and he ran for them. He would not fail his men again. Never again. Taennen came from behind the attackers as the wildmen attacked a trio of Maquar soldiers. The Maquar durir dragged his khopesh across the back of one barbarian, his blade slicing through the man's leather armor. The soldiers pressed their attacks harder with the arrival of reinforcements. One of his comrades felled another attacker with a series of quick strokes. Taennen bashed his shield into the face of a third enemy, but he took a shallow cut on his shoulder from another at the same time.

A strange noise rang through the air, deep and bellowing. All over the courtyard, the attackers began backing their way toward the open citadel gate, coming together in groups to fend off the Maquar and Durpari. Taennen cursed the wizard Khatib to himself. Why had he opened the gates?

Taennen saw Jhoqo at the front of the defending forces where he was exchanging mighty blows with a man covered in dark animal hides. The invaders continued their retreat, covering one another as they streamed out the gate into the plains. One of their number fell and was picked up by others who dragged his body with them. Perhaps two dozen of them remained. They split their formation well, archers in the back covering their escape.

Jhoqo and his men pursued them for a few hundred paces out the gate, trading blows, until the Maquar commander ordered his troops to desist. Everyone returned to the citadel, closing the gates behind them. Taennen barked orders to the men around him. Those still able-bodied moved to the wall while the injured helped one another to the center of the courtyard for healing.

Taennen looked up at the impressive height of Neversfall tower and wondered about Khatib. Despite his confidence before the battle that he could wield the tower's weapons, Khatib hadn't managed to keep the gates closed, let alone fire off the flurry of missiles he'd promised. Taennen scowled.

He would need to get a better sense of what Khatib could and could not do with the tower before another attack.

"Haddar!" Taennen called. The muzahar trotted over and saluted. "Send your men out to find Khatib. We need him to help search the bodies of the attackers. You four"—Taennen gestured to a group of Durpari—"go check on the prisoners. There's no telling what happened to them in all that chaos. Secure them and make sure no one's hurt."

✚
chapter seven

"Sir, are you well?" Taennen said to his commander as Jhoqo approached, waving off the attentions of one of the Durpari healers. Blood trickled from his right wrist, the crimson stain spreading through the colorful silk cuff of his undershirt. Adeenya approached looking weary but otherwise well.

"A few cuts," Jhoqo said. "And you, son?"

"Same, sir, but nothing serious," Taennen said. He had received worse in his time, but the wounds ached already. His stomach wound had reopened in the battle. With the rush of battle over, he was fighting to move past the pain. By morning it would be debilitating without aid. "I can wait. And you, sir?" Taennen said, looking to Adeenya.

"Fine, Durir, thank you," she said.

"Get a count of our liabilities, Durir," Jhoqo said. "We need to know where we stand as soon as possible."

"What in the . . . ." Adeenya said, turning around.

"Sir?" Taennen said, his hand going to the hilt of his khopesh.

"Where are they?" Adeenya asked.

"Who, Orir?" Jhoqo said.

"The bodies. The attackers we just killed."

97

Taennen released his weapon. "I saw them collecting some of the fallen as they fled."

"But why pause for your dead when you're being pressed?" Adeenya said. "And how did they get every one?"

Taennen shook his head. Recovering fallen comrades was a priority, but given the circumstances of the routed attackers, their care with their dead was surprising. Taennen turned when he heard Loraica curse behind him. The woman stood next to Haddar who limped out of the central tower with Khatib's lifeless body cradled in his arms.

Taennen stared at the corpse of the wizard with whom he had spoken only a short while before. Haddar's broad chest served to miniaturize the man's body. Khatib's face was pale, his blood lost through a slit in his throat. The wound spanned the breadth of his jaw, leaving a flap of skin hanging wide open.

Taennen stood silently and took the corpse from Haddar when the soldier offered it. Loraica ordered Haddar to have his leg examined. Haddar saluted and shuffled away, his head hanging low.

Taennen felt the damp coolness of more blood along Khatib's lower back, and his fingers found a wide, deep gash there. His digits explored the cavern of their own will, Taennen's bile rising. Though he had never felt particularly close to the wizard, the man's death, so cowardly in its execution, angered him, and he felt a pang of loss for the comrade whose excitement about the workings of the tower he had found so engaging just moments before.

"They breached the tower," Jhoqo said, staring hard at Khatib's body.

"This . . ." Taennen started. "This can't be."

Jhoqo reached over the wizard's cradled body and patted the younger man on the back, but Taennen shrugged it off. "No. I mean, he was safe. He locked himself inside the top of the tower," Taennen said, taking a step back.

"What?" Loraica said.

"The tower. The room at the top can be magically sealed. I was with him when the attack started. He locked the door behind me."

Jhoqo looked puzzled. "So someone broke in and killed him."

"No," Taennen said. "He said someone would need to know the proper way in once it was locked. There was a passphrase." He lowered his voice and looked to Jhoqo, forgotten hurt resurfacing. "He said you told only him what it was."

Jhoqo's lips twisted tighter into a frown. "He must not have locked it, or perhaps the damnable invaders had a more powerful arcanist with them."

"If that's so," Loraica said, "we are in a lot of danger without Khatib."

"We will avenge him. Do not doubt that," Jhoqo said. He stepped in close, placed his hand on Khatib's head, and whispered something so soft that even Taennen could not hear.

"Get me the counts, Durir," Jhoqo said. "Terir, liaise with the Durpari dorir to ensure that the healing needs of everyone are met as well as we can accommodate."

"Aye, sir," Loraica and Taennen both barked.

"Sir, permission to follow the invaders," Adeenya said.

Jhoqo looked at the woman for several moments but said nothing.

"Not to engage them, sir. To scout the area, to figure out where they are coming from so that we might launch an attack of our own when we muster our forces," Adeenya said. She stood straight and tall, her face solemn, as though she were not asking the impossible.

"Reconnaissance, then?" Jhoqo said. "Very well. Take a small contingent of both forces. Do not be seen, Orir, and do not go far."

"Aye, sir. Thank you, sir," she said.

Jhoqo nodded and took a step before Adeenya stopped him.

"Sir, one more thing."

"Yes, Orir?"

"Sir, the halfling. He told us he was a woodsman who knew this area. He might be able to help," Adeenya said.

"You want me to release a prisoner, Orir?"

"Not release, sir. Just make use of a resource on hand in a bad situation, sir."

She was clever, no doubt about that, Taennen thought. Jhoqo could not deny her request of a useful resource given the circumstances. Taennen had not realized until that moment how brave Adeenya was. And clearly it had worked. She had done the impossible.

Jhoqo squinted at her a moment before chuckling a little. "Very well, Orir. Take the halfling, but I hold you responsible for the safe return of the prisoner. We hold their safety in our hands, after all."

Adeenya nodded. "Yes, sir. Thank you sir." She saluted and turned to gather her forces.

After Jhoqo had walked away, Taennen looked to his friend and said, "Something's not right, Lori."

"Agreed," she said solemnly. "Let's check the tower."

Taennen placed his hand on Khatib's forehead, uttering a prayer to the Adama. He set the wizard's body beside the half dozen others laid out in the yard, ordering a nearby

Durpari soldier to give the man a burial proper for his order and position.

"No rank. He was a wizard."

"Yes, sir," the Durpari soldier said grimly, then added, "Bad day for magic users."

Taennen looked down at the bodies. Two of them were Maquar clerics. Taennen swore and turned back to Loraica.

Taennen walked beside Loraica to the central tower. The courtyard was alive with activity, but the air was heavy with caution and fatigue. They had been surprised and significantly damaged in a fortress that they had believed was theirs. The attackers had come in undetected, despite the measures available to prevent such an ambush.

As he pushed open the door to the tower, Taennen faced Loraica. "Kill anyone you don't know."

Loraica nodded and drew out her heavy falchion. Taennen crept up the stairs, listening after every few steps for the sounds of anyone moving around at the top of the tower. His pace increased as he continued. They reached the top of the tower to face the door he had seen for the first time earlier that day. The door no longer sparkled with the glow of possibility and mystery. Instead it hung open, dull and uninviting.

"I saw him close it," Taennen said.

Loraica knelt on one knee, examining the door and its jamb. "It doesn't look like it was forced. They must have figured out the passphrase," she said.

Taennen shook his head. "Khatib said one had to know it ahead of time."

"Do you think the invaders tortured the phrase out of the last regiment?" Loraica asked.

"If so, then why not occupy the citadel? Why keep to the woods?"

"They are wildmen, sir," Loraica said.

"You saw them fight, Lori. They're no wildmen."

She conceded the point. "They did seem too organized, didn't they?"

Taennen nodded.

"What is all this?" she said, motioning around the room.

Taennen smiled, thinking of Khatib's enthusiasm for the crystals. "This is the heart of Neversfall."

"Well, how does it work?"

"It needs a brain."

"It doesn't have one?" she asked.

"He's being buried right now," Taennen said, leaving the room. "There's nothing here to see. Coordinate with Marlke, Lori. I'm going to get a count of our losses."

Evening was consuming daylight as Adeenya stalked the plains. Even with Neversfall within sight behind her, she felt conspicuous and naked in the open. The Aerilpar was nearby, promising no end of dangers, yet that was where the tracks of the invaders seemed to lead.

She sought not only an end to the attacks and revenge for her dead but answers to a personal mystery that took precedent in her mind. Not long after the battle had ended, Adeenya discovered that her pendant, the magical device she used to communicate with her superiors was missing. The attackers who groped at her were not interested in her body but her pendant.

She remembered their probing hands and wished she could hack them off. How could they have known about the pendant? What did they want with it? True it was magical, but its power was not difficult to come by. Other than her own soldiers and the sly wizard Khatib, no one had known about the pendant. Khatib was dead, which left only her own soldiers under suspicion, and Adeenya did not want to travel that road. She refused to believe that random chance had allowed the attackers to find her pendant. She would be all the more wary until she could figure out for certain how they had known.

"Here, Orir," Corbrinn said, interrupting her thoughts. "Two dozen or more."

"More than two dozen? You're sure?" she asked the halfling, who crouched on the ground before her examining tracks.

Corbrinn stood and nodded before continuing toward the forest. "At least two dozen left the citadel on their own feet," Corbrinn said. "Some of these are deep, too heavy. Those are from the ones carrying fallen comrades on their shoulders."

Adeenya motioned to her squad to follow and prompted the halfling to lead the way. At the edge of the woods, huge, dark trees loomed overhead and seemed to speak to her of the many lifetimes that had passed before their watch.

Violent lifetimes, she thought, keeping an eye out for the Aerilpar's monstrous inhabitants.

Tall undergrowth in every shade of green blocked their way but also showed signs of recent passage, indicating the attackers had fled this way. A few of the soldiers cut a path with their swords, but the going was slow.

Corbrinn seemed frustrated, climbing to the low branches of a tree to look further into the forest, confirming the path they followed. He hopped down and pushed to the head of the line. "Out of my way, boys," Corbrinn said, taking the lead.

The small man seemed to be swallowed by the plants all around him as he plunged forward. Adeenya followed closely behind so as not to lose track of their guide.

She followed the squirming weeds in front of her for several paces, and she was growing concerned about finding their way back. She could no longer see the edge of the woods behind them, and she did not much care for the notion of getting lost in the Aerilpar forest.

The brush before her stopped moving and she bent down, pushing some of the plants from her path. Corbrinn was there on all fours, and he looked over his shoulder at her, a finger to his lips. She squinted to look past him into the murkiness, the forest canopy letting in very little light by which to see. She jerked back when she saw motion, but she didn't think her movement had been detected. With hand signals, she ordered the troops behind her to move back quietly before crawling away herself.

Corbrinn was right behind her, and after a short distance he spoke. "A clearing ahead. It's them. Maybe a dozen or so."

Those were the types of odds she liked. She began to stand but stopped, a thought nagging at the back of her mind. Only a dozen?

"You said two dozen came through here, didn't you?" she asked.

The halfling nodded.

"Trap?" she asked the halfling.

Corbrinn shrugged in response.

"Can't be certain in all this brush."

She had no choice. They needed more information, and if this bunch were alone, she could wipe out a large number of the wildmen in one quick sweep. Passing the word quietly through the ranks, she waited until it reached the last of them before holding her spear high and dashing forward past Corbrinn. The undergrowth pounded her face, the edges of the leaves making tiny cuts across her nose and cheeks. She set foot into the clearing and whirled her weapon high over her head in an intimidating flourish.

She felt her stomach drop to her knees as she looked around and saw nothing but more trees and dense plants. The soldiers with her came to a stop and fanned out to search the clearing. The halfling entered with a confused look on his face.

"They were here. Right here," he said, bending down to examine the tracks.

After a few moments he stood, his face flushed. "I just don't understand."

"You lost the trail?" she asked but could not make herself upset. The ground here was muddy. The interior of the forest was far moister than the fringe where they had entered, but even that could not account for the wet ground. The forest floor looked more like a soup than a trail riddled with tracks.

"No!" Corbrinn said, with a huff. "I lost nothing. It just ends here."

Adeenya spun all around, looking for any clues at all. The men they'd been following had simply disappeared, it seemed. At Corbrinn's insistence, she gave the halfling more time to examine the area, but she was not hopeful that they would find any sign of the vanished band. She looked at the faces of the men with her, all of them hungry for revenge, knowing that she could not sate their hunger that day.

"We should return," Adeenya said.

A soft click answered her.

"Run!" Corbrinn shouted as he brushed past her leg.

Adeenya spun to face the direction the halfling had come

from to see bright orange flames rising from the ground and growing steadily stronger. She moved to follow Corbrinn, shoving some of her soldiers along with her until more flames appeared before them and on every side.

"Yes, it's a trap," Corbrinn said over his shoulder.

The flames formed a nearly perfect circle. Several of the soldiers lobbed mud at the wall of flames chasing them to no avail. The fire was not spreading on the moist forest floor but that was little comfort to those trapped inside the burning circle.

"I'm sorry, miss," Corbrinn said. "I should have smelled the oils."

"Let's just get out of this," Adeenya said. "Ideas?"

Corbrinn stepped past the soldiers and stopped a few steps from the fire. His hands moved in strange patterns, and he mumbled something indistinguishable. Above the blazing orange light, a large quantity of water appeared, hanging in the air for a moment before crashing down, extinguishing the flames and creating a plume of smoke. A gap large enough to accommodate their passage opened before them, and several of the soldiers thanked Corbrinn as they fled the trap.

The circle of fire still burned, and although the plant life there was mostly protected by the moisture, leaving the forest ablaze seemed unwise. "Spread out, douse the flames with mud and dirt as best you can from the outside, and then we head back to Neversfall," Adeenya said. "We can't let it spread to the citadel."

"And the invaders?" Corbrinn said.

"They're gone. We won't find them this day."

"How do you know?" the halfling asked.

"If they were still here after that fire," she said, "they wouldn't have left us alive."

Taennen and Loraica's examination of the tower had revealed no clues to Khatib's death. When they returned to the courtyard, word was waiting for Taennen to join Jhoqo in the formians' prison.

By the torchlight, Taennen saw Neversfall with all its dancing shadows. He found that he had no taste for the place. He accepted the salutes of the four guards outside the low stone structure and pushed the heavy door open. The smell inside nearly caused him to retch, and he took a step backward.

"Close the door," Jhoqo's voice came from the dimness of the interior.

Taennen lifted an orange silk sash to his face and tried to breathe through it, hoping to dull some of the stench. His eyes adjusted to the low torchlight, and he saw the formians divided among cells. Their feces and waste were in one corner of each cell and, although there was very little of it, the stench burned Taennen's nostrils.

"We'll get them outside for that in the future, sir," Taennen said, indicating the mess.

Jhoqo shook his head. "They stay in here. Under no circumstances are they to leave this building."

One look at Jhoqo's face told Taennen not to argue the point. He acknowledged the order with a nod and turned his attention to Guk.

"Has he said any more?" Taennen asked.

"He's talking. In fact, he'll answer nearly any question you ask him."

Taennen's eyebrow went up. "Do they know who attacked us?"

"Ask him," Jhoqo said, anger rising in his voice.

Taennen knew the anger was not directed at him, but he wondered what the formian had done to provoke Jhoqo. He turned to the big formian. "Do you know who attacked us?"

"It does not matter. You and they will all become part of the hive," Guk responded. He looked smaller, locked in the cell. He was still bound and blindfolded, the gag hanging loose around his neck.

Jhoqo snorted. "That's his response to everything," he said.

"It is the truth," Guk said, his grating voice setting Taennen's ears vibrating.

"They weren't involved with the intruders, sir," Taennen said, risking his commander's ire.

Jhoqo spun to face him. "How do you know?"

"Because the attackers didn't head for these cells at all. They weren't here to free the prisoners. I doubt they even knew of them."

Jhoqo's eyes narrowed, his lips pursed. "They did not get the chance to," he reasoned. "We know what these things can do, if the halfling and the other humans and even your experience are to be believed. And we've established that these things aren't foolish. Their rescuers were outnumbered and ordered to retreat."

Taennen had not considered that the intruders might be slaves of the formians. He knew the ant creatures had the ability to control the actions of other creatures. Guk stood passively as the two men discussed the situation. The formian's ease and lack of expressive or readable features disturbed Taennen more than he could admit. But his gut still told him that the creatures were not involved in the attack on the citadel.

"It won't matter," Taennen said. "Adeenya will find the

bastards, and we'll hunt them to the ground this time."

"Let us hope so, Durir," Jhoqo said. "We're not getting anywhere with these beasts."

"Sir, a moment, please," Taennen said.

"Yes?" Jhoqo said.

"Sir, why didn't I know about the tower? You told Khatib but not me," Taennen said. He felt young and small again, but he needed to hear the answer.

"You didn't need to know," Jhoqo said as though he had been waiting for Taennen to ask the question. "The phrase was shared with me in the mission briefing. I knew that as our only arcanist Khatib would be using the tower, so he needed to know it. No one else had the information, not even the orir," Jhoqo said.

"What about the lost company, sir? Who among them knew the phrase?"

"Their commander, certainly, and their arcanists," Jhoqo said. "I don't know who else. I knew that regiment's commander. He was a good man and wouldn't have revealed the phrase even under duress."

"And their mage?" Taennen asked.

"I don't know," Jhoqo said. "Perhaps that's the answer— the citadel's former wizard was captured and revealed the phrase under torture. Or perhaps he had been on the intruders' side all along."

"That's possible, sir," Taennen said. The answer seemed too easy to Taennen but, as his own father had said, often the easy answer was the right answer.

"It's more than possible. Much as I hate to doubt the fellow, it's the only logical answer," Jhoqo said, turning toward the door. "Come to my office at first light, Durir. We have plans to discuss."

Taennen looked to Guk a few moments after the door

closed. "We'll see that removed," he said, pointing to the fecal matter.

"It does not matter," Guk said.

"It does to me. It isn't healthy," Taennen said.

When no response came, Taennen turned for the door. As he grasped the iron handle, his gooseflesh leaped again at the sound of the formian's voice behind him.

From her watch position on the southern wall Loraica studied the empty plains that unfolded before her eyes, seeming to roll on endlessly. Even with their patrol time before the mission, Loraica was accustomed to life in the cities of Estagund, and she missed the smells of civilization, even the unpleasant ones. At Neversfall, she could smell only the nearby woods, and the Aerilpar held an odor of rot and decay mixed with the usual clean smells of foliage that she found unsettling, unlike any forest she'd ever experienced.

She scanned the ground below her in the darkness. Twice she believed she might have spotted something before picking out the movement as some sort of prairie rodent scuttling along the ground. When she spotted the creature again, she was tempted to fetch a bow to make a meal of it for the morning, but she decided to let it go about its foraging. It was nocturnal, much like herself, after all, and she honored that kinship.

"Report."

Loraica spun, sword in hand in a flash, to face Jhoqo, who had approached her from behind. She did her best to settle her racing heart and school her face against the shock.

"No report, sir," she said.

Jhoqo nodded and leaned against the outer wall, looking out into the vast night.

"You heard that Orir Jamaluddat returned?" he asked.

Loraica affirmed, sheathing her sword. "I haven't heard the details."

"They say a trap was set for them," he said, jerking his chin toward the forest, "a ring of fire that erupted around them. But they escaped."

"Are they all right? What happened?" Loraica said.

"They're fine. Two of the wall guards earlier did report seeing some smoke from the forest interior," he said.

"So they did not find the invaders?" Loraica asked.

"No," he said.

"If they attacked the citadel simply to set a trap for us in the woods, they are foolish. They lost several men in the fight," she said.

"Whose bodies we can't even examine because they took the damned things," Jhoqo said.

Loraica nodded. "Sir, I beg your pardon if I'm too bold, but what's on your mind?"

He looked up from the floor and smiled. "Very well. I can always count on you to get to the heart of the matter, Terir. I need your help," he said, looking her in the eyes.

"Anything, sir," she said.

He blew out a long breath, leaning against the walls once again, and looked out into the dark plains. "Watch her. Tell me what she does, who she talks to, where she goes."

"Sir . . ." she started but didn't know how to finish. He was asking her to spy on Adeenya. She couldn't think of anything less becoming a Maquar, let alone an officer.

"I know. I don't like it, either, but I've put a lot of thought into this."

"Tell me," she said.

Jhoqo smiled a little at her boldness and stood straight again. "Wait a moment, Terir. Maybe this is premature. Did you see her during the battle with the intruders?"

Loraica thought back to the fight and shook her head.

"Now a mission that she led to find the invaders failed," he said. "And she was very eager to speak with the form-ian prisoners. And she took that halfling prisoner with her on her mission." He stepped away from the wall, looking stern. "And she seems too friendly with our durir, doesn't she?"

Loraica could see the thought process on his face and knew his mind was working furiously through a puzzle. "Sir . . . collusion with the enemies? Leading her troops into a trap? Trying to divide our command?"

Jhoqo patted his hands in the air. "I just don't know what to make of any of it, and I want to be sure of her and her soldiers. Maybe I am being too cautious, but I'd rather be too careful than not careful enough."

Loraica fell silent for a while in the darkness. "Didn't Khatib examine her troops when we first met up? I thought he found them to be acceptable. Did he study her as well?"

Jhoqo shook his head. "It would have been an insult to examine her. Khatib may have secretly checked her out, but he's no longer around to ask," the commander said ruefully.

Loraica considered for a few moments. She didn't know Adeenya and had no reason to trust her, but spying still felt wrong. She looked into Jhoqo's face and thought about how many times his clever thinking had saved her life. Her decision was made.

"Aye, sir. I'll watch her."

Jhoqo smiled, clapping Loraica on the shoulders before turning to leave the wall. She resumed her patrol and spotted the rodent on the plains again. Whom did it trust? Whom did it doubt? Probably no one, she thought and envied the furry creature.

✠
chapter eight

"You will free us," the formian said.

Taennen turned back and faced Guk. His strange, alien face, somewhat obscured in the dimness, was devoid of curiosity or hope. Taennen thought about what to say and decided on the truth. "I don't know."

"You will free us," Guk said, again with no question in his voice.

Of course Taennen would free them. They didn't need to be held any longer. Taennen nodded and began to speak. His mouth opened but no words came out. He could feel his mouth moving, trying to form the word "yes," but something was stopping him. He reached for the cell door to release Guk, his mouth still moving without sound.

His hand stopped shy of the door, his fingers trembling. He couldn't remember why he was going to release the formian. He was sure he was going to do so, but why? He turned and faced Guk, who cocked his head to one side with a twitch of his neck.

Thoughts of why he was doing what he was doing flitted across his mind. Taennen tried hard to grab those fleeting thoughts, but they felt slippery and flew away each time he reached out for them. He closed his eyes and took several deep breaths.

Images of the formians free in the courtyard played themselves out before his mind's eye, but beyond those images he couldn't seem to find the explanation. Reason and sense seemed to be images of their own, sharp-beaked birds pecking away at those scenes of the freed creatures. Suddenly the formian images shattered in his mind, and Taennen's eyes popped open and he stared at Guk.

"What did you . . ." he said. "How?"

Guk's antennae twitched and his head straightened, but the formian did not speak or otherwise move. Taennen realized that the thoughts and images had not come from his mind but from Guk's. Somehow the formian had attempted to convince Taennen to free him and his comrades. Taennen felt in control of himself again but knew he had come close to freeing the creatures.

"You're loose," Taennen said, seeing that Guk had broken the bindings on his hands and had partially removed the blindfold. When had that happened? How long had he been under Guk's influence?

"We'll double the bindings this time," he said. Taennen turned for the jail door, wanting nothing more than to leave, when Guk spoke again and stopped him in his tracks.

"You want the one that killed the wizard," the formian said, his voice softening from its usual vibrato.

Taennen focused his mind against further intrusion. "How do you know about that?"

"We hear. We see. We are prisoners, but we are not stupid."

"What about the wizard, then?" he asked, uncertain why he bothered. He strained to search his mind again, making sure the thoughts were his own.

"We know who killed him. It was not the invaders."

"What?" Taennen said. The statement could not have caught him more off guard.

"We saw the one who killed the wizard," Guk said.

"Who then?" Taennen asked.

"When we are freed, we will tell you," the formian replied.

Taennen turned for the door again. To his surprise, Guk did not scramble for him to remain. Either the formian was telling the truth, or he was a far better gambler than one might think. His bluff called, Taennen faced Guk again.

"How do you know who did it?"

"We saw someone enter the tower."

Taennen cast his eyes around the room as the other formians watched him intently. There were many eyes between them. Maybe some of them had been watching the battle. And maybe one of them had seen something. The windows in the structure were small and high, but it wasn't impossible.

"Tell me, and I'll speak to my commander about freeing you."

"Free us first."

"You know I can't agree to that," he said, deciding that sometimes in a bluffing contest only the man telling the truth could win. It sounded like one of his father's adages.

Guk's mouth appendages clacked together as Taennen stared at the creature. The other prisoners stared at him with similarly stolid expressions on their faces. Taennen would have given a finger for a hint of insight into the minds of these strange formians. With no response forthcoming, Taennen decided that his only choice was to fold his hand. He shrugged and headed for the door.

"We do not lie," Guk said behind him.

Taennen continued through the door, not looking back. Even if the formian knew who killed Khatib, that did not change his position. He could not promise the ant creatures freedom even if they could grant his fondest wishes; it simply was not within his power.

He emerged into the courtyard and grabbed one of the guards by the shoulder. "The big one is free of his bindings. Get at least three others and bind him again," Taennen said. "This time do it right and double it, if not triple it! Do not, under any circumstances, let anyone in there alone with him." The durir turned in the direction of his bunk for much needed rest. His stomach wound still ached and nothing would do for it what sleep could.

Adeenya woke to the smell of roasting meat. Her stomach's rumblings urged her from her new quarters toward the cooking fires in the courtyard. The bright morning was warm, the citadel walls effectively blocking the fierce plains winds she could hear whistling above her. She was pleased to see Maquar and Durpari soldiers breaking their fasts together, sharing tales and tactics, telling one another about their respective homelands.

She could not deny her disappointment from the night before, but she felt confident that they had done their best to track the attackers. The halfling, Corbrinn, intrigued her, and she felt badly that he had been returned to the holding building. She dared not broach that topic with Jhoqo yet, certainly not so early in the morning.

She settled down with a plate of food, thanking the soldier who'd cooked it. She couldn't identify the meat, but she knew a Durpari fikrie sauce when she smelled one. The tart and spicy flavors coated her tongue and pried her tired eyes wide open.

Taennen approached and motioned to the ground next to her. Heavy eyelids, puffy cheeks, and other signs hinted that he had chased sleep through the night yet it had eluded him. She waved to him, and he sat beside her. They ate together in silence for a short while, the sun warming her neck and shoulders as it rose higher in the sky behind her.

"Good sauce," he said.

"It's made from two different fruits and more spices than I can remember," she replied.

"Congratulations on the expedition."

She turned a curious eye on him and was rewarded with a genuine smile. "We didn't find much."

"Any expedition where everyone returns unharmed . . . ." he said, leaving the sentence unfinished as he bit into a piece of meat.

Adeenya couldn't stop a chuckle and agreed. "And what about here, Durir? Any news? I've not spoken with the commander yet."

Taennen's face turned dour. "Twelve dead, Orir. Seven Durpari and five Maquar."

Adeenya bowed her head, offering a prayer of balance to the Adama, asking for the powers that be to replace what had been taken.

"Your dorir can give you the list, sir," Taennen added.

"How did the invaders get in?" she asked. "Even opened, the gates should have forced them all into one spot."

Taennen blew out a long breath. "We still don't know. And then there's Khatib."

She placed her plate on the ground and turned her body square to his.

"He was locked in. I've no doubt about that," Taennen said.

"Then they found a way to break the lock?" she said.

"It isn't that simple," Taennen said. "Jhoqo believes the attackers got the passphrase from the citadel's former wizard."

"A traitor?" Adeenya said.

"Maybe," Taennen said, "or they may have tortured the phrase out of his or her mind."

"That makes sense, I suppose," she said. "But you don't seem certain."

Taennen glanced around and said, "One of the prisoners told me that Khatib's murderer was not one of the attackers."

Adeenya's head swam with too many questions. She did not know where to begin. "Which prisoner? How did they see?"

"The big formian," Taennen replied as he looked at the ground. "Guk."

Adeenya sighed. The word of the formians meant less than nothing. "You can't be serious. Who does he say is the traitor?" she asked.

"He won't tell me until I free the formians."

"Who do you think did it, if Guk's not just spinning tales?"

Taennen dropped his fork to his plate and set both on the ground. "I haven't any idea. There are over two dozen people in this camp that I do not know. It could have been any of them."

"You assume it was one of my people?" she replied, turning to see the man's face turning red.

"I . . ." he stammered.

Taennen stared at her for several moments before

holding out his left hand, palm up. He gripped his left wrist with his right hand and closed his eyes while lowering his head. Adeenya was humbled by the gesture, remembering its roots. Before Southerners learned of the Adama they lived very differently by often savage rules. If a man stole or even offended someone, a common punishment was the removal of his hand. Offering one's hand in such a gesture as Taennen was doing was a sign of great apology and acceptance of wrongdoing.

"Besides, it probably wasn't anyone here," he said. "Jhoqo is right. The last wizard of this place probably died right after revealing the passphrase. Poor soul."

Adeenya nodded, but she just wasn't sure. She debated telling him about her pendant. "Why would the formian lie?" she said.

"For his freedom, of course," Taennen replied.

"Yes, I suppose. He just . . ." she said.

"What?"

"He just doesn't seem dishonest," Adeenya said. "Frightening in his goals, yes. But not dishonest."

Many moments of silence passed between them. All around the courtyard, soldiers from both armies went about their duties, some on watch, some inspecting the small buildings, others hauling the dead bodies toward the citadel gate. They would be taken outside and burned some distance from the fortress.

"Time to start new," Adeenya said, quoting the founder of the Adama.

"The beginning is the beast," Taennen said.

"What?"

He turned toward her, a weak smile on his face. "My father used to say that every time he was working on a new spell or making a new piece for a customer."

Adeenya agreed. "He was full of quotes. You said he was good."

Taennen nodded. "He was the best enchanter in Estagund."

"Then I'm not sure I understand what you said about him needing the coin. He must have been a wealthy man if he was that good."

Taennen shook his head. "He refused to use his magic on weaponry or armor."

Adeenya lifted an eyebrow. "In Estagund, I'd imagine that limits one's business opportunities tremendously."

Her companion affirmed her thought. "I should have known before I did," Taennen said. "Who makes an honest living putting charms and dweomers on jewelry and decorations?"

She still could think of nothing else to say about the topic. Taennen had lost one father and gained a new one in the same day. The idea of making such a choice at a young age was beyond her. Knowing that Jhoqo had taken the boy in should have made her feel more warmly toward the man, but Adeenya still found the whole situation unsettling.

She decided to change the subject. "So where do we start on Guk? Where does the beast begin?"

"If Jhoqo is right about the former wizard of this place, then we have nothing to do, no leads to follow."

"You might have guessed this about me, Taennen, but I don't like to sit idle," she said. She wasn't going to tell him about the pendant, she decided. She couldn't trust him with that part of the puzzle. She hated the feeling, but Adeenya felt little reason to trust anyone at that moment.

Taennen grinned and said, "I figured as much."

"So even if Guk is a dead end, even if he's just trying to con his way to freedom, it's still a lead worth following simply because it's there. If Jhoqo's right, then it won't lead us to this supposed mystery person of Guk's, but we might find some other information of use. We both know that the formian knows more than he's saying," she said.

Taennen considered for a moment before saying, "I think we can arrange to interview him more carefully on the matter. I can talk to Jhoqo."

"That won't get us anywhere," she said. "You know that. You've seen how hard Guk is. He won't crack."

Taennen nodded.

"I have an idea," she said. "But I don't think you're going to like it." Before he could reply, horns sounded, and Adeenya noticed a commotion at the gate. They both ran toward the front of the citadel, pushing through the crowd of soldiers as they went. As expansive as the place was, Adeenya fought against the feeling of being hemmed in as she waded through the crowd. She lost sight of Taennen for a moment, but found herself standing behind him an instant later, as he stood stopped in his tracks. She moved next to him as he shouted for the onlookers to stand back.

On the ground before them lay the bodies of four soldiers at the feet of another five. Three of the dead were Durpari, the other Maquar, while two Maquar and three Durpari still stood. All bore scratches and were smeared with dirt. Adeenya shouted for a healer to be fetched.

Taennen stepped forward to face one of the Maquar who did not bear a serious wound. From the sweat and mud on his brow, he had clearly been in battle. The two men stood silently there another moment, Taennen's eyes locked onto the man before him, while the wounded man stared at his fallen comrades on the ground.

"Report," Taennen said, his voice a growl.

The soldier shook his head and lifted his eyes to Taennen,

giving his superior officer a look that Adeenya might expect to see on a dead man's face when asked how things fared.

"We were attacked, sir," the man said.

"By whom? Where were you?" Taennen asked.

"On patrol, sir. The men who attacked the fortress before . . . it was them."

"You were outside the citadel walls? By the gods, man!" Taennen roared. "What in the hells were you doing out there with such a small force?"

"On the urir's orders, sir," the man said firmly.

Taennen seemed to shrink before Adeenya's eyes. The color drained from his face, leaving a pale palette begging to be filled in again.

Adeenya fought the urge to pull her remaining soldiers out and march straight back to Durpar. The Maquar urir had overreached yet again. Jhoqo had ordered men outside the walls, and now more of them were dead. That did not surprise her. She hadn't been told about it. That did not surprise her, either. It angered her, but in no way did it surprise her.

Taennen hadn't known about the patrols, though, and that surprised her. She expected a certain level of secrecy on Jhoqo's part. She was an outsider, after all. But Taennen was like the commander's son, not to mention his second in command. He should have known about the patrol.

The durir of the Maquar stepped away from his soldier as healers pushed through the crowd to tend the wounds of the injured warriors. Taennen took several steps backwards, the throng parting for him as he went. His eyes remained locked on the bodies of the men on the ground for several long moments before he looked up and found Adeenya's face. Taennen turned from the gathering. She darted after him and found him on the far side of the crowd. She caught up to him easily and fell into step beside him.

"He should have told you," she said.

Taennen shook his head. "No."

"You're his second."

Taennen stopped and looked straight at her. "He was right to leave me out of it. I've been a joke of an officer on this mission, and I have lost the right to be in on those decisions."

"That's not—" she started.

"Stop. Please," he said, holding up his hand. "I don't deserve his respect, but I will. From now on, I remember my place."

Adeenya shook her head. "So you'll just do whatever he says? Blind to what it might mean? Sending those men out there was foolish and he should have known better."

"I led my men into that massacre, I failed to stop the attackers, and now I'm following up on the words of our enemy who is trying to deceive me?" Taennen said. "Trust that formian? I must be mad. Jhoqo's right to leave me out of this until I get my head straight. I need to regain my focus."

Before Adeenya could speak, Taennen started off again, his gait determined. She had no idea what to say and even less idea of how to say it. She let him leave. If he wanted to wallow in self-pity she would not stop him.

Adeenya turned toward her quarters. She stopped when out of the corner of her eye she caught sight of Loraica standing nearby, looking out of place. Adeenya did not doubt that the Maquar terir had been trying to eavesdrop on the conversation between her and Taennen. She considered reprimanding Loraica, but the plan she had in mind could not be accomplished alone. She needed help. She could not approach Jhoqo, and Taennen had chosen to remove himself from participation. Adeenya smiled at Loraica. She would do.

But first, there was a more pressing issue to deal with. Adeenya made her way through the courtyard to Jhoqo's command building. She took long, determined steps and kept her focus on the approaching door. The guard there didn't even attempt to stop her, instead opening the door for her. Adeenya stepped into the dim room and looked for the Maquar urir.

Jhoqo sat in a chair on the right side of the room, several scrolls lying around him in a mess. He looked up when she entered and waved her in. If he was surprised or upset at her arrival, he did not show it.

"Yes, Orir? May I help you?" Jhoqo said.

"Sir, you are in command here," Adeenya said.

"I'm glad we agree," Jhoqo said, rising to his feet.

"But that doesn't excuse your decision not to inform me that you were sending my people out on a scouting expedition," she said. She held herself still and poised.

"I had hoped that by sending out the party quickly and without much fuss, perhaps they could have slipped out unnoticed and caught our enemies unawares in the woods," Jhoqo said.

"I'm not questioning your tactics, sir," Adeenya said.

"Then what, Orir?" he said.

"You did not consult me or even tell me what you were doing. My people are dead and I never even knew where they were," she said.

Jhoqo's shoulders sagged. "They are back then? It did not go well?" he said.

"I'm sure they'll inform you, sir," Adeenya said, "but that's not why I'm here."

Jhoqo watched her for a moment. "Then tell me, Orir, exactly why you are here," he said.

"Sir, I'm here to tell you to not let it happen again," she

said, stiffening her posture. "If my people are to be sent somewhere, I expect to know ahead of time."

"Orir, you said I was in command, didn't you? The resources in this citadel are mine to utilize," Jhoqo said. "And that includes your forces."

Adeenya relaxed her stance and looked the man in the eyes. "Never again without my knowledge, Urir. Never."

Before Jhoqo could respond, Adeenya left the building, leaving the door wide open behind her. She felt better. She wished Taennen could experience what she just had.

Taennen strode through the courtyard, ignoring the salutes as he went. They meant nothing. The men giving them had not believed in the gesture since before their fight with the formians. That fight was why Taennen had lost the respect of both his men and Jhoqo. His feet felt heavy and part of him screamed to stop, but he moved forward simply to be away from anything.

"Taennen," Loraica called. She jogged toward him, her leather armor creaking as it tried to contain her mass through the jostling motion.

"Terir," he said.

"Can we talk a moment, sir?" she said.

"Of course. Walk with me."

"I'm concerned about you, Taen," she said.

He stopped and looked at her. His oldest friend's brow was creased, her eyes big and alert. "I'm all right, Lori."

"Are you sure? You don't seem all right. I saw what happened at the gate."

"I was angry and ashamed. I'm dealing with it."

"I'm glad," Loraica said.

"What is it, Lori? There's something else bothering you." Taennen had shared more with her than anyone else in the world. Stories of his childhood, hopes for the future, bruises, blood, tears, and joys. There was likely little they could hide from one another.

"You just seem different on this mission," she said.

Taennen thought about her words. "I suppose so. This is unlike any other mission we've been on, isn't it?"

Loraica shrugged. "I guess, but. . . forgive me, but I'm not sure I trust the orir, and you're spending more time with her than might be necessary," she said, her body stiffening to stand at attention.

"I'm not sure what to say, Lori. I'm glad you said something, but I don't think that's the case. I trust her so far, but I hope you can trust me when I say that I'm being cautious."

"I do, Taen. You know I do," Loraica said, a smile overtaking her face. "Oh, speaking of the orir, she asked me to tell you that something's come up in her ranks, so she'll try to catch up with you later."

"I see. Thank you. Can we break our fasts together on the morrow? I feel like we haven't had much time to relax together since we got here."

Loraica smiled. "You're on, *sir*. See you then."

✠

chapter nine

Adeenya faced west, standing atop the wall, watching the vastness of the plains stretch out before her. She had asked Loraica to join her, but she could not guess what the Maquar woman would do.

When at last Loraica approached, Adeenya did not give any indication that she had heard the other woman coming near. They stood in silence for a few moments, both staring to the west. Adeenya turned to face the terir and, for the first time, appreciated Loraica's true size. She stood at least two heads taller than Adeenya and was nearly twice as broad through the shoulders. Her skin was darker, her features less distinguishable in the soft light. A foe to be reckoned with, but now, she hoped, an ally.

"Thank you for coming," Adeenya said. "I have a plan, but carrying it out requires your help."

"Why me?" Loraica asked. Some would have asked what the plan was first.

Adeenya smiled. "I'll be honest with you and admit that I had wished to convince Taennen to help me, but he seems . . ."

"Distracted," Loraica finished, and Adeenya agreed. "And why not go straight to Jhoqo?"

128

Adeenya weighed her options and chose honesty. "The urir seems . . . less than pleased by my participation in serious decisions here," Adeenya said.

Loraica looked to the west again and said nothing for a few moments. "What's this plan, then?" the Maquar asked.

Adeenya hid her surprise at the woman's lack of protest over her characterization of the Maquar leader. "Taennen was informed that someone inside the citadel, not an attacker, killed your wizard," she said.

"Who?" Loraica said, stepping back, her face wrinkled in confusion.

"His source didn't tell him," Adeenya said. "But if it's true, that person is helping the attackers and we must stop them," Adeenya said.

Loraica arched an eyebrow and said, "And who is this source?"

"The formian," Adeenya said, continuing to speak so as to cut off Loraica's objections. "Yes, I know. It's probably nothing. They're probably just angling for their freedom. But what if he did see something? Isn't it worth trying to find out? We could all be in grave danger."

Loraica shook her head but said nothing.

Adeenya could not say the words she truly wanted to say: The Maquar, bastions of law and order that they were, could not see what Adeenya saw. It was only her perspective as an outsider that told her for sure that Guk was not lying. She didn't think the beast capable of it, actually. In perhaps the biggest twist of irony she had ever seen in her life, Adeenya knew that the Maquar and the formians had a great deal in common. They both cherished law and hated disorder. But she doubted the Maquar would see it that way, so she painted her plan in a more hypothetical light.

"We need to lure that person out," Adeenya said.

"Lure them out? Why not just interrogate the formian?" Loraica said.

Adeenya stared at the woman for a moment before saying, "Do you honestly believe that would help after having met the formian?"

Loraica shook her head. "But if there is no one, if the formian is lying, then how do you lure out someone who doesn't exist?" Loraica said.

"Then we're not luring them out. We're proving Guk is lying and that Jhoqo is correct. And, if Jhoqo is right, then what harm docs it do? We can't do anything about a dead wizard who broke under torture, but we can do something if there is a traitor," Adeenya said.

Loraica rolled hcr cycs and turned away, saying, "This is pointless. There is no traitor."

Adeenya reached out to stop the Maquar woman and placed a hand on her shoulder. "There's something else," she said.

"What?" Loraica said, eyeing Adeenya's grip on her.

"Something was stolen from me during the fight. Something no one should have known about," Adeenya said.

"What was it, Orir?" Loraica said.

"A pendant."

"Well, I'm sure it was valuable or held meaning for you, but—" Loraica began.

"No, no. It was magical. I used it to communicate to my commanders back in Durpar," Adeenya said.

Loraica looked at her for a long moment and said, "Go on."

"It was hidden away in my pocket, but they knew exactly where to look. They restrained me specifically to look for it," Adeenya said.

Loraica nodded and said, "I've always been told that items like that give off some sort of aura if you know how to see them. They probably just saw that aura when they looked and decided to take it."

"No," Adeenya said, shaking her head. "They specifically came after me. They knew what they were looking for, I'm telling you."

"Who else knew about this pendant?" Loraica asked, leaning in closer.

"Only a handful of my own soldiers and your wizard," Adeenya said.

Loraica jerked back at the mention of her comrade. "Khatib? How?" the large woman said.

Adeenya shook her head. "I'm not really sure. He approached me shortly after I used it to contact Durpar. He made it clear he knew about it, but said nothing else."

"This doesn't make any sense," Loraica said, easing herself against the wall.

"I agree, Terir. That's why I need your help. I don't believe any of my soldiers would have given out that information. Nor am I suggesting that Khatib betrayed us," Adeenya added, cutting short Loraica's objections. "But he knew about it and now he's dead. Perhaps whoever killed him didn't want him able to talk anymore."

Loraica drew herself to her full height again and spoke. "If the formian is telling the truth, then who would be fool enough to show themselves as Khatib's killer, regardless of what lure you use?" Loraica said.

Adeenya said, "I find foolishness is never in short supply." Before Loraica could respond, Adeenya continued. "They'll reveal themselves if they think we already know who they are. If we spread the word that the formian knows who did it, then Khatib's killer either takes the chance that he or she won't be discovered . . . or eliminates the threat the formian's knowledge represents," Adeenya said.

Loraica shook her head. "No. Jhoqo would never allow it. We're responsible for the prisoners and their safety."

Adeenya agreed and said, "There's no doubt that it's risky, but if there is a traitor among us, isn't it worth risking the life of a prisoner?"

Loraica continued shaking her head. "As a Maquar, a true soldier, we understand that the way we treat our prisoners indicates our own worth," the large woman said, folding her arms across her chest.

Adeenya took a deep breath and released it, holding back her barbed retort, before saying, "We do not kill our prisoners, and many Durpari have died protecting their prisoners in the past, as I'm sure have many Maquar. But we're talking about *risking* the formian for the safety of everyone in this citadel."

"This plan is the same as murdering the formian. He would become a target for Khatib's killer," Loraica said.

"For the traitor," Adeenya said. "Remember that. If there is a traitor among us, we need to lure him or her out before this goes any further. Before anyone else dies." She paused, letting her words sit on Loraica's mind. She wished she could make Loraica see what she saw, but knew it just wasn't possible. Adeenya cherished freedom and righteousness but knew that sometimes, the rules needed to be bent to achieve them. That was something a Maquar could never see.

Adeenya continued. "We will do everything we can to protect the formian until the traitor reveals himself. What's the other alternative? You agree we must reveal the traitor if there is one, yes?"

"Of course," Loraica said, pushing herself away from the wall to stand upright.

"And it seems quite possible that there is one, given Khatib's death, the attack, and my pendant, right?" Adeenya asked.

Loraica rolled her head from one shoulder to the other and ran a hand through her dark hair. Her lips curled and she asked, "And if we cannot protect the formian? If it dies?"

"Then we will have failed," Adeenya said, pausing for a moment. "But we'll have our traitor. It doesn't matter anyway, does it? There is no traitor." Adeenya grinned. "Right?"

Loraica's face showed her struggle with the idea. Adeenya wanted no one to die, but she was willing to let the formian die if it meant revealing the traitor.

"What would I need to do?" Loraica asked at last.

"Just tell a few of your soldiers that one of the formians knows who killed Khatib. Word should spread easily enough from there. And, before you ask, I'm not suggesting that it was one of the Maquar," Adeenya said.

"If the prisoner dies it will be on your head," Loraica said before turning to leave.

Adeenya watched her go, wondering if she had made the right choice in sharing her plan with Loraica. Adeenya did not doubt that Taennen would also have disliked her plan, so her odds of succeeding were about the same either way. Adeenya sighed and walked the opposite direction along the wall, headed toward the stairs that would lead to her quarters. It had been a long day, and she looked forward to some dinner and a chance to set aside her troubles.

Adeenya exchanged pleasantries with the guard at the northwest corner before descending the stairs. The fading light of the setting sun and the soft glow of Lucha gleamed on the polished stones of the citadel walls. She emerged into the courtyard. A Durpari soldier named Obeidat passed her, offering a salute, which she returned. Her movement was interrupted when she heard a dull thud behind her and spun on her heel to find Obeidat lying on the ground, an arrow shaft erupting from an eye socket. She sucked in a breath to shout an alarm, but was cut off by another arrow passing within inches of her face. She threw herself to the ground and shouted an alert. Her eyes cast about, looking for the source of the attack. When she found it, any doubts about her plan to ferret out the traitor flew far from her mind, and her resolve firmed.

Taennen sprinted forward, dirt flying into the air under his swift feet. Bringing his left arm up to cover his face with his shield, he reached out to grab Adeenya's belt. One arm would not carry her, but his momentum dragged her from her place out in the open courtyard just as an arrow struck the space. She continued to shout an alarm to the rest of the citadel.

Taennen dragged her several paces, stopped, and yelled for her to regain her feet. He looked over his shoulder to see the attackers, perhaps a dozen of the same masked invaders as before, in the middle of the courtyard. They carried long bows and loosed their arrows in every direction, showering the interior of the fortress with deadly shafts. They stood back to back in small groups, covering every direction, protecting one another from unseen reprisals. The invaders looked like statues in the garden of a wealthy merchant.

"Get down!" Adeenya knocked Taennen's leg from underneath him, toppling him to the ground. An arrow struck the building nearby. The archers had spotted them.

"Move!" she shouted. He rolled to his feet, and they ducked into the cover of the nearest building.

Taennen peered through to the other side to find two of the enemy archers had fallen to bowshots from the defenders, but sprawled about the courtyard at least three times that many Maquar and Durpari were dead or injured. Taennen stood flat against the wall again and forced a deep breath. His eyes came to rest at the top of the northern wall where he saw Loraica positioning Maquar archers. He made hand signs indicating that he would try to make it to the western wall to muster more fire power from there. Loraica nodded at this communication and turned her attention back to the men with her.

"Get to the eastern wall. I'll head for the western," Taennen said to Adeenya.

Adeenya nodded. She patted his shoulder and ran east, leaving the safe cover of the structure. He watched her dash across the courtyard, arrows thunking into the dirt behind her as though she were dropping them as she ran to make a trail she could follow back.

Loraica's archers loosed enough arrows to cover Taennen as he made his move to the western wall. He breathed a sigh of relief as his foot made the bottom step of the northwest stairwell. He scanned the area for ally troops and saw a pair of Durpari soldiers running toward him. Taennen waved the men on and ordered the two to follow him up the stairs.

When they reached the top of the wall, they found that more of the enemy bowmen had fallen, but over half a dozen still remained. Taennen ran along the wall, the Durpari soldiers following him. He stopped at a point from where the two soldiers with him would have clean shots to the center of the courtyard and barked the order for them to attack. Farther down the wall, several Maquar were already loosing their weapons at the invaders.

At least ten Durpari and Maquar soldiers were dead in the courtyard, having attempted to charge the enemy archers. An arrow sailed high toward the wall, and Taennen shouted for the two Durpari men to lie flat. The missile flew wide of its target and bounced off the wall behind him. The Durpari men found their feet, offering their thanks for his intervention, and set about firing at the invaders.

Two more enemies fell. Their attack would have to end soon. One of the invaders made a noise, an unintelligible shout to the others. Two of the archers shouted back and pulled arrows from their boots, firing the missiles perhaps twenty paces from their position, straight into the ground. The courtyard suddenly filled with an unnatural darkness, which covered a large portion of the interior of the fortress from the ground to halfway up the walls. The citadel defenders stopped firing, no longer able to see their targets within.

Many tense moments passed before the uncanny darkness dissipated. Taennen loosed a breath and felt his shoulders relax, though only a little. He looked to the two men with him. "That was excellent work, men. Well done," Taennen said.

"Thank you, sir," they said in unison.

Taennen took in the scene around him and shouted to all within the sound of his voice, "Hold the wall! Keep your eyes alert both inside and outside the citadel. We cannot be surprised again."

Returned shouts of "Aye, sir!" came to him and he headed to the courtyard, offering more complimentary words to those he passed. Adeenya and Loraica were headed toward the courtyard from their perspective places on the wall as well, and each offered him a nod as they approached.

All around him in the courtyard were the bodies of his comrades and those left alive tending to them. He walked to where the attackers had been cloaked in their darkness and crouched to examine the ground.

"That was damned effective," Loraica said, standing next to him.

"How in the hells are they doing this?" Adeenya asked. "The darkness is no real feat. Any arcanist worth his salt can do that. But how do they enter so easily?" Her voice dropped. "Do you think someone is letting them in?"

"Twice they've hit us here in the supposed security of our citadel," Taennen said as he stood. He noticed a few other soldiers standing nearby had heard him and listened to his words. He raised his voice for more to hear. "Twice, they've invaded our safety. They will surely come again," he said.

One of the nearby Durpari blurted out, "No! We can't let that happen."

Taennen nodded at the man. "He's right. We can't let them do that. We can't do that to ourselves. We will figure this out. We will stop them," he said.

Several heads nodded but a few muttered amongst themselves, their reservations clear.

"There is nothing we cannot do if we stay united, if we stand up to what appears to be hopeless," Taennen said. "Trust in me and I will trust in you, friends. That trust will be a wall that these heathens will not break, will not pierce. They will assault it and be turned away by its strength."

Subdued cheers came in response and more heads nodded. That was the most he could hope for The coming night would be a long one as the dead were identified and sorted out. Hope would be important.

"Make sure shifts are changed every six bells. I can't have anyone missing something because they're exhausted," Loraica said to a subordinate soldier as they both looked over a duty roster. Several more names had been crossed out.

The man affirmed her orders and left for the wall.

"What have you learned?" Jhoqo said from behind her.

Loraica turned to face Jhoqo, reminded of the last time he had sneaked up on her. His face was plain, his gaze locked onto hers. His stealth wasalways disconcerting no matter how long she'd known the man.

"Sir, I have important news from the battle. I was just coming to see you."

"First, what have you learned about the orir?" Jhoqo said.

"Sir, before the attack, I saw Taennen and the orir talking extensively," she said. "After they separated, the orir approached me and told me of a plan to lure out a possible traitor that might have killed Khatib. She wants to spread word through the ranks that one of the formians witnessed the killer—one of our own—entering the tower during the fight."

"That would be pointless. There was no traitor," Jhoqo said, resting against the wall. "That doesn't make any sense."

Loraica agreed. "Yes, sir, but the orir thought it worth a chance in case there really was a traitor, and she said that if there wasn't one, then there would be no harm done. And an item was stolen from her during the battle."

"What item?" Jhoqo said.

"A magical trinket used to contact her commanders," Loraica said.

"Hmmm. That's unfortunate, but I don't see how that figures into these attacks," Jhoqo said.

"Sir, she thinks it might mean that someone knew about her device, and might have betrayed us," Loraica said.

"Nonsense. They're wildmen. They just saw something shiny and valuable and took it," Jhoqo said.

Loraica nodded. Jhoqo might have been right, but Loraica found all of the pieces of the puzzle harder to deny than he did. She decided to think on it further and said, "Sir, I think the orir just needs to feel useful, to be honest with you."

"You've done well, Loraica. You're a fine terir," the man said.

"Thank you, sir."

"Does Taennen know of this plan?" Jhoqo asked.

Loraica shook her head and said, "I do not believe so, sir." Her guts wrenched, and in that moment she knew why. She wanted to tell Taennen, to let him know that she hadn't gone over his head by approaching Jhoqo directly, that she wasn't excluding him over his mistakes. She tried to comfort herself with assurances that she had done so on a direct order from her commanding officer.

"Let's keep it that way for now. I'll approach him with this," Jhoqo said. "This mission has been a struggle for him. You know that, don't you?"

"Yes, sir," Loraica replied.

"You also understand that this plan of the Durpari woman is unnecessary, don't you?" he said.

"Yes, sir," she said, uncertain for the first time in a long while.

"Good. Where would we Maquar be without our honor? Our prisoners are as good a measure as any by which we gauge ourselves," Jhoqo said. "Using them as bait, even when we feel there's no danger . . . it's just not right."

Loraica nodded, hoping she could share her news soon.

"With this latest attack, morale will be low," Jhoqo said.

Loraica agreed. The soldiers of both nations would be demoralized by their inability to understand how the attackers had twice gained access to the citadel and how they remained so well hidden in the wilds.

"We need to strengthen the resolve of the soldiers to protect Neversfall and everything it stands for. We must defend our position regardless of the cost. This is too valuable an asset to our nations to let it slip through our hands," Jhoqo said. "We need to figure out how these barbarians are gaining entrance to the citadel and how they killed Khatib."

"Sir, that's where my other news is important."

"Of course, Terir. Please, what is this other news?"

"Sir, I believe I saw some of the invaders coming from one of the buildings in the courtyard."

"Hmm. You're sure?"

"Yes, sir," Loraica said. "Very sure."

"Maybe they were raiding it, or hiding there?" he said. "Well, it's circumstancial, I suppose, but definitely worth looking into. Which building, Terir?"

Loraica turned and pointed to one of the smaller vacant quarters.

Jhoqo nodded. "I hope you're right, Terir. If so, we can stop the orir's nonsense about a traitor. The idea of a traitor in our midst only hurts morale more. If you're right about that building, then we can firm up morale by reassuring everyone that the threat does not come from within," he said. "And if the men discover for certain that the enemy is on the outside, they'll stay alert and anxious to exact retribution."

"Yes, sir," Loraica said. "But it could be possible that they have an accomplice inside. It's unlikely, but possible. Shouldn't we at least consider it?"

"When you are a leader of men, Terir, you realize that belief is a stronger tool than truth," Jhoqo said. "Uniting men in a cause by appealing to their morale is the single most effective weapon a commander has at his or her disposal. Remember that. Sometimes that means giving them all something to care about. Other times it means taking that something away."

They stood there, facing one another for a long time before Jhoqo spoke. "You have wall duty this night?" Jhoqo asked.

"Yes, sir."

"Good. I will sleep more soundly knowing that," Jhoqo said with a smile, and he clapped her on the shoulder. "I will order an examination of the building you suspect is the invader's entrance. Until we can prove something, though, please don't share this with anyone else. I don't want a panic, tearing buildings down looking for the attackers."

"No, sir."

"Good. Thank you, Terir. I believe firmly that morale will benefit if you are right. But if we get hopes up among the troops only then to dash them if we find nothing, I fear a greater plunge in spirits," Jhoqo said. "Let me know if you learn anything else. Have a good night."

"Yes, sir."

Jhoqo smiled again and walked away. Loraica looked back at her dwindling list of soldiers' names and pondered what the man had said. She had expected him to show a little excitement at her discovery, instead of launching into one of his speeches.

She sighed. If holding her tongue for a short while would

keep the list in her hands from growing shorter, then that's what she should do. But she wasn't sure it would help to pretend there was nothing strange going on.

In the end she had made a commitment to Adeenya. With any luck, Jhoqo was right and it was pointless, but if he were mistaken, something needed to be done. Loraica settled into her pace atop the wall, watching the stars come out and wishing she had answers. Moreover, she wished she didn't have the questions.

chapter ten

The dim light of the morning peeking through the high windows in the small stone room made Marlke's frown difficult but not impossible to see. His lips were as square as the stones that made up the walls.

"Are you sure, sir?" the dwarf asked as he knelt to continue lacing his boots.

"Yes. The formian was very clear," Adeenya said.

The room was clean and orderly. Marlke was discipline incarnate and always kept his quarters neat, as all soldiers were required to do in training, but few managed once they were in the field. He said it was good for morale, and Adeenya figured if it worked for Marlke, he was welcome to it.

"I don't know," Marlke said. "It sounds too convenient to me, Orir. They're prisoners looking for a bargaining chip."

"We can't take that chance. They saw the traitor," Adeenya said. "Until we can pry the identity from them we need to be on guard for treachery—all of us. Getting the information shouldn't take too long."

"It's risking a lot on nothing," Marlke said. Adeenya raised an eyebrow and the dwarf added, "Begging your pardon, sir."

"I agree that it's risky," she said, "but it's what we must do."

Marlke grunted and shrugged before saying, "Fine, sir. I'll spread the word this morning during the meal."

Adeenya nodded. Withholding information, especially from her own second, felt wrong and unbecoming to a leader, but she saw no choice given the circumstances. She had considered letting Marlke in on her plan, but had decided that the fewer people who knew, the better the chances of the plan working. And the plan needed to work. The mystery of her missing pendant still burned in her mind. She hoped she would not cross the boundary between caution and paranoia.

She thanked the dwarf for his cooperation and took her leave of him. The sun had just passed the horizon, but the morning air still bit at her cheeks as Adeenya strode across the courtyard toward her meeting with some of the jail guards. She paid no heed to the soldiers around her who were still cleaning up the mess from the previous evening's attack. The dirt was still black where her comrades had fallen. She mouthed a prayer and continued on her way.

Adeenya moved around the side of the structure built to serve as the armory, reaching her quarters. The gray stone matched her mood. She disliked subterfuge and resented having to play at it. She passed through her door and sat at the desk on the right side of the room. Its light wood, polished to a high sheen, shone in the sunlight streaming in through the eastern windows.

She had found no rhyme or reason to the placement of buildings with different features in Neversfall. Some had tiny windows, others were normal. Some had heavy, solid doors and locks while others were secure but minimally so.

neversfall

Adeenya sat at her desk to review her schedule for the day. After her meeting with the jailors, she would speak to the supply officer and then the cartographer. Every officer in her unit knew their job and did not need to be managed, but Adeenya had found her people often appreciated it when their she checked in with them. There was a fine line between going too far and riding one's subordinates to the end of their wits and letting her presence be known. She made every attempt to make her expectations clear and her support obvious without crowding anyone's efforts. A quick meeting once a tenday kept her informed and her subordinates on their toes.

She set her papers aside when a knock sounded on the door. "Enter," she said.

Two jail guards entered and stood attention. The first was a tall Maquar, lean and trim with a seasoned and disciplined stance. His face was clean-shaven and his hair short and trim. The personnel records on her table showed his name was Initqin, though Adeenya could not recall having met the man.

The Durpari guard next to him was named Muria. She had joined Adeenya's command more than a year before and Adeenya enjoyed the woman's company whenever she found time. Muria was shorter, bulkier, and less meticulous in appearance than the Maquar.

"Good morning, sir," Muria said.

"Good morning, Muria. Initqin," she said with a nod. "Both of you, please have a seat."

Initqin saluted and relaxed his stance. "I'll stand if that's all right, sir."

"Whatever you like," Adeenya said. Her dreams of joining the Maquar when she was a young girl came back to her in that moment—the proper demeanor, the strict order.

Adeenya enjoyed her Durpari comrades, but sometimes she longed for more formality from them.

Muria sat facing Adeenya and rolled her eyes toward her Maquar companion. Adeenya smiled at the woman and shuffled through her papers for a moment.

"We'll try to keep this quick. Do either of you feel that any guard changes are needed? Anyone having trouble with the duties? Does it seem like the prisoners are getting to anyone?" Adeenya said. "I know none of this is easy, even under ideal conditions."

"Sir, for my part I think everyone's doing pretty well," Muria said. "We're tired and shaken, but you know that."

"Sir, I believe Bhariq could use a break from the jail duties," Initqin said.

"He's okay, really. He's just a little tired," Muria said. Adeenya was pleased by Muria's defense of Bhariq but felt the need to dig further. Solidarity between soldiers was wonderful, but not at the cost of overlooking someone's well-being.

"Muria, can you fetch his papers for me? They're on the shelf back there," Adeenya said. Duria nodded and headed toward the back of the room. To Initqin, she said, "Can you give me some specifics?"

"Well, sir, he just seems overly irritable. Yesterday he shouted at one of the human prisoners who was being persistent about being released. We all want to release them, and we all have to listen to them whine—" The man stopped, drawing the sword from his belt as Muria screamed.

Adeenya leaped from her seat, tipping over her chair and letting it clatter to the ground. She ran toward Muria who stood leaning against the bookshelf at the back of the room. Muria showed no wounds or signs of injury—only shock.

Adeenya scanned the room. She saw a thin line of dark, dried blood on the floor and followed the trail to the corpse of Loraica tucked behind a chest and partially covered by Adeenya's spare bedroll.

Adeenya's ears rang with a low tone as her knees began to wobble.

Initqin appeared at her side and looked past her to the body of the Maquar terir. "What in the name of all the One?" he said.

"Muria, get help. Initqin, search the rest of the room," Adeenya said as she began searching the area around the corpse. Whoever had killed the terir was long gone, no doubt, but there might be clues. Finding them quickly would be crucial before the room filled with more people coming to the call for assistance. Muria nodded and ran out the door.

Adeenya pulled the blankets back from Loraica's body. Her flesh was cold and dry. She had been dead for some time—hours, at least. Adeenya froze. When had the body been hidden there? Had she slept in her room all night with the woman's corpse nearby, or had it been concealed during the her visit to Marlke's quarters? Loraica's throat had been cut, much like Khatib's. The line was smooth, made by a sharp weapon. Loraica's hands and arms showed no immediate signs that she had struggled.

Adeenya pushed the corpse on its side to look under it. As she had suspected, there was also a deep wound in the woman's back. Loraica had been attacked from behind, and then had her throat slit.

"Do you see anything, Initqin?" Adeenya asked as she moved a chest away from a wall. "There must be a clue somewhere."

"Sir, drop your weapon," the man replied.

147

Adeenya turned to face the Maquar who held his sword a few handspans from her side. "What are you doing, soldier?"

"Placing you under arrest, sir. Now please, drop your weapon."

Adeenya felt a rush of adrenaline and fought off the urge to attack the man or flee for her life. Her military training kicked in and she saw the earnest look in the man's eyes. He would try to kill her if she did not comply.

"Stay calm, Initqin," she said, letting her sword fall to the floor. She held her arms out low to her sides.

"I will, sir. Thank you for disarming. Please remain still until reinforcements arrive," Initqin said. Adeenya noted and appreciated his calm tone and demeanor. His commanding officer was dead several paces behind him, but he was collected and professional. Another soldier might have killed her where she stood.

"I'm going to sit down if that's all right. We'll sort all this out when Jhoqo gets here," she said. She needed to sit. She needed to think. Loraica was dead in her room. If Adeenya had seen such a sight in someone else's quarters, then she would have acted as Initqin had.

Adeenya glanced back to the rear of her quarters as though Loraica might rise and be well if she only longed enough for it to be true. But it wasn't. It never would be. Adeenya ran a hand through her hair and returned her gaze back to Initqin who returned her stare and readjusted his grip on his sword.

"I'm not going to run, Initqin. I've done nothing wrong," she said. "You really believe I killed that woman?"

"It hardly matters what I believe," the man replied.

In her time with the Maquar, Adeenya's childhood admiration for them had dwindled but never so much as in that moment. Duty, a fine thing, a tradition the Maquar held most sacred, was blinding the man before her.

She could see in his face that he did not believe she was a murderer. But his sense of duty made it impossible for him to choose to lower his weapon and help her reason out what must have occurred. He could come to her defense when Jhoqo arrived on the scene. He could but he would not. Initqin would stand there, weapon readied, and watch Jhoqo accuse Adeenya. That was duty.

"You can lower your arms, soldier," came Jhoqo's voice as he entered the building.

Initqin complied and stood at attention.

Jhoqo strode to the back of the structure and knelt next to the corpse of his terir. "By the gods, Lori," he said.

Several moments passed, Initqin still staring Adeenya down, before Jhoqo rose and took a seat across from Adeenya. "Tell me everything," he said.

Adeenya met his eyes. "I was here, discussing reports, when her body was found," Adeenya said. "I have no idea how she got here."

"You deny killing her then?" Jhoqo said.

"Of course I deny it. I didn't do it!"

Jhoqo nodded and patted Adeenya on the knee. She held herself and did not flinch at his fatherly reassurance. Certainly that would not have helped the situation at all.

"Then what did? Are there any clues?" he asked.

Adeenya was puzzled by his question, his lack of accusation. "I didn't have a chance to look for them," she said, looking to Initqin.

Jhoqo nodded. "Well, rest assured we will come to the bottom of this. When is the last time you saw Loraica?" he asked.

"Last evening atop the wall," Adeenya said.

"To what end? What did you discuss?" he asked.

"The situation with the invaders," Adeenya said, seeing no reason to tell the entire truth. "And the possibility of the formians' involvement. She was concerned, the same as I am, that there could be a traitor among us."

"I see," Jhoqo said. "Please find some different quarters for the time being. Take a few of your essentials and move them there. We'll need to thoroughly investigate this place."

"I am to go, sir?" Adeenya asked.

Jhoqo shrugged as he stood. "If I were to hold you over this incident, I would have riotous soldiers—namely yours—on my hands. Also, truth be told, Orir . . . I'm inclined to believe you."

Adeenya stood and nodded, too stunned to speak.

"If I am wrong, we will soon find out." Jhoqo smiled nastily. "Besides, my dear, look where we are. If you were guilty and wanted to run, where would you go? The wilds of the Aerilpar? That's a death sentence, and I know you're well aware of it."

"Where is he?" Jhoqo asked, as he strode away from Adeenya's quarters through the courtyard.

The Durpari woman he spoke to said, "The durir, sir? I saw him near the big tower, sir."

Jhoqo quickened his pace, turned a corner around the central tower at a jog, and spotted Taennen walking toward him, a puzzled look on the younger man's face. Jhoqo stopped and waved the durir to him.

"Sir? What's wrong?" Taennen said, the confusion clear on his face. He had not heard yet. That was fortunate, Jhoqo thought.

"Son, come with me," Jhoqo said and walked to the door of the largest tower. He pushed the door open and stepped inside. There were many windows in the tower, unlike most of the buildings in the citadel, so the interior was bright with morning light. Jhoqo pointed to the steps and asked Taennen to take a seat.

"Sir, please, what's the matter?" Taennen asked. "You look disturbed. What's happened?"

"Taennen, we're losing this citadel," the urir said. Taennen's body went rigid, and he shook his head. "It's true, boy. The men are furious and helpless but have nowhere to direct their anger. That's a horrible combination, one that always begs for trouble."

"Sir, we'll figure this out," Taennen said. "All isn't lost."

Jhoqo shook his head. "This is a critical time, son. We must be strong for our troops. We have to rally them and point them in the right direction."

Taennen nodded and narrowed his eyes. "Why do you say these things to me now? What's happened?"

Jhoqo stared hard at the man he considered his son. He looked into Taennen's dark eyes, watched as the younger man's cheek twitched in anticipation. He saw the boy he had raised as much as he saw his second in command.

"We have to remain strong, Durir. Remember that," Jhoqo said. "The men will look to us."

Taennen nodded as he rose to his feet and said, "Tell me."

Jhoqo sighed and lowered his head before saying, "Loraica was found dead this morning."

All color fled Taennen's face. His muscles gave out all at once, and he toppled to the steps, his hands flailing out behind him for purchase.

Many moments passed as Taennen stared out the doorway

151

and Jhoqo watched him. The urir never imagined feeling someone else's pain so strongly.

"How?" Taennen asked, his lips quivering.

"Murdered," Jhoqo said.

Taennen fixed him with a hard stare. "How was she murdered, sir?"

"It does not matter," the urir replied.

Taennen stood, fierceness fueling his voice. "How was she murdered?"

"Her throat was slit." Jhoqo said.

"Who?" Taennen asked, his voice tremulous.

"We don't know," Jhoqo said.

"Who found her?"

"The Durpari orir."

"Adeenya?" the younger man said.

"I'm afraid so," the urir replied.

"Where was she?" Taennen asked.

Jhoqo sighed. "In the orir's quarters."

Taennen shook his head and said, "Surely she could not . . ."

"I hope she could not, too, son," Jhoqo said. "We'll need to question her further, but I decided it would be bad for morale if I threw her in a cell. It's not as though she can go anywhere."

Taennen swayed as he stood. His forehead wrinkled as though he might cry.

"You understand what I said about the troops?" Jhoqo asked.

Taennen nodded, but his eyes were unfocused.

"Very well, then. You're dismissed—just remember what I said," Jhoqo said.

Jhoqo stepped out of the way as Taennen strode past him without a word. Loraica and Taennen had worked together and been friends for as long as Taennen had been in the Maquar. Nothing Jhoqo could say would soothe the boy.

Jhoqo recalled the first time he had seen the two together and smiled. Loraica had been large even then, twice the bulk of Taennen at the same age. She had taught Taennen how to fight. Jhoqo had watched them many times as they figured out new maneuvers to try on one another. Even full days of training with the troops had not exhausted them enough to skip their own training sessions.

Jhoqo sighed and walked toward his quarters. It would be a long day, he knew. He went over what he would say to the troops in his mind and found nothing adequate. Nothing that seemed worthy of Loraica, nothing that would transform grief into enough motivation and morale to turn things around. But as commander of the fortress, it was his duty to make the best of the situation. Loraica had served the Maquar well in her life, and if he had anything to say about it, her death would prove just as useful.

Adeenya paced back and forth outside Taennen's quarters. The image of Loraica's pallid corpse was etched on her mind's eye, and she could see little else, no matter how hard she tried to think other thoughts. She had rushed to Taennen's quarters and waited for him to return instead of searching the entire citadel for him. She had wanted to be the one to tell the man about his friend, but he had already gone by the time she arrived.

"I saw you talking to her yesterday evening on the wall," Taennen said from behind her.

Adeenya spun to face the man. His shoulders were slumped, his head cast down. His hands hung at his side, and his cheeks and nose were red. Adeenya could think of nothing to say, so she nodded. "Yes."

"Both of you were tense. I could see it," he said. "You were arguing? She was angry with you?"

"Angry? No. What are you saying?" Adeenya asked.

"What did you tell her?"

"Did Jhoqo send you?" she asked.

"What did you tell her?"

"My plan to lure out the traitor," Adeenya said. His closest friend was gone, but Adeenya hoped he could not think her responsible.

Taennen's face wrinkled. "What plan?" he said.

Several of the soldiers had gathered nearby, likely attracted by the tension that leaked from Taennen. Adeenya waved them off as did Taennen when he noticed them. The warriors moved away.

"Let's talk inside, shall we, Durir?" she said.

Taennen nodded and followed her into his quarters. The room was like most of the others in the citadel, plain and unadorned with small, high windows that let very little light into the room. Taennen closed the door and stood before it, his arms across his chest, and he said, "Tell me, now."

"Durir, I would remind you of your place," she said.

Taennen stiffened and stood at attention. He trembled, looking like nothing so much as a scarecrow being tousled by the wind. Adeenya sighed and motioned toward a chair as she raised an eyebrow. When Taennen nodded, she sat. All the muscles in her body seemed to coil and tighten at once before releasing, leaving her feeling like a puddle of mud.

"I tried to tell you about my plan," she said. "When you were not responsive, I approached Loraica instead because I knew I would need help to find the traitor."

"How, sir?" he asked, punctuating the honorific.

She told him of her plan and every detail of her conversation with Loraica. Adeenya watched his eyes harden and his face sour from his tight lips to his wrinkled brow. His response was not unexpected.

"It violates every principle that the Maquar hold dear," he said, looking as though his personal honor had been insulted. "Loraica turned you away when she heard it."

"I see no alternative," she said. "And she disliked it for the same reason you do, but she agreed to it in the end when I told her about my pendant.

"I had a magical device to contact my superiors. It was my only way to reach the outside world, to get us help here, to do anything. It was stolen, deliberately, in the attack. They came straight for me and took it," Adeenya said.

"So?" Taennen said.

"Khatib and a few of my soldiers are the only ones who knew about it," she said.

"Khatib?" Taennen said. He stared at her a moment longer before nodding. "That's a lot of evidence."

Taennen crumpled to his bed where he sat, head in his hands. He loosened the straps of his leather armor with a sigh. He ran his fingers through his short hair for several moments. Neither of them spoke.

"She agreed willingly after hearing all of that, Taennen."

"I would have, too," he said after a long moment. "You found her in your quarters?"

"Yes." She studied his face, but found it unreadable. "You came looking for me believing that I killed her?" Adeenya asked. "Taennen, forgive me for being blunt, but there was almost no blood in my quarters. She couldn't have been killed there."

"So she was moved," he said softly. "You could have moved her, the same as anyone."

"No," Adeenya said. "Loraica could have moved me with no trouble, but I couldn't have moved her without help. And after all that trouble, why would any killer put the corpse in her own quarters? I'd have to be a fool to do that."

Lifting his head with what appeared to be great effort, Taennen locked eyes with her and said, "You're not a fool."

"So you believe me?"

Taennen shrugged and offered a small nod.

"What now?" she asked.

"I don't know," he said, lowering his head into his hands again.

"The plan Loraica and I discussed is already in motion. There's nothing to stop it now," she said.

Adeenya stood, facing the door. "You may not like it, but could you just keep your eyes open? Watch the cell building where the formians are kept as much as you can without looking too obvious," she said. "It's not a great plan, but it's what we have."

"Loraica died for that plan," Taennen said, looking up at her. His eyes were red-ringed moons of sorrow in the dim light of the room. "Her pyre will burn this night," Taennen said.

"Rest until then. I'll watch for the traitor," Adeenya said, moving to the door to leave.

"Does Jhoqo know about this plan?" Taennen asked.

Adeenya shook her head. She wanted to ask him not to share it but knew Taennen would do what he would, regardless of her requests. Her only choice was to hope that he didn't choose to share it.

Out in the courtyard, several soldiers of both armies watched her, curiosity plain on their faces. She strode past them, each step a declaration of her innocence.

Taennen shambled across the courtyard toward the funeral services. The shadows were just beginning to disappear with the dwindling light of the evening. In a short while, the torches would be lit and new shadows would be brought to life. Taennen's neck was jelly, unable to hold his head up. His arms dangled at his side as his stiff legs stepped, pushed, lifted, and stepped again, moving him forward. Taennen did not want to see his friend's body. He didn't want to hear people talk about her in the past tense. Taennen did not want to do anything at all. He wasn't sure that he even wanted to be at all.

He had spent most of the day in his quarters staring at a wall, the eastern one, he thought, but could not be sure. Memories of his time with Loraica had replayed in his mind during that time, but mostly he stared. He stared and focused on not thinking, not feeling, not being. If he didn't think or feel or exist, then Loraica wasn't dead. If Loraica was not dead, then he would see his friend again.

As he approached the pyre where her body rested, the crowd parted, letting him pass. Only because of her honored rank was Loraica to be burned inside the citadel itself. Taennen did not look at her, casting his eyes aside to rest on Jhoqo instead. The short man stood atop a pyramid of crates, holding a torch. He wore his dress uniform. The white silk reflected the light of the torch in his hand. Jhoqo motioned for Taennen to join him. The durir's legs seemed to move of their own accord. He climbed atop the crates and stared at the face of his commander.

"You have words, I assume?" Jhoqo said.

"I can't . . . sir," Taennen answered, the look on his face never changing.

Jhoqo nodded toward the men and took Taennen in an embrace, placing his mouth close to Taennen's ear and saying, "Gather yourself, son. Remember what we talked about earlier. These people need your words."

Jhoqo released the embrace and faced the gathering again. Taennen turned and scanned the crowd. He realized that only Maquar were present. Across the courtyard he saw some of the Durpari looking on from a distance. Taennen knew Loraica had made friends among the Durpari, and he wondered why they did not come forward to mourn her.

Jhoqo stomped on the crate, jarring Taennen's bones and rattling his teeth. The urir waved his arms to get the attention of those gathered at the pyre. He lifted his palms to the sky and then fanned them out before bringing them together in a tight clasp. The mourners mimicked the gesture, which symbolized the spirit of a loved one dispersing and returning to the oneness of the Adama where all souls belonged.

Jhoqo waited for the crowd to focus on him again and said, "Friends, brothers, sisters, we have a sad duty today, but one that must be done. One, I must say, that she whom we are here to honor would not shirk from if it fell to her."

Claps against leather leggings came in response. The sound echoed in Taennen's ears like rain on stone.

Jhoqo motioned for silence and continued. "Loraica was the absolute finest soldier I have ever had the pleasure of serving with and commanding. I know that commanders always say that, but without causing offense to anyone here, I feel the need to stress how true that was of Loraica.

"If she was given a task, it was her duty, and Loraica never shrank from a duty. She did everything at least twice as well as it could ever need to be done. If you told her you needed a fortification built that could hold back ten men, she'd build one that could hold back twenty!"

Cheers rose this time before Jhoqo again silenced the crowd. "She will be missed. She will never be replaced in spirit. It is not possible. But we must continue. Loraica loved being a Maquar, and she knew that what we stand for is vital to Estagund."

Shouts of affirmation filled the air, and Jhoqo had to shout over the din. "Let us continue in her tradition and fulfill our duty beyond even her lofty expectations, always!"

Taennen stood in silence as the cheers rose, fell, and rose again as someone from the crowd added another cry. The stares of those gathered should have felt heavy, he thought. To his surprise, he felt layers of confusion and sadness peel away under their eyes and cheers. His chest rose, his chin lifted, and he felt as though he might begin to float. His thoughts still clung to Loraica, but instead of pitying himself he began to wonder what she would want him to do, what she herself would do. Taennen straightened further, imagining himself as tall as his departed friend.

"Loraica saved the life of every person here at least once," Taennen said. "Above all else, Loraica believed in loyalty to one's self. We are taught to make decisions by examining a situation and choosing the most sensible course after weighing all the facts. Loraica knew this and believed in it. But," he said, raising his volume, "she also had a heart and knew when to use it. We are Maquar. We are of Estagund and the South. That is all true. But we are also of the oneness all around us. Let us not forget that. For Loraica never did!"

Cheers and shouts buzzed in his ears, and Taennen felt separated from the moment in one instant and enveloped by it the next.

Jhoqo brought the noise to an end with a wave of his hands and spoke again, "Before we return to our duties, I need to inform you that, due to the last attack on Neversfall and the loss of our brothers and sisters these barbarians have caused, I sent word for reinforcements. The further loss of our beloved terir today only convinces me that I was right to do so."

The thought that Jhoqo had not informed him of these reinforcements flittered through Taennen's mind, but it did not gain purchase in that roiling place. Help was coming. He was ready to accept it and found himself surprised that Jhoqo was as well. Normally very stubborn, Jhoqo had always said that his troops could handle anything and never needed help.

"It will take more Maquar and Durpari forces some time to get here, but the noble rajah of Estagund and the estimable chakas of Durpar have seen fit to provide us with trusted help from a wandering troop that has served the government of Estagund before," Jhoqo said.

Murmurs whipped through the gathered crowd, and many eyebrows arched. Several of the Durpari moved closer to the gathered Maquar, having overheard the man's words. Jhoqo nodded, waving his hands in the air, and said, "I know, friends. I know. I, too, wish we could simply wait for our Southern brethren, but we do not have that luxury. Our duty to protect this citadel is at stake, and we must never shirk our duty. Fear not—the soldiers they are sending us have a long relationship with the South and will aid us in our struggles. But now, my friends, we must say goodbye and return to our duties. There is much to be done."

With those words, he set his torch to the pyre. A brand of straw ignited a bundle of sticks, and soon the flames quickly spread to the full structure. The heat rose rapidly in the warm air, causing sweat to bead on Taennen's brow. He watched the yellow-orange monster devour the wood, but

✠
chapter Eleven

Taennen woke to the smell of fowl cooked with dried dates, the sweet and tart aromas, and the smell of roasting meat permeating the air. The dish basked in a thread of sunshine that crept into the room from the small high window. Taennen rolled out of bed, grasped the plate, and opened the door. He made it almost five steps before thinking of Loraica, but he did not stop or falter when he did. The image of her face in his mind helped to drive his step. He would avenge her.

Outside, the sun had already baked away the morning mist. Half a dozen soldiers from both forces milled around the courtyard, listening to one of their fellows who gestured excitedly but spoke in hushed tones. The troops nodded their agreement or made clear their dissent with hissed objections. The speaker was a Durpari, one of the men Taennen had led to the wall during the last attack. He was a fine archer, and by the look of things, the same could be said of his oratory skills.

Taennen walked toward the gathering, and the Durpari archer stopped speaking and greeted Taennen with a salute from some distance away, while motioning for the others to disperse.

"Hold there, men," Taennen said, returning the salute, his dish still in his hand.

The soldiers all obeyed and held their salutes. "What's this about?" Taennen asked no one in particular as he paced toward them.

"Nothing, sir," one of the Maquar barked.

"Of course it's 'nothing, sir,'" Taennen said. He stopped and looked each soldier in the eyes. "I need to know before I can help."

The Durpari archer stepped forward, now standing crisp and tall as a soldier should, and said, "Sir, I was telling them that we shouldn't be sending out more scouting parties."

"Of course we shouldn't," Taennen said. "The first one was slaughtered. We're lucky to have any of them back."

"The first two patrols, sir," the archer corrected.

Taennen stopped moving and looked to the Durpari man. "Two? More soldiers were sent?"

The man nodded. "Very late last night, sir."

"How many?"

"Three Durpari and three Maquar, sir," the man said, his gaze holding Taennen's. "Two of them survived, sir."

Taennen turned back toward his quarters, dismissing the gathered soldiers over his shoulder. They scattered in all directions, pleased to be excused. Taennen closed the door to his quarters and hurled his plate at the opposite wall. Dates splattered against the stone, sticking to it like smashed bugs.

Taennen stood in his dim quarters and danced with a choice. He could go about his duties, or he could confront his commander about the man's tactical error, for surely it could be called nothing else. Sending small units outside the walls was getting them killed by the strange intruders.

Taennen thought of the formians and suppressed a shudder. Were the Maquar fools for keeping them alive? The beasts had proven themselves dangerous. They might be controlling the attackers this time. Taennen thought about Adeenya's plan. The troops were surely whispering about the rumor she had started. If one of them were a traitor, he or she would have to make a move soon. Taennen hoped Adeenya had been able to watch the prison. He would have to find ways to do the same himself.

Taennen dressed, hastily fastening his armor, slipping his boots on over his muscled calves, and sinking his khopesh into the sheath at his hip. He opened the door to the courtyard once again and took a deep breath. The air was dry and hot and stank of burnt wood from Loraica's pyre. As he crossed the courtyard toward the building where Jhoqo had made his command headquarters, Taennen heard Loraica's name whispered more than once, but he never broke his stride. Each utterance spurred him on harder. He arrived at the door and knocked.

A passing Durpari soldier stopped and saluted. Taennen returned the gesture and faced the door again, waiting to be greeted by Jhoqo.

"Sir, no one is in there," the Durpari said.

"Where's the urir, soldier?" Taennen asked, facing the younger man.

"On the north side of the central tower, sir, welcoming the new arrivals."

"New arrivals?"

"The reinforcements, sir. They were sighted a short while ago. The urir will be introducing them soon."

Taennen dismissed the man if for no other reason than to hide the look of shock that he knew must have been riding his face. Jhoqo had sent for reinforcements only a day earlier—at least that was the earliest Taennen had heard of it. Taennen walked toward the central tower. He was comforted to see his face was not the only one showing surprise.

His shock was replaced by doubt as uneasy thoughts crept into his mind. The newcomers were quick to arrive. Who could these reinforcements be? How did they arrive so quickly? He had not known of any military presence this far in the wilds.

Then again, Taennen reminded himself, no one had known there were barbarians and man-sized ants roaming the area either.

Adeenya saluted the guards and grasped the handle to the door of the prison housing the humans and the halfling. A pair of Durpari soldiers stood to either side of the door, looking tired.

"Sir?" one, an older woman named Nooawala, said. "You won't be attending the announcement of the new troops?"

"No. Someone has to keep on schedule around here," Adeenya said. The truth was, Adeenya needed to keep herself circulating near the formian cells to watch for trouble. The formians were guarded, of course, but Adeenya was unsure whom she could trust.

Adeenya pushed the door open with a creak and stepped into the room. The sun poured in through the door. The men and women inside all looked her direction, shielding their eyes from the brightness. The small windows in the building kept the structure cool but were not made for lengthy time spent indoors. The prisoners flinched in the sunlight.

Some of the prisoners greeted her and all appeared to be in good health. Though many glared at her as their captor, they seemed to be making the best of their situation, having divided the duties of daily life among themselves. One corner of the large room was for washing clothes, another for dishes, each making use of large buckets of grimy water. Everyone seemed to have a duty to attend. All except one.

Corbrinn Tartevarr sprawled across his bed, as much as a halfling could sprawl, soaking up the sunlight streaming in through the door. Adeenya approached him, leaving the door open for the prisoners to enjoy the light and fresh air. None of them would try to escape. They were safer inside the confines of Neversfall than they would be out in the wilds, and they all knew it.

The halfling still wore his hides but had stowed his furs somewhere, likely due to the heat. His eyes were closed, and he wore a broad grin as though dreaming pleasant dreams. His chest rose and fell rhythmically, but Adeenya knew he was not asleep. His stubby toes wiggled as she sat on the bed next to him.

"You've heard about the second expedition being killed?" she said with little question in her voice.

Corbrinn nodded but did not open his eyes or otherwise move.

Adeenya watched the halfling, wondering if it was wise to consult him. She had believed him when he had claimed that he had lived most of his life in the wilds and knew Veldorn well. Adeenya felt too alone and isolated both inside and outside the citadel's walls. Someone of Corbrinn's experience was valuable, at least as far as the space outside the walls mattered.

"Have you ever heard of a group of humans living in the

forest?" she asked. "How could they survive, let alone thrive enough to raid this fortress?"

Corbrinn pulled himself up with a grunt and locked eyes with her. They shared the look for a few moments before he raised his eyebrows with a shrug as if to say "Good question."

"That's what I thought," she said, and gave him a pat on the leg before adding, "Thanks."

She rose to leave but was stopped by the halfling's hand on her wrist. She turned back to look at him and saw his face held a serious demeanor.

"They'll pick you off a few at a time if you don't find them," he said.

She nodded.

"I can find them," Corbrinn said.

She nodded again before turning to leave. Behind her, she heard the halfling's bed creak as he lay back down and groaned a little as his back stretched.

Adeenya faced Nooawala and said, "Be sure these prisoners get some fresh air and a little time out in the sunlight."

Nooawala began to object but stopped when Adeenya raised her hand. She headed toward the greeting of the newcomers to catch a glimpse. She could get close and still maintain her surveillance of the formian cells. With most of the fortress personnel distracted by the arrival of the reinforcements, this would be the ideal time for the traitor to make a move against the prisoners.

Jhoqo bellowed his greeting to the gathered crowd—a crowd that had grown noticeably smaller since their arrival at Neversfall. Taennen did not know who to blame for the anger he felt at the deaths of his friends and comrades, so he chose to blame the citadel itself. Neversfall, its magical walls and towers, beacon of security and free trade. Taennen nearly spit as he scanned the stone walls of the place. Some good these walls had done the men and women who had died here, he thought.

Jhoqo quieted those in attendance and began to speak. In a mellow, baritone voice he said, "Brothers and sisters, please hear me on this day. We have suffered much in our duty here in Neversfall. Undoubtedly, we shall suffer more still. But we are soldiers. Soldiers have duty, and we shall not fail in ours!"

Subdued applause from the Durpari and palms slapping leather from the Maquar responded. Jhoqo hopped atop a crate he no doubt had had placed there so that he might look into the faces of everyone listening to him. He threw his arms out wide and puffed out his chest.

"But we cannot do this alone. And thanks to the illustrious rajah, the government of Durpar, and of course, the All and the One, we need not. Today, friends to both Estagund and Durpar join us. With their help, we shall prevail in our mission here!" Jhoqo said with a flourish.

He waved his arm in a beckoning motion, and three dozen men stepped into view from behind one of the nearby bunkhouses. They all wore black leather armor with thin cloaks in the shade of blue that the sky attains between dusk and nightfall on a warm summer night. Most wore thin beards and were fairer of skin, having a more honeyed hue.

Taennen recognized them immediately: Chondathan mercenaries from the west on the Sea of Fallen Stars. He had met a few in his time.

Instead of marching in rank and file, they walked in

a triangular pattern with one man at the front and rows successively widening behind him. The foremost man was about the same height as Taennen, but he had a more muscular frame. His beard was trimmed and neat and he sported no moustache.

Jhoqo motioned the man forward as waves of murmurs rippled through the gathered Maquar and Durpari. A nearby soldier caught Taennen's eye and gave him a confused look, as if imploring his durir to explain what it could mean that western foreigners were meant to be their saviors. Taennen nodded to the man, unsure what else to do, and looked back toward the stranger.

The newcomer joined Jhoqo on the crate and smiled, offering a tight wave much too practiced to be genuine. The Durpari were called mercenaries, but at least they worked for their government and people exclusively. The Chondathans, on the other hand, worked only for the right price, no matter whose gold paid them. They were truly mercenaries, soldiers-for-hire. Taennen's mouth filled with a tang he found sickening. These men had no place in Neversfall.

The murmurs quieted, and the stranger spoke in a thick accent of soft consonants and tight vowels. "Greetings friends. I am Bascou, commander of the *rakrathen* you see before you. We are honored to assist the great nations of Estagund and Durpar in their time of need."

At first, no response came. Jhoqo clapped alone in slow, measured beats until more joined in, and then nearly everyone's hands were applauding. Taennen's arms hung limply at his sides.

"Bascou, may I present my second in command, Durir Taennen Tamoor," Jhoqo said.

Taennen stepped toward the man and nodded, not

offering his hand. His face was blank and he did not speak. Jhoqo narrowed his eyes at Taennen but never shed his smile. He turned to the crowd and said, "Please make our new brethren comfortable. Treat them as you would any comrade among you. Maquar, treat them as you would any other Maquar, Durpari, the same as you would another of your comrades-at-arms."

A tidal wave of whispers and murmurs rushed through the assembly. Soldiers huddled together in hurried dialogues, some gesticulating, others looking stunned. Jhoqo ignored the reaction, clapping Bascou on the shoulder, dismissing the man and motioning for one of the Maquar to show the newcomers to their quarters. Jhoqo and Taennen stepped down from the crate, and Jhoqo placed an arm around Taennen's shoulders, walking with the younger man. Jhoqo smiled and waved at the gathered troops who were now whispering among themselves.

Still smiling, he growled into Taennen's ear, "That will not do, Durir."

Taennen glanced over his shoulder to see the crowd dispersing, breaking into small clusters of soldiers, all still talking among themselves. Looking back to Jhoqo's face, Taennen saw his phony smile, but he did not miss the anger burning in the man's eyes.

"That was inappropriate," Jhoqo said.

Taennen flashed back to his youth, to Jhoqo schooling him in proper etiquette while he was being introduced to the upper echelon members of the Maquar. Taennen felt all the more confused by the regression of their roles. Confusion gave way to frustration. Frustration hinted at anger like red skin around a wound hints at infection.

"Excuse me, sir?" Taennen asked, more loudly than he intended.

Jhoqo stopped their stroll and turned to face his second. "Your behavior was unacceptable. Bascou and his men are here to help us, yet you just treated him as though he were somehow outside the oneness, something less than part of the whole."

Jhoqo's face softened as he spoke the last words, but Taennen did not relent. He slid the man's arm from his shoulder and said, "Sir, you just told your men—the brothers you trust with your life—to extend that fellowship to complete strangers."

A snarl overtook Jhoqo's face as he said, "I am your urir. You will show me and those I deem worthy more respect than that."

"Are we done, sir? Am I dismissed, sir?" Taennen felt like a child again, frustrated by his father's answer of "because I said so."

Jhoqo took a step back, letting out a deep breath. He turned soft eyes to Taennen and said, "Son, I need your help on this. I know my command may not make sense, but we must have unity with these new men if any of us hope to survive. You see that, don't you?"

"You've known your men for years and these Chonda-thans for moments, sir."

Jhoqo nodded and said, "I know, but I see no other way to do this. We need to trust these men, and they need to trust us."

Taennen's stance relaxed as he said, "Yes, sir. Am I dismissed?"

"No," Jhoqo said. "We are sending out another patrol expedition."

"Sir?" Taennen said. He could not hide his surprise. "Is that wise?"

"You heard me, Durir."

Arguing would get him nowhere, Taennen knew. Instead, he did the only thing that might help the situation. "Let me lead it, sir."

Jhoqo cocked an eyebrow before shaking his head. "I don't think so, son."

"Let me prove myself, sir. I know I've been out of order, and I want to fix that," he said. If Jhoqo insisted on sending out more men, then Taennen would make sure they all came back alive. Jhoqo got his scouting mission, Taennen a sense of control returned to him. Everyone would win.

Jhoqo stared at him for a long while. His face softened, and his voice was low. "You may join the expedition, but you will not lead it."

"Who will, sir?"

"Bascou," Jhoqo said.

"Is the Chondathan to outrank me in operations here at Neversfall?" Taennen asked.

"You are my durir, Taennen. You know that," Jhoqo responded. "But Bascou leads this patrol. We need to establish him and his men among our ranks. I see no better way right now."

"Yes, sir. I will serve him as best I can."

Jhoqo's lips curled into a small smile. "I know you will, son. I have no doubt."

"When does the patrol leave, sir?"

"Next bell," Jhoqo said, a softer gaze locked on Taennen.

"I'll do a quick check of things around here, sir, and then I'll convene with the Chondathan. Will he be picking the patrol members?"

Jhoqo thought for a moment. "Why don't you select four Durpari and four Maquar for him? You know the personnel better."

"Yes, sir," Taennen said.

Jhoqo placed his hands on Taennen's shoulders. "You make me heartbright, son."

"Thank you, sir," Taennen said. Jhoqo's eyes did not hold pride. They looked sad. Jhoqo returned Taennen's salute and moved toward his quarters.

Taennen needed to speak to Adeenya. She would be continuing her surveillance of the prisoners. He was more certain than ever that her plan should be carried out. Even if fruitless, her plan was trying to accomplish something important. What was Jhoqo's plan doing? Taennen didn't know. He hoped his commander did.

✛

chapter twelve

Several moments after Jhoqo had stopped speaking, the crowd dissolved like sugar in water, but Adeenya stood rooted to her spot, the whispered conversations of the passing Maquar sizzling in her ears. At first, she thought they were about her, suspicion about her role in Loraica's death, but she soon realized that was not the case. The stunned faces around her, the angry tones and white knuckles—even if they believed she had betrayed them, her traitorousness would not garner such rage. Only treachery by a trusted friend could bring about these wild looks and fevered whispers. The Maquar felt daggers at their backs, and Jhoqo was the wielder of the blades.

The Maquar commander had pulled Taennen aside for a few moments and, once the younger man had left, Jhoqo crossed to the leader of the new arrivals, the man named Bascou. The two men spoke into one another's ears. Bascou nodded, his eyes on the ground until suddenly they flicked up and locked onto Jhoqo, who nodded. Adeenya glanced over her shoulder one last time and saw that Bascou was speaking to one of his men, while Jhoqo was nowhere to be seen.

She scanned the dispersing crowd for Taennen and

spotted him walking away. He nodded for her to follow, and she did. The durir had not struck her as the sort for secrecy, so she knew it must be urgent. She fell into step behind him.

"I'm to join the Chondathan on another patrol," Taennen said without looking at the woman.

"How many soldiers on the patrol?"

"Eight of ours, plus me, the Chondathan leader, and however many of his men he takes," Taennen said.

"You have a plan?" she said.

Taennen grinned but his eyes were sad. "Not as such."

Adeenya forgot her response when she heard a low humming sound that caused the insides of her ears to tremble and her jaw to clench. She thought the ground itself might shake, and she remembered stories of buildings collapsing and cracks forming in the ground beneath people's feet. She stopped and watched a nearby building as a guide. It did not move, nor did she, but still she vibrated, and the pressure in her ears grew. The confused look on Taennen's face told her that she was not alone in noticing the unusual sensations.

"What could that—" she started.

"Come on," he said, dashing toward the prison cells.

She ran to catch him. He barreled past the soldiers guarding the prison building and disappeared into the darkness of the room beyond.

"Cease!" she heard Taennen say from inside.

She heard a grunt followed by a muted growl as she plunged into the darkness. Her eyes slowly adjusted to the low light. Another grunt of effort came, and she saw a Maquar poking one of the dog-sized formians with a spear. The creature scuttled to a corner to avoid the strikes. The guard spit a curse before stepping toward the big formian who stood still, bound and blindfolded.

Taennen lunged forward, grabbing the man's shoulder and pulling him back. The spearman shrugged off Taennen's grasp but halted his progress toward the formians. "You are dismissed, soldier!" Taennen shouted.

"Sir, the prisoners were planning something. Didn't you hear it?" the man replied. "It was terrible. My ears felt as though they might ignite."

"Soldier, the Maquar do not harm their prisoners, regardless of the noises they make. You're new to this outfit, but surely you know that," Taennen said.

The man nodded but quickly replied, "Yes, sir, but the sound . . . Sir, it was making me crazy, and the leader of the new men heard it as he went by earlier and said if it were up to him, he'd do something about it."

"Bascou told you to do this?" Adeenya asked.

The Maquar man blanched and stammered, "Well, he didn't order me to. But . . . well, you know . . . he sort of . . ."

"Enough. Your orders come from me, the orir, or the urir. Do you understand, soldier?" Taennen said.

The man nodded, and Taennen dismissed him, suggesting that the soldier get some rest. The man skirted past Adeenya on his way out the door. She closed the door behind him.

Taennen went to one knee and looked to the assaulted formian. The young man stood after a few moments and approached Guk. He stared at the large formian for a few moments as though the blindfold were not there.

"We'll see the wounds are tended to," Taennen said.

"What do you think the sound was?" Adeenya asked.

"I don't know, and I don't really care. They're free to make noise. It's not harming anyone," Taennen replied.

"True enough," she said. She wanted the prisoners to be

well treated, but the sound had unnerved her.

"Your plan is working," Taennen said in a low voice, stepping in close to her and pointing at the formians. "Word they might have seen someone in the tower is all over the citadel."

"What next?" she said.

"You keep watch, and I'll see what the Aerilpar holds for us," Taennen said.

"Good luck, Taennen," she said. "Watch your back."

"You too."

Before she could reply, Taennen moved out the door, his shadow blocking the light that barely touched the darkness of the interior of the prison.

He was right not to linger. It might look strange to an observer if they stayed in the company of the formians for too long. Besides, the strange ability of the creatures to manipulate those they came in contact with was nothing she felt like struggling with at that moment.

Adeenya followed Taennen and stepped back out into the sun. He motioned the two guards outside the building to him and nodded as Adeenya indicated she would be leaving. He told the soldiers that no one was to mistreat the prisoners unless they wanted to deal with him. The guards nodded vehemently and answered every question with affirmatives.

Loraica's warnings came back to Adeenya. Maybe her plan did put the formians at risk unnecessarily. Whoever had killed Loraica was heartless at best. That person would not hesitate to kill alien enemies. If there were a traitor and the prisoners died in that room alone and defenseless, how would she feel? She had no love of the creatures, for certain, but the thought of them being executed by some assassin made her grim. The rumors had been circulating for a while. Surely the traitor would strike soon. Or perhaps the saboteur was wiser than that. Perhaps he or she would let anger and frustration boil over among the ranks. Maybe the sinister soul knew that eventually the soldiers would succumb to loss and infuriating helplessness until they reached the point where they would take care of the formians themselves in an attempt to ease the call for vengeance and action they all craved.

Adeenya glanced over at Taennen. The man was distracted, lecturing his soldiers. The guards nodded, their backs turned to her.

Adeenya ducked into the prison again and looked around. In the corner opposite where the formians huddled, she found a stack of stone blocks like those used to make the dividing walls in the room. She dashed behind them, pulling them in to make a snug space against the wall. She knelt down, hidden from the rest of the room. The formians had seen her, no doubt, but anyone else entering the room would not be able to.

Every bad idea she had ever had flooded into her mind, but that tidal wave of feeling was turned away when she considered the guilt that would weigh her down if her plan led to the deaths of the formians. She would hide here and protect the creatures. She almost laughed at herself, the utter ridiculousness of the plan occurring to her. But impending guilt, duty, and a need to solve the mystery anchored her to the floor. She peered over the stones to see Guk's head turned in her direction. Adeenya sank back to the floor and sat, waiting, hoping she was there for no reason.

Taennen clasped hands with the young guards, a pact of trust forged between them. He disliked lecturing them, but he knew that tensions were running high. If one of their own had been willing to discipline a prisoner the way the spearman had, things were out of hand. He gave them a smile, confident that his words would be heeded, and left the two to guard the prisoners once again. He ordered them to see to the small formian's wounds but otherwise to grant the creatures privacy. Taennen walked away from the building, his mood dark after the disappointing incident with the spearman and the nearly devastating interaction with Jhoqo earlier in the day.

Groups of soldiers, Maquar and Durpari, huddled here and there in the courtyard. No doubt the newcomers were the cause of the whispers. Even Jhoqo's impassioned speeches weren't enough to put the Maquar at ease. As much as Taennen agreed with his soldiers' discomfort, it was better to have the Chondathans working with them then not to have anyone. The midday sun beat down on him, but Taennen's skin absorbed it hungrily and he enjoyed the warming sensation. It burned at the edges of his bad feelings, its warmth a kind of forgiveness he would not earn from any other source.

Taennen saw Bascou speaking to one of the Chondathan men as a group of Maquar stood nearby. Bascou, clearly aware of his observers, offered them a smile and salute. When Muzahar Haddar sneered back in response, Taennen saw an opportunity to set the proper tone. He bolted to stand before the Maquar and took satisfaction in their rigid salutes.

"You will show the proper respect, Muzahar," Taennen said.

Haddar eyed him hard, never one to hold his tongue.

"They are darkblades, sir," he said. "Foreign sellswords. Even the Durpari have more honor than they do. At least the Durpari serve their own country and only their own country."

Taennen glared at the man, long enough for Haddar to notice and become quiet. When he did, Taennen looked him in the eye before doing the same in turn to each of the other three Maquar gathered there. "Do you believe in the ways of the Maquar?" he asked Haddar.

The man blinked but maintained his gaze straight ahead at attention before saying, "Yes, sir. Of course, sir."

"The Maquar are my family. Are they yours?"

Haddar nodded.

"A family must be willing to change and grow. After all, people die, marry, have children . . . isn't this so?" Taennen asked.

Again, the man nodded.

"A family must also stand united, or surely it will dissolve. They may disagree, of course, but they must come together in times of need, yes?"

Taennen did not wait for the man's response before continuing. "The head of your family has asked of you all that he must—no more, no less. We are in trouble, brothers," Taennen said, turning to look each man in the eyes. He added, "We must save one another. We are in a strange land, and we are overwhelmed. A good warrior must know when this is true and admit it to himself.

"There is no shame in it. Jhoqo knows this and so has done what was necessary," Taennen said, pointing toward the sellswords. "To protect his family," he added, indicating the men standing before him.

Haddar nodded and said, "Of course, sir. My apologies, sir."

Taennen dismissed them, the men all too glad to be on their way. He was not fond of the Chondathans either, but orders were orders, and, since the newcomers were already here and not going anywhere, inhospitality would only make things worse. Jhoqo knew what he was doing. They needed to trust their commander. *He* needed to trust his commander.

Taennen turned toward the stairway to his quarters but stopped when someone called his name from behind him. He turned to see Bascou coming toward him, his hand extended. His long, thick hair seemed cumbersome. Taennen could imagine a hundred ways to use that hair against an opponent in a fight. It did not seem beneficial to a soldier. His plain dress also bespoke more stealth than battle prowess, and Taennen wondered at the tactics employed by the sellswords. He stuck out his arm and accepted the man's clasp, returning it with a small squeeze.

"Thank you, friend. Your help is appreciated," Bascou said.

Taennen nodded, wondering at the man's accent. His vowels were stressed and accentuated, and his tongue rolled on his consonant combinations.

"I know this is a difficult situation for your men, needing help from outsiders," Bascou said.

Taennen replied, "Yes, it is hard for some."

"I wonder, though, if your message was received by them," the sellsword added, his lips parting in a smile that reminded Taennen of a teacher asking a question he knew a student could not answer correctly.

"They're good men. They'll come around."

Bascou's smile widened as he said, "Of course, of course. It is interesting to see how others lead, is it not? For instance, if one of my men had insulted you so," Bascou said, waving his hands before his face as if to ward against that situation, "I would have killed him and set an example for the rest of my men."

Taennen felt uncertain whether he should laugh at the man's posturing or take him seriously. He chose to stare ahead, attempting to show no reaction whatsoever.

Bascou's smile went crooked as he let out a small chuckle. "Very good, my friend," he said, grasping Taennen's forearm. "Thank you again."

"Of course," Taennen said, realizing he did not know by which title he should address the man. It did not matter, and he did not care. He wanted nothing so much as to be away from the man.

"I will see you in one bell's time at the front gate. It will be a pleasure to watch you at work," Bascou said with a slight bow. "It will be my honor to lead you into the wilds."

It seemed Jhoqo had found time to inform Bascou that Taennen would be joining him.

"I understand that you will be picking our party yourself," Bascou said.

"That's right."

"Good. I look forward to meeting the men and women you trust with your life," Bascou said.

"And your men? How many of them will be joining us?" Taennen asked.

"None," Bascou said.

"Excuse me?"

"Jhoqo insisted that I lead only you and the Durpari. He believes it will lay a foundation of trust between us, a bridge, you know," Bascou said. "And that it will show me your legendary skills."

"I see," Taennen said. "Very well. I will meet you at the front gate."

✛

chapter thirteen

After what felt like an eternity of sitting behind the rough stone blocks in the corner of the dark prison, Adeenya was well past doubting her decision, her mind mired in regret. When the Maquar's cleric had entered the room with a pair of guards and administered her healing power to the injured formian, Adeenya had been convinced her ruse was about to be discovered.

Since that time, Adeenya had sat with her ear pressed against the front wall of the small building waiting— *hoping*—to hear the guards outside step away from their duty for a moment so that she might sneak away from her mistake. Duty, the goal she had held loftiest her entire life, was to be her undoing. These guards would never shirk theirs, would never leave their posts. Yet that was what she had to wait for. To leave, to simply stand and walk out the door when no one was aware of her presence in the structure would surely cause suspicion, and Adeenya knew all too well that she carried too much of that on her shoulders since Loraica's death. Adding any more might mean she would leave Neversfall as a prisoner instead of a soldier, if she left at all.

She glanced over the piled stones to see the big formian,

Guk facing her direction despite his blindfold. The absurdity of their mutual inaction, their refusal to interact with one another while locked together in the small room, struck her. She sat cross-legged, her back stooped and sore, waiting. The same duty that trapped her—those loyal guards—would also foil any attempts by the supposed traitor. She could not get past the guards to get out, and the traitor would have a hard time getting in. Unless, of course, the guards were part of the betrayal. If there even was a traitor, she reminded herself. But there had to be. Khatib, the pendant, the attacks—there was too much incongruity there to deny as coincidence.

The door to the building creaked open. The midday sunlight, highlighting the sheen on the carapaces of the formians, was dimmer than she expected. She had been in the room longer than she had realized.

She heard boots scrape against the stone floor, but the door blocked her view of the newcomer. The door shut, and as her eyes adjusted to the utter dimness of the prison once again, she fought the nerves igniting her entire body. They screamed at her to spring from her hiding place and run for the door, ruined purpose of duty or not, for surely a foiled plan would be easier to live with than being caught by the room's newest visitor. To her surprise, it was Jhoqo.

Jhoqo latched the door shut behind him. His eyes seemed locked on the formian prisoners. A long time passed before he stepped toward them and offered a greeting. None of the formians responded or even acknowledged his presence. Jhoqo withdrew a short sword from his belt and, through the bars, poked the piles of food left for the prisoners on the floor. He seemed to be checking to ensure their adequacy or freshness. He did the same to the small troughs of water provided for the prisoners.

Jhoqo looked back at the creatures and knelt down. He

scrutinized the smallest and spoke, "You appear injured. How is this so?"

The silence after his deep voice was an enormous canyon, impossible to cross. He stood and hung his head with a sigh. "I have come on the most important matter between us. That is, of course, what we can do with you," Jhoqo said.

Again, no response came, and Adeenya leaned forward, anxious to hear more of the man's words. After keeping the information he had gathered about the formians from her, she wouldn't be surprised to find out he was still hiding more.

"I've come to learn that you may have seen something during the attack on this place. Is that correct?" Jhoqo asked.

Guk gave no response.

Jhoqo shook his head. "I cannot help you if you do not speak to me," he said. Jhoqo swayed from one foot to the other for several quiet moments before turning to leave. His face was in a tight scowl as he approached the door.

Adeenya watched him through a small crack between some of the stones. His eyes drifted toward the piled rocks but did not tarry. He grasped the door handle and left the room. Adeenya shifted to place her ear on the wall again. She heard Jhoqo's voice as he spoke with the guards outside.

"Get some rest, soldiers. You've done well. I'll have your relief along shortly," the man said.

The guards affirmed the orders. Adeenya heard feet shuffling as they all moved away from the door. If the shift-change was so close, then she had lost track of time by more than she'd suspected. She thought about taking the chance to slip out, but her plan might have a chance to succeed now. With no guards outside the cells, the traitor might make a move. Adeenya stretched her tired legs as well as she could and readied herself.

The sun was past its zenith for the day, but still it poured the midday heat down upon Taennen as he marched behind Bascou. The Maquar durir glanced back toward the fortress. Though it was still only a few hundred paces away, he felt the tether of safety it provided him snap in his mind. To judge by the faces of the Maquar and Durpari with him, he was not alone. Eight soldiers plus himself and Bascou made a small force, especially with an enemy lurking somewhere just out of sight.

"There, do you think?" Bascou said, pointing to the border of the Aerilpar in the nearing distance.

He indicated a narrow parting in the otherwise thick, unrelenting line of trees at the edge of the forest. The trees to either side of the path stood tall and straight at their bases, their tops leaning in toward one another with centuries of branches weighing them down. The opening looked like nothing so much as the mouth of some cursed cave, beckoning fools to enter.

"It is the only break in the trees. Surely it must be what the invaders use to gain entrance to the forest," Taennen said.

"Exactly. We will find them quickly, will we not?" Bascou said with a smile.

"But they will know the area and could be expecting us to take the most obvious path to find them. If we cut a path through another part of the forest, we could come at them from a different—" He stopped when the Chondathan leader waved him off.

"Quicker is better. We will find them faster if we go this way. We will go this way," Bascou said.

Taennen could think of a hundred arguments against the idea, but all were quelled by his training and, he could not deny, his thoughts of earning back Jhoqo's trust. Taennen nodded to Bascou and fell into step behind the man, marching toward the mouth of the forest.

As they entered, the dense foliage of the trees blocked the light, making the interior of the woods a world of night in the middle of the sun-drenched plains. They pushed through underbrush that, while mostly cleared, slowed their progress. As their eyes adjusted, the darkness was not as deep as it had seemed at first. Trickles of light filtered down through the canopy, and their ears filled with the sounds of the wild. On the plains silence reigned, but in the forest the sounds of beasts none of them had dreamed of held court. Men were trespassers in that kingdom.

Chirping, squawking, buzzing, and something akin to the tittering of tiny children filled the air as Taennen brushed broad leaves from his path. Bascou navigated the lush forest well, flattening very little of the underbrush under his feet. Some of the other men were not as delicate, but Taennen did his best to follow the Chondathan leader's example. The shafts of light from above illuminated motes of pollen that scattered across the ocean of murky green. Insects—some so small they could not be seen, some species as large as a man's finger—darted through the air all around them, occasionally getting swatted away for having flown too close.

"I think I can see some sign of passage here," Bascou said in a low voice as he continued into the forest.

Taennen squinted and bent down to examine the underbrush as they passed, but he could not discern what signs the other man might have seen. The exotic plants rising from the ground looked defiantly intact, though the dim light made further detail difficult to discern. Their perfumes were overwhelming, some close to the scents of familiar spices, others so foreign and new that his nostrils flared in confusion at their scent.

Taennen stooped to examine the petals of a yellow flower the size of his fist. Bascou gripped his shoulder, stopping him, and motioned for him to stand. Seeing the man's fingers to his lips calling for silence, Taennen looked over Bascou's shoulder. The Maquar durir held his left hand up in a clenched fist, signaling to the other men to hold and make no noise. Focusing his eyes through the darkness, Taennen could not make out what Bascou saw. Perhaps the man was not sure himself. That notion was lent weight when the Chondathan man dropped to the ground before him.

Taennen dropped to a crouch in a blink and heard the thud of an impact behind him. Staying low, he turned to watch one of his fellow Maquar fall to the ground, a spear lancing his gut. One of the Durpari men fell next, an arrow piercing his cheek. The man's cry of pain was muffled by the arrow shaft blocking his tongue and clacking against his teeth. The rest of the soldiers all dived for the ground before scrambling toward the source of the projectiles, not ready to be motionless targets for their opponents.

Taennen stayed near Bascou, ready to defend the man. It was the place of any second-in-command on any given mission. He held his shield over his head and pulled his khopesh into his right hand. Sweat stung his eyes as he crawled through the foliage. He heard a volley of arrows followed by another shout of pain. Still on his belly, Taennen rounded the tree where he figured the spearman would be hiding, but he found nothing.

He scanned the immediate area for any sign of the enemies. Suddenly, one of his men's arms was struck by an axe lashing out from the darkness behind a low tree branch. The soldier's arm fell to the ground as he screamed and collapsed to the forest floor. The axe flashed again but missed a second soldier, who had thrown his weight backward and fallen to the ground to roll and come back to his feet a few paces away. Taennen dashed toward the tree, his shield and khopesh at the ready.

Taennen leaped for the branch, swiping at his foe with his blade. The enemy's axe rang out against Taennen's shield. At the same time, the khopesh dug into the soft flesh of the man's thigh. Pulling down hard as the man fell from his perch, Taennen slid his sword through flesh and sinew before wrenching it from the man's leg. His opponent hit the ground on his feet. The man was dressed in the same dark colors and mask as the invaders from the earlier attacks. The barbarian seemed not to notice his leg wound. He growled and charged Taennen.

Taennen deflected the first swipe of his opponent's axe with a clang. He sent the back of the khopesh across the barbarian's stomach, sending hot blood pouring over his hand. The enemy unleashed a howl of pain. Taennen stared down the axeman, who was barreling toward him with a bloodied blade in his hand. Taennen could hear the struggles of his companions all around him. He needed to end the fight quickly.

The barbarian's bright green eyes shone in a patch of light, peering above a kerchief that obscured most of his face. All of the wildmen wore similar masks.

The man came in for another blow. Taennen feigned a wide swing. His opponent rushed the opening, and Taennen easily dodged the man's axe. Sidestepping the blow and switching his shield to his right hand, Taennen reached out and yanked hard on the face covering with his left hand. His shield crunched into the man's shoulder. In the dim light, Taennen couldn't distinguish anything specific about the man's face—just that he was too pale for a southerner, and bearded.

Holding his shoulder in pain, the barbarian turned and ran into the forest. Taennen let the man go and dashed through the ground cover toward his men locked in combat.

Ahead of him, one of the remaining Durpari took a spear to the stomach. Taennen leaped and kicked the enemy's chest, sending him tumbling away. Taennen landed and headed for a tall spear-wielder who menaced one of the Maquar.

The spearman thrust at Taennen, ignoring his previous target. Taennen swept his weapon toward his enemy's gut, but he missed. He brought the concave edge of his khopesh around and down hard on the spear shaft. The wood of the long weapon splintered and shattered with a snap.

The wildman's eyes widened, but his surprise did not stay his hand. He dropped the remains of his weapon and drew a short sword from the back of his belt. Before he could bring the blade to bear, Taennen swung his own weapon up, twisting it in his hand. The end of the khopesh bit into the man's groin, eliciting an inhuman yelp, and sent the man to the ground. Taennen bent and slid the rounded side of his blade across the man's throat to end his pain and the threat to Taennen's squad.

✚

chapter fourteen

Not long after Jhoqo had gone, the door squeaked open. Adeenya tensed the muscles in her legs, ready to spring. Footsteps, heavy by nature, slow by effort, tapped across the hard floor at a pace that indicated no hurry. Adeenya leaned toward the low stone wall, moving slowly so as to produce no noise. She closed her left eye and peered through a crack between the blocks.

A stubby man with light hair greeted her eyes, the familiar armor recognizable even from the back. She could not see his face, but she had no doubt. There, wielding his axe a pace from the big formian, was Marlke. He shook the wrist of his free hand and popped his knuckles. Marlke moved to the heavy ring of keys hanging on the wall farthest from the cells.

Questions about his motives ripped through Adeenya's mind, but she knew no answer would satisfy her. She wanted to see the dwarf's face, hoping that he was staring at his intended victims with remorse even before the deed was done. Though she had not known her second-in-command long, she had grown to trust the moody dwarf. It might have been selfish, but that betrayal was what hurt her the most.

Adeenya sprang from her crouch and over the stone wall in one motion, already running when her feet hit the floor. "Stop!"

Marlke spun, his axe dropping to his side in one hand. He looked at her as she stopped a few paces away and drew her sword. He shook his head and pushed a disgusted sigh past his thick lips. His weapon still hung at his side, the axe head clunking to the floor as he growled, "Girl, what are you doing here?"

"Stopping a traitor," she answered.

The dwarf looked over his shoulder at the formians before returning his eyes to her. Marlke's knuckles went white as he tightened his grip on the handle of his axe. He took a step forward and brought the large weapon before him, gripped in both hands. "That's a shame."

Adeenya sidestepped the dwarf's blow. His axe rang off the stone floor. Her body moved by instinct, her thoughts coming too slowly to save her. Marlke's axe split the air arcing toward her. She hopped back a step, avoiding the strike. Coming to her senses, the anger of Marlke's betrayal settling over her like a persistent fog, Adeenya hissed. She launched her knee straight up into the flat of his axe and sent it high and away from her. At the same time, she thrust her sword low and right to score a hit in the dwarf's abdomen. He cursed aloud and sprang backward from the biting weapon.

"Always too clever for your own good, weren't you?" he said, adjusting his grip on his axe.

"The Maquar wizard?" Adeenya asked.

"Aye," Marlke replied, a grin creeping onto his face.

"Who are the attackers to you? Why would you help them?"

The dwarf laughed as he circled to his right, spinning

the axe in his hand. The head of the weapon caught one of the few beams of light in the room, and the resulting flash caused her to squint for a moment. Marlke leaped forward at that instant with a sweeping blow. She avoided the thrust with a twist of her body.

"They're nothing to me," he said, circling to his left.

Adeenya matched his pace and counter-circled. "Then why help them?"

"Why? For the coin, of course. Why else? Well . . . that and their help with killing my uncle," the dwarf said.

Adeenya knew that Marlke was the only heir to the Gemstone Chaka's ruler. Were the venerable Stoutgut patron to die, Marlke would inherit complete control of the Gemstone Chaka's considerable holdings, not the least of which were their newly discovered mine and a seat on the ruling council.

"Why not just betray your uncle and kill him yourself? You're more than capable," she spat.

Marlke rolled his eyes and said, "Oh, yes, clean and easy is your view of me, isn't it?"

He stepped in, drawing the axe across her body in a short span. The blade bit at her armor, catching enough to send her into a half-spin. She recovered her feet and responded with a wide blow.

"Ah, but there's so much more at stake. That's your problem," Marlke said. "You're so busy fussing over the details of a thing, you can't see the big picture. Well, hear me when I tell you things are never that simple."

"You'll forgive me if the lessons of a mad killer don't hold much weight with me," she said, feigning another strike.

The dwarf did not oblige her attempt and merely chuckled. "See, there you go again!" he said, slowing his pace and changing directions. "A lesson is a thing to pay heed to, no matter where it comes from. And what's so mad about making coin?"

"Blood coin," she said.

"Don't be so dramatic," the dwarf replied, ceasing his circling. "You've spent your fair share of the stuff that your daddy earned."

Adeenya centered herself on him and stopped. Marlke gave her a grin before charging, pulling the axe back for a swipe. She drove forward to meet his charge until she saw his swing come toward her from behind his back. His face showed the strain of power he was putting into the blow. Her sword was no match to parry the axe with the dwarf's full strength behind it. Adeenya threw herself on her side, the world tilting in her eyes as she plummeted to the floor. The axe rang against the stone floor where she had been only a moment before. She landed hard on her right shoulder but twisted immediately to her back. She drove her short sword into the dwarf's belly between two horizontal bands of his layered armor before rolling away and finding her feet.

Marlke let go of his axe, the weapon clattering on the floor, and placed his hands on his wound as he staggered back. Adeenya came forward with her sword drawn back, ready to cleave his head from his shoulders if he came after her again. The dwarf stumbled and slid to the floor. Adeenya heard the door open behind her. Marlke's face turned from pain to amusement as his eyes looked past her. She spared a glance over her shoulder to see Jhoqo closing the door behind him.

"You've done well," the Maquar urir said.

"Thanks, but she got me pretty good," Marlke said.

Jhoqo shook his head and walked to stand next to Adeenya. "I am sorry you were betrayed by this filthy *ojbadu*," Jhoqo said to her.

Adeenya caught her breath, befuddled by the dwarf's answer to the man. She turned her gaze from Jhoqo's kind face to see Marlke coming to his feet, his brow furrowed. His eyes were not on her but on Jhoqo. She turned to look at the Maquar but suddenly her head was falling forward and a sharp pain shot across her neck. She hit the floor, face first, her head bouncing like a child's ball. Her final glimpse before blackness overtook her was Marlke's grin.

"To your left!" Taennen shouted to one of the Durpari soldiers still standing.

Too late. The man howled as a barbarian cleaved into his shoulder with a heavy axe. Taennen barreled into the attacker. The two fell in a tangle of limbs and weapons. Taennen rolled from the fracas to his feet before his opponent. With a quick slash, his khopesh took the barbarian's life.

Taennen spun to watch a Maquar, a man he'd known for four years, being run through with a spear. The durir moved toward his falling comrade, watching in horror as blood spouted out his mouth in gouts. Taennen dived blade-first into the attacker, sinking his khopesh in deep before springing away and into another barbarian. His new opponent landed a solid blow. Taennen's armor absorbed most of the damage though his ribs crackled with pain. He kicked his opponent's stomach. The man fell to the ground, breathless. A quick slice of Taennen's khopesh made certain he'd stay that way.

The coppery tang of spilled blood filled the small forest clearing. Taennen crouched in the dim light that filtered through the trees, sweat dripping from his brow.

The forest around him had grown silent, only the buzzing

of insects to be heard. All around him the bodies of allies and enemies alike sprawled in the dirt and leaves. Only Taennen remained standing.

He found a pair of his Maquar comrades, sprawled near a tree, and was pleased to see they had found their ends fighting next to one another, defending one another until the very end. He offered quick prayers over their bodies, though he was no holy man. At a quick glance he counted eleven dead barbarians and his eight allies.

"Come, friend Taennen, we should return," Bascou said behind him.

Taennen spun and faced the man, weapon in hand, unsure where he had come from. "Return? We must search for signs of where they make their camp. Surely there are tracks or something to indicate where they came from," he said. "They killed our entire party. We have greatly diminished their numbers for certain. Now is the time to strike."

Bascou shook his head and said, "No. We are in sorry shape. We need more men."

Taennen looked Bascou over and saw no wounds at all. The man's sword dripped with blood, but he looked as whole and hearty as when they had entered the forest. Taennen began to protest, but quieted when Bascou held up his hand.

"We return."

"Our dead. We need to bring them back," Taennen said.

"I am returning," Bascou said. "You may do as you wish."

Left with little choice, Taennen followed Bascou in shock. Soldiering was Taennen's entire life, but he was accustomed to orders being sensible. Bascou's unwillingness to make fruitful the loss of so many lives was baffling. And his leaving fallen was an abomination.

Taennen walked beside the man but kept a wary eye on him. Nothing about the expedition had been right from the start. Now the Maquar and Durpari numbers were even further depleted, and Bascou did nothing about it. Did Jhoqo know Bascou was this type of man?

"How did you fare in the battle? Are you injured?" Taennen asked.

"Four fell to my blade," Bascou said.

"And your health?"

"I am uninjured. You appear unharmed as well," Bascou said. Taennen shook his head and pointed to several wounds. Bascou nodded. "You were brave indeed. That Maquar spirit—it is something to see."

The late afternoon sun washed over Taennen out on the plains, and he soaked in the warmth, glad to be in the open again, away from the dark forest. The woods felt like his mind had for the last two days: murky and dark, full of things he did not understand or want to see. Things that, no matter how he resisted, held sway over his actions, forcing him into situations he couldn't get himself out of. Though the grass was no higher than his knees, Taennen felt each blade as if it were a dark tree looming over his head.

✚

chapter Fifteen

"Very tidy," Jhoqo said, prying the sword from Adeenya's limp hand. He nudged her body on the floor of the holding cell with his foot and sighed.

Marlke groaned as he rose to his feet, the motion causing his gut wound to spill forth a new gobbet of blood. "How was I to know that wench was here?" he asked, wobbling on unsteady legs before continuing. "I asked around for her, but no one had seen her. I figured she was off somewhere bossing someone else around, and this was the best time to handle things. I was trying to think ahead."

"Thinking is exactly what you weren't doing," Jhoqo said.

"It doesn't matter now. She's out of our way. You know, I can't say I'm sorry to see her go. Acting an underling to that one . . ." Marlke screwed up his face.

"Give me some rope. We need to bind her before she rouses," the Maquar said as he knelt to position Adeenya's arms behind her back.

"Tie her? Just kill her," Marlke said.

Jhoqo said nothing.

Marlke pulled a coil of rope from his belt and tossed it to the man. Jhoqo proceeded to tightly tie the unconscious woman's wrists together. The dwarf slumped against the wall, his face taking on a dull pallor. He glared at the formians who stood silently in their cells as if the scene before them had not just played out.

"I'm going to enjoy gutting them too," the dwarf said.

Jhoqo finished his knots, tugging on the bindings a few times, and stood, pleased with his work. He removed a pouch from his belt and fingered through its content for a moment before fishing out a small vial of brackish liquid. He placed the pouch back on his belt and uncorked the vial. His placid face wrinkled as the fumes from the vial hit his senses. He held the slender glass at arm's lengths but still suffered from the scent. It smelled of cockroaches, like the acrid tang that comes from insects who live, eat and survive on death and filth.

"What are you doing?" Marlke asked.

"She could wake at any moment. We do not want that," Jhoqo replied. "This will keep her down."

The Maquar commander rolled Adeenya onto her back and moved his hand along her jaw, tracing the lines of her face. He pulled her chin down to open her mouth and tilted her head. Still shrinking from the nauseating odor of the vial himself, Jhoqo inclined the vial until a drop fell into Adeenya's open mouth. Jhoqo gently closed her jaw and settled her head back to the floor.

"There. Now she won't bother us for a while," Jhoqo said. He turned to Marlke. "I find it hard to believe that working with her would have been unpleasant. By my observations she's a fine officer, possessing a good head on her shoulders and strong—though certainly misled—morals."

"Aye, good—she's a wonderful person," Marlke said. "Now, give me a hand, will you? I know you've got a lovely elixir somewhere in that pouch of yours. Let's have it."

"No," Jhoqo said without looking at the dwarf. His eyes were trained on Adeenya, his hands on his hips. "I don't think that would be prudent."

"No? I'm bleeding out here," Marlke said.

"How do you suggest I deal with this?" Jhoqo asked, pointing at Adeenya.

Marlke's face wrinkled as he said, "Deal with . . . you kill her, of course!"

Jhoqo shook his head. "Why would I do that? It will turn the rest of the Durpari against me and draw unnecessary attention," he said. "Besides, she's a fine officer, and that's a terrible thing to waste."

"Her men? Her? Once she's dead, they're my men!"

"Yes, I suppose that's true," Jhoqo said. "Do you feel that you've earned the responsibility of leadership?"

"What are you doing?" Marlke said. "Give me that potion . . . I'm dying! I can already see two of you." Marlke tried to climb to his feet, but his shaking arms would not lift him from the floor. He flopped back to the floor with a moan. A long moment passed as the dwarf rolled onto his side to once again look upon Jhoqo. The flush of his anger slowly drained away as his body lost blood. The puddle of his own gore grew around him, expanding every moment. The smooth stones resisted the fluid, spreading the crimson stain.

"Are there three of me yet, or does it only go to two?" Jhoqo asked. "I wouldn't know as I've never died before. But that's obvious, I suppose."

"Help me," Marlke stammered.

"Now, why would I do that?" Jhoqo asked. "If I let her live, I gain the chance to train a fine officer and show her the truth of the world. She's partway there. I feel confident I can guide her the rest of the way."

"If you let her live? What are you saying? She'll tell everyone it was me in here, trying to kill the beasts."

"Of course she will. It's the truth."

"They'll lynch me!"

"It's difficult to punish a dead man," Jhoqo replied.

Marlke squinted and tried to push himself to a seated position, but his hands slipped in his own blood, slamming his chin hard to the floor. He rolled his head to one side and pleaded, "He won't like me being dead, and you know it."

Jhoqo smiled, ignoring the remark and said, "Besides, you do not have the trust of her men. Why would you? You're incompetent. If she dies but you live, I will certainly lose control of them. They will be none too happy when I accuse her of being a traitor, but she will be alive to face a fair trial. That should keep them civil enough."

"But you cuffed her on the head. Had to be you, she'll see that," Marlke said.

Jhoqo nodded and began to pace as he said, "True. I suppose. But then, to everyone else's eyes, I wasn't sure if both of you were involved or not. I was doing what I had to in order to protect the lives of our prisoners. I think they'll understand. Even she'll have to understand that I meant no harm."

Marlke's lips, turning a purplish blue, moved but no sound came at first. After a few attempts he managed to speak. "You can't . . ." he started but was interrupted by a cough. "You can't kill her, can you? He won't let it happen," he said through a bloody laugh. He licked the liquid life from his lips as his eyes fluttered. "Figures. Sentimental fool, that one."

Jhoqo said, "True enough. You're not entirely an idiot. You know what I dislike most about you, though? Your greed. It is boundless."

At that, the dwarf's eyes shot open. "Me? What about you? You're not getting paid?" he said, his words slow and beginning to slur.

Jhoqo paced back and forth in a tight circle before the dwarf and said, "Of course I am. I would be remiss in my duty as a citizen of the South to perform a job without compensation. However, you are a different matter. I am trying to open commerce, to see that every man, woman, and child in the Shining South gets an opportunity to seek their fortunes with a new and powerful ally and source of untapped wealth."

Marlke coughed, trying to respond.

Jhoqo nodded and continued, "But you—you, dwarf, merely wish to control as large a portion of the wealth as you can get your hands on. You would decrease worker wages, buy out competitors, and drive up your own prices, no doubt blaming the rise on growing production costs."

"He won't like it," Marlke whispered, returning to his earlier line of reasoning.

Jhoqo ceased walking, knelt outside the puddle of blood and said, "I am confident that, were our employer here, he would agree with me. You are just not the patriot we thought you to be, and your service is no longer required. Besides, there won't be much to be done about it in a few moments, will there?"

Taennen followed Bascou back toward the citadel. The grass on the empty plains smelled dead and defeated under the scorching sun. Taennen glanced over his shoulder many times as he followed the man before him.

As they approached to within an arrow shot, the front gates cracked open for them. Bascou sang the praises of the fallen men to those gathered just inside the citadel, proclaiming Taennen a warrior of unmatched prowess. The observers joined in his praise.

Their forces were waning, and soon there would be none of them left unless they could stem the tide of the invaders' attacks. Taennen's prowess didn't matter if they were outnumbered and outmaneuvered. He ignored the remarks and strode past Bascou, headed toward the building Jhoqo had designated for citadel operations.

Taennen's mind wandered as he walked through the courtyard. He needed to have his wounds dressed, and his sword needed to be cleaned or he would risk damaging the fine blade. He needed to write letters to the families of the men lost on the patrol that day. He pictured Loraica's face along with the rest of his fallen friends' and focused his attention. Right then, he needed to speak to Jhoqo.

The list of concerns to bring before Jhoqo formed in his mind. He chose his words carefully to tread the fine line between being too lightly critical of Bascou, whom Jhoqo clearly believed in, and smearing the man unnecessarily to the point of closing Jhoqo's mind to the possibilities he would present.

Thoughts still whirling, he knocked on his commander's door. There were no guards on duty—not surprising, given the dwindling number of bodies still upright and breathing in the citadel. Jhoqo's voiced beckoned him enter.

The late sun found every crevice it could to leak through and the room shone. Jhoqo sat behind the planning table, still covered with maps and notes on the geography and vegetation of the area. The commander held his head in his hands, not raising his eyes to greet his durir.

Still not moving, and speaking very slowly, Jhoqo asked, "Do you have word of the mission?"

"Aye, sir," Taennen replied. "It's not good."

Jhoqo lifted his face. "Taennen."

"Aye, sir."

"I am glad you are well, son. Report."

Taennen cleared his throat. "We lost all eight men."

"And Bascou?"

Taennen wanted to roar in the face of his commander. Four of his own were dead, and their commander cared first and foremost about the foreigner?

"Alive, sir," he said.

"You found them, then?" Jhoqo said.

"A contingent, not their base of operations if they even have one. Sir, we had the opportunity to learn more, but Bascou decided not to pursue the tracks of the enemy. That's why I came, sir, I don't think he—"

"I'm sure he had his reasons. Unfortunately, further issues have arisen," Jhoqo said.

"Sir, we lost—"

"I heard you, Durir. Now, listen to me," Jhoqo said as he slumped back into his chair. He pointed to another seat, but Taennen declined the offer. Jhoqo ran a hand through his dark hair and said, "There was a traitor in our midst, a saboteur. Two of them, it seems."

Taennen stood silent. Jhoqo continued before the younger man could ask the obvious question.

"Marlke's dead. Killed by his conspirator, whom I captured," the commander said.

Taennen responded before the words had finished leaving the man's mouth, "Who?"

"I'm sorry, son," Jhoqo said, and Taennen felt his knees soften. "I know you had grown close with her."

✦ ✦ ✦ ✦ ✦

Adeenya's eyes flew open and then slammed closed just as quickly when a shaft of light in the room lanced them, sending a sharp pain through her skull. Her head jerked away from the brightness, eyes cracking open again. She pulled herself up to a sitting position on the floor. Her head ached, but a check at the source of pain showed no blood or severe injury, though a bruise would doubtless fill the space. There was blood on the floor, and her face throbbed. Her fingers found a large, sore crevice of a wound on her chin as well as a split lip. Her right cheek and eye were swelling even as she felt them. Her mouth tasted terrible.

The wall behind her was rounded, a half circle that met with the flat wall before her, and a single covered window was set in the wall instead of small openings close to the ceiling. She was in one of the towers of Neversfall, she realized.

The moments prior to finding herself in that place began coming back to her. Marlke was the traitor—he had been about to kill the formians, but she had stopped him. After that, she was unsure what had happened. She had wounded the dwarf, almost certainly incapacitating him.

Adeenya glanced around the spartan room, deciding she had not been taken here for medical attention. Even the most unskilled healers would place a patient on something other than the floor, and at the very least would have cleaned her wounds. Gray walls met bare floor that held only dust. She was a prisoner, then.

Marlke's face came to her mind, his eyes looking past her, his lips turning up in a smile even as blood poured from the wound she had given him. As if it were a stone thrown at her by a giant, Adeenya felt the truth crash down upon her. Jhoqo had knocked her unconscious while she stood over Marlke.

She shuffled to her feet and checked the window. Crossed with wooden planks, it was well sealed. She pushed and pulled on the boards but to no avail. Perhaps if she had a weapon, she could work her way out, but she counted herself lucky to be alive, never mind armed. Her chin throbbed worse as she loosed a small growl.

"The door it is, then," she said.

"There's no mistake, Taennen. The Durpari dorir is dead by her sword. The prisoners nearly died as well," Jhoqo said, rising from his seat. The smaller man passed Taennen, motioning toward the door with his chin as he said, "Come, we must tell the others now that you and Bascou have returned."

Taennen had not yet spoken since Jhoqo had revealed the second traitor. He could feel his tongue in his mouth, but it felt transitory, temporary, as though his first attempt at speech would cause it to streak from his mouth and fly away, never to return. He felt like a child again, confused beyond cognition. Marlke? Adeenya? Why would Adeenya have launched such an elaborate campaign to discover the traitor if it were her?

They crossed the courtyard, Jhoqo shouting for the men to gather in the center. Word spread in ripples, one man shouting to the next, so on and so forth, until even the guards on the walls were sprinting down the stairs. The crowd fell in behind Taennen, murmuring among themselves about what the commander might say. Bascou's voice could be heard over the whispers, telling soldiers to get out of his way as he moved to stand beside Jhoqo.

Jhoqo stopped and raised his arms high, patting his

hands in the air. He called for silence and, after several moments, had it.

"Friends, I have news. News that is tragic," Jhoqo said.

Shouts issued from the audience, prompting the man to continue.

"We have been betrayed, brothers," the urir said.

Loud protestations and utterances of anger boiled forth before quieting at Bascou's insistence.

Jhoqo nodded his thanks to the Chondathan leader and continued, "But there is good news. The traitors have been found!"

The Maquar slapped their leather armor and whistled, until Jhoqo again called for silence and added, "Know this, friends, had it not been for this treachery, our other brethren who are lost to us would surely be standing with you now. Without the help of these betrayers, surely no foe could begin to harm us!"

The last several things his commander had said began fitting together in the durir's mind. Taennen looked out over the gathered crowd and saw what remained of the Durpari soldiers. What would they say when Jhoqo proclaimed their leaders as traitors? How would they react? What would a Maquar say or do if someone accused Jhoqo and himself of treachery? By sheer practice of duty, Taennen steeled himself for trouble.

Jhoqo stood tall and went on. "I know that you all wish vengeance upon those who have betrayed us, but I beg your stay in this matter. These filthy dogs should be tried, publicly acknowledged as being in violation of the Adama, in their homeland. Their faces will be spat upon by their former friends and family, and they will know the true depth and consequences of their treachery."

Cheers came in a short burst, the crowd anxious to hear

the names. The Durpari seemed to be moving toward one another in the crowd, massing together as if sensing what was about to be said. Surely they had noticed that neither of their leaders was present.

Jhoqo moved toward the Durpari, asking Maquar and Chondathan alike to part from his path. When he reached the first Durpari, he raised his arms and said, "Brothers and sisters, please understand it is with great regret that I lay before you the names of the traitors. Please know they will receive every benefit our legal code has to offer."

A few of the Durpari nodded, while the others stood silently, hands away from their weapons. They had no doubt seen the caution on the faces of everyone else present.

Jhoqo nodded and motioned the Maquar and Chondathans to back away. "My Durpari comrades, I am afraid you have been deceived. Your leader and her second have betrayed us all, and the dwarf lost his life by Adeenya's own hand."

Taennen's eyes moved at lightning speed across the scene before him. When Jhoqo finished his sentence, one of the Durpari drew his sword, the steel singing against the scabbard. Taennen's khopesh was in his hand and arcing up as he moved to intercept the Durpari.

"Halt, for your own good!" Taennen shouted. "We will resolve this without steel. She will be treated fairly."

The Durpari who had drawn his sword froze, surprise etched on his face. He held out his hand, palm facing front, and bent to place the sword on the ground. Rising, he nodded to Taennen, who lowered his own blade.

The Durpari looked to Jhoqo and said, "Consider my blade on the ground a gesture of our cooperation. While we do not believe our honorable leader to be guilty of the crime you accuse her of, we wish for no further bloodshed or treasonous behavior. We will continue to serve with the righteous Maquar and help you secure this citadel. We will await her trial back home in Durpar."

Jhoqo smiled as the Durpari motioned to his comrades to keep their weapons sheathed. "Thank you, brothers. You honor us with your trust. The orir's trial will be adjudicated fairly, I promise you this."

The speaker for the Durpari nodded and herded his men out of the crowd, leading them back to their barracks, no doubt to discuss what to do next. The Maquar in attendance muttered amongst themselves until Jhoqo dismissed them. The Chondathans present returned to their duties, all except Bascou.

The bearded man approached Taennen and Jhoqo, his head shaking. "I cannot believe this," he said with a smile. "She seemed such a good soldier."

Taennen wanted to slit the man's throat even though his words complimented the woman. The young Maquar's blood boiled at the thought of the Chondathan speaking of Adeenya at all. She was a soldier, and he was a darkblade unworthy of even her company. Taennen stayed his hand, however, staring straight ahead. He knew without a doubt that Jhoqo's eyes were on him, and he needed to measure his actions. Jhoqo answered the Chondathan's comment with something Taennen did not bother to hear.

Taennen's mind struggled with the idea that Adeenya was the traitor and wouldn't accept it. He was more certain about her than he was about anyone else in the Citadel. If she had not betrayed them, then Jhoqo had been misled in what he had seen.

Bascou said something else and offered a parting salute to the Maquar commander. Taennen fell in beside Jhoqo as the shorter man headed toward his command center. The courtyard, bustling with activity only a few days earlier, now felt deserted. The bulk of the troops had been assigned to the wall, watching the forest and plains around them in shifts, wary of the savages coming once again. They were hens trapped in a coop, but at least they were armed with swords to defend against the foxes. Neither spoke on their short trek to the command post, both knowing they would speak privately there.

Jhoqo waited for Taennen to clear the doorway before closing the door. He sat in his chair near the map-covered table in the center of the room. He waved to a chair for Taennen, who refused, preferring to stand, arms dangling at his sides.

"Speak," Jhoqo said, undoing the upper chest strap on his armor.

"Sir, are you—"

"She is responsible for the dwarf's death, son. Of that I am certain," Jhoqo said.

"She couldn't have," Taennen said.

"I've had time to think this out," Jhoqo said. "During the first fight here at the citadel, as we fought for our very lives, did you see her during the battle? Did you see her killing our enemies as our Maquar and Durpari brothers and sisters died?"

"No sir, but I could not see the entire battlefield," Taennen objected. "And neither could anyone else."

"I'm no fool, Taennen. I've spoken with others, and no one else saw her during that fight," Jhoqo said with a sigh.

"No one, sir? You've asked everyone?"

"Don't patronize me, son," Jhoqo said. "And the night our own Loraica died? Where was she then?"

Taennen shrugged, wishing he could answer the question.

"And where did we find Loraica's body?" Jhoqo asked.

"Sir, Lori could not have been killed in Adeenya's quarters. There wasn't nearly enough blood there. Besides, only a half-wit would store her victim in her own quarters."

"I hoped that she had simply been mired in a dispute with the dwarf and that his death was an isolated incident," Jhoqo said. "But the more I looked, the more I thought, and the more I realized the earlier tragedies of our betrayal seemed to fall into her lap."

Taennen did not move or speak.

"You still don't believe me?" Jhoqo asked, standing up and walking to meet Taennen face to face.

"Sir, it's just—"

"You trusted her," Jhoqo finished for him. "She didn't seem capable of it."

Taennen nodded.

"I know," Jhoqo said. "The best thing we can do with this is take it as a lesson, son. People can always fool you. I know you liked the woman. Whether I showed it or not, I did too. I still think there's hope for her, if you hear me out."

Taennen looked at the slight smile the man's face held and asked, "Hope? What hope could she have?"

"The Durpari might never allow her to serve again after her trial, but I would gladly find a place for her in our ranks, maybe even as our terir," Jhoqo said.

Expecting to feel pleased and relieved by the man's words, Taennen was taken aback by his simmering anxiety and uncertainty. A former Durpari soldier, let alone soldier turned criminal, would never be allowed to serve in the Maquar, even if Jhoqo made the request to the highest echelons of command. Even considering such a thing was beyond the scope of reason.

"Why would you do that?" Taennen asked.

"We all have the capacity to change and grow and learn from everything we do. She can learn too," Jhoqo said, taking a seat at the table.

Jhoqo stared at the table before him, the look on his face caught somewhere between concentration and contentment, as though he were about to solve some great puzzle. It was a look Taennen had seen on his father's face countless times as the man teased out new spells or formulae. In his right senses, Jhoqo would never make such an offer. Something was very wrong. If Adeenya was a traitor in league with Marlke, why would she go to such lengths to set a trap for him?

"Is she with the other prisoners?" Taennen asked.

hoqo shook his head. "That didn't seem prudent."

They stood in silence several moments longer before Taennen took his leave. In the courtyard, the evening meal was being dished out, but he had no appetite. Clouds with bellies full with the promise of rain floated through the dark blue sky. The small gatherings of soldiers scattered about were quiet, conversation an art best left to those who were not awaiting more bad news.

Taennen noticed a Chondathan soldier idling near the eastern tower that had been designed to serve as guest and dignitary quarters. Since arriving at Neversfall, the troops had not used it. Jhoqo would not have locked Adeenya away in one of the accessible buildings to prevent her own men from attempting to free her. Their goodwill would only last so long, Taennen knew, and if he knew, then Jhoqo knew. Eventually the Durpari would try to free her.

There could be no other reason for the Chondathan's presence near that tower. The man was trying to be inconspicuous but failing miserably at the pretense.

Certain Jhoqo would have his rank for it, Taennen strode

toward the door, deciding that hearing Adeenya's side was worth the risk. The rules of his duty felt constricting. He needed to look at the bigger picture. For that, he needed to hear from Adeenya. Fairness in all things, as his father had often said.

Taennen's legs gained strength beneath him as they propelled him forward. He pushed past the door and strode up the stairs. He heard the Chondathan outside the tower scrambling toward him from behind, but he did not stop.

The stone steps unwound before him. He climbed one level, passing the platform that led to the first set of rooms, then another, and then he stopped counting. He would know the door he sought when he found it. More Chondathans would be there. His boots thundered on the stone, the echoes bouncing off the cylindrical walls and back to his ears in strange waves. As he approached another level, he heard the voice he had been expecting. "Turn around, young one," Bascou said, starting down the stairs toward him.

"I will speak with her," Taennen said.

"I'm afraid not," Bascou said, as a pair of Chondathans peered over the walkway, weapons exposed.

Taennen stopped. "What business do you have with her?" he asked.

"It is not my business, but your own commander's business that brings me here," Bascou replied.

"Jhoqo's business is my business," Taennen said.

Bascou smiled and said, "Then perhaps you should talk to Jhoqo."

"I am his second-in-command," Taennen replied. "Everywhere I step is with his authority."

"Perhaps your steps can no longer bear the weight of responsibility?" Bascou said, shrugging as a grin spread across his face.

Taennen turned and paced down the stairs. He would not fight them until he knew what was going on. Any action he took other than walking away would be divisive and dangerous.

Emerging into the courtyard below, Taennen was faced with several questions in his own mind. Was Adeenya a traitor? Was he misinterpreting all the evidence that cleared her? Was Jhoqo trying to oust him from his duties? Did his commander no longer trust him? Why would they deny him access to Adeenya? What could conversation with her possibly hurt? The final two questions decided all the rest for him. If she was guilty, there was no reason to hide her away. Only the voices of the innocent needed to be silenced by those they could harm with their words.

chapter sixteen

On unsteady legs, Adeenya crossed the squared-stone floor to the door. She eased herself to her knees and put her ear to the door, its cool smoothness soothing to her aching head. When no sound greeted her, she bent lower, attempting to look beneath the door through the narrow gap between floor and portal. Two pairs of boots stood a few paces away to the left of the door. Twisting her head, she put her ear toward the gap and heard voices, just above a whisper. Their unfamiliar tongue grated on her ears with guttural syllables and fricatives sprinkled throughout.

Adeenya rose to her feet, doing her best to be quiet. Her slow speed made her muscles strain, adding to her fatigue. She glanced around the room again, hoping she had missed something on her first check, but she saw the same bare walls and empty floor. Adeenya leaned against the wall and took several deep breaths before knocking on the door with the flat of her palm. The voices outside stopped, and scuffling boots sounded on the stone floor. Quick words were exchanged, and the door opened inward revealing two Chondathan soldiers. Both were of middling age, with the typical dark hair and heavy moustaches common among the newly arrived troops.

"What?" one of them asked, his sword in his hand but his posture relaxed.

"Why am I here?" Adeenya asked.

"Traitors belong in cells," said the other, his accent much less thick than his partner's.

Adeenya focused on the second man, noting his distinctive green eyes and soft, round face. "Traitor?"

The green-eyed man nodded and added, "Yes, traitor. We know you work with the savages."

"By whom have I been accused?" Adeenya asked, knowing the answer but wishing to keep the men engaged as long as possible so that she might discern more information.

The other man sneered and said, "The Maquar leader saw you kill the dwarf, girlie."

"He died, then?" she asked. She knew the wound she had delivered was not a small one, but it would have been possible to heal it.

The round-faced man nodded while the other chuckled, spitting something in his native tongue. Adeenya stepped back, her head shaking. The green-eyed man, the better speaker of the two, stepped into the room and put a hand on her shoulder. She lifted her head and looked the man in the eyes.

"It will be all right. You will receive judgment. They will only make you work," the man said. "In our country, it would be much worse for you."

His emerald eyes smiled at her, nearly withdrawing her attention from the man behind him, who stood laughing at her plight. Adeenya placed her hand over the one on her shoulder and looked the man in the eyes. A snarl flashed on her lips as she squeezed his hand with all her strength and jerked his arm downward.

The smile fled the man's lips as Adeenya's knee slammed

into his face. His wrist cracked under her grip. His head bounced off her knee, straightening his forcibly bent posture. Before the man could steady himself, Adeenya followed her assault with a fist to his nose that sent him spinning away behind a flowering spray of red.

She whirled to kick at his companion who was already on her. Her strong, slender leg arced toward the grinning man who caught her foot and gave it a hard yank with his left hand. He dropped his sword from his right hand and sent a balled fist into her gut. The force of his punch stole every bit of breath her lungs held.

He tossed her leg aside and punched her again, and this time his aim found her jaw. Gasping in pain, Adeenya fell to the floor. A gray dimness encircled her vision and grew darker each moment she held onto consciousness. As the darkness closed in around her, the first man with the kind green eyes stood and dusted himself off. Red-faced from his compatriot's chuckling, the man kicked Adeenya in the ribs with a resounding crunch.

The door slammed shut before her. Outside, she heard her chuckling assailant say to the green-eyed man, "That is twice now, my friend. You are slipping."

Adeenya pulled herself against the nearby wall and tried to relax her muscles. The pain was easier to take than she had expected. Her ribs ached. Her head throbbed. Had she a mirror, Adeenya was certain she would find bruises on the side of her face, likely blooming bright and colorful. They would fade into purples, greens, and then yellows. Would she still be trapped in this place then? Would she be alive long enough to see those ugly marks diminish?

The room had become very dark, not granted even the meager light that made it past the boarded window before her assault. Evening had settled. She wondered if the guards had changed. Even if so, it would do her little good. The previous guards would have warned the newcomers of her attempt to escape, making them wary of any further efforts.

Adeenya pulled her legs in tight to her chest, resting her forehead on her knees. She thought about all the times other warriors had told her that they felt naked without their armor and limbless without their weapons. She craved her armor worse than even her favorite food, but she did not feel naked without it. She desired her weapons more than any lover she had ever taken, but she did not feel limbless. Anger pervaded her mind, leaving room for little else and granting her protection and fury.

A voice outside the door spoke. She started when she heard a familiar booming voice answer the first. She uncoiled her body but stayed seated, ready to move quickly if necessary. Other voices answered the first and feet shuffled. The door before her opened, and torch light poured in, chasing away the darkness. Her anger seethed at the sight of the entrant as he placed a torch in a sconce on the wall.

"Good evening," Jhoqo said, closing the door behind him with one hand, the other riding the hilt of his sword. He wore a slight smile and soft eyes. He was in full dress—armor, rank insignia, and Maquar silks.

Adeenya met his gaze and did not falter, even when she heard the men on the other side of the door moving away, their feet pounding as they went down a flight of stairs. The muscles in her jaw flexed rapidly as she clenched, the pressure on her teeth growing almost unbearable. For his part, Jhoqo knelt and nodded toward her, as if he understood and forgave her reaction.

"I can only imagine what you're feeling now," the man said.

Adeenya sprang forward, her hands reaching toward the Maquar's neck. Jhoqo's head shook as he stepped into her attack and drove a fist into her stomach. She crumpled back to the floor, sputtering and gasping for air. He withdrew and crouched, watching her closely. She forced away the pain and drew a deep breath as she pushed herself back up against the wall. Her eyes found his again, his dark skin shimmering in the firelight from the torch.

"Please do not do that again," Jhoqo said. "I have no wish to harm you."

"Only to knock me out from behind? To blame me for Marlke's death? And what else?" Adeenya said. "What other invented crimes have you charged me with?"

"A few, all necessary," Jhoqo replied. "His death is the only one that you are guilty of."

"I was trying to stop him! Your interference is what killed him. Or maybe you finished him off yourself!"

"You caused his death," Jhoqo replied. "Whether directly or indirectly, you were the cause of his death. Had you not insisted upon setting a trap for the traitor, you would never have discovered Marlke at his work. Had you not found him, he would not be dead."

"That's the logic of someone seeking absolution if I've ever heard it," she said.

Jhoqo shrugged again, unimpressed with the distinction. "I let him die. You killed him," he said. "There is a difference."

"By the One and the All . . . you are mad," Adeenya said, her feet unconsciously pushing against the stone to move farther from the man.

Jhoqo smiled halfway and nodded as he moved himself to rest against the door, sitting opposite the woman. "Your words do not surprise me, but let me ask a question. Why did you become a mercenary?" he asked.

When she did not answer, he continued, "Did you wish to serve something greater than yourself? Though Durpar does not have a military institution in the same sense as my country, you mercenaries fill that void. Is that why you made your choice?"

Adeenya thought about the question and nodded. She saw an opportunity and could not pass it up.

"It is the same for most of us, I think," he said, offering a larger smile.

"Most of who?" she asked.

"Patriots, like you and I," he answered. "That's what we are, Adeenya. We love our countries, our people, our ways of life."

Her eyes wide, Adeenya said, "You're a murderer. You're no hero!"

"I said patriot," he replied, and added, "though I think history will remember me as a hero as well. How do you wish to be remembered, Adeenya? As a hero or a traitor?" Jhoqo asked, leaning toward her.

Adeenya hesitated, Jhoqo's grotesque nature growing clearer to her by the moment. Talk of patriots and heroes, love of country and fellow man—it made her stomach heave in protest to think of the man before her believing such things about himself, while the blood of his subordinates soaked the ground. His eyes shone back at her in the torchlight, and he clearly expected a response to his question.

"I'm no hero, " Adeenya said, "and I don't yet deserve to be remembered as one. Maybe I never will be," she said with a shrug before continuing. "And if you're what passes for a patriot, then I'd not call myself one in this life or any after."

Jhoqo nodded, easing away from her. He stared at her

in silence for several moments before standing, his knees grinding a little and causing him to sigh. The short man moved to the wall against which she rested and placed his hand on the stone. Running his fingers along the rock, he smiled, tracing the tiny gaps where one stone met another.

"Do you know what makes stacked stones stand together as a wall?" Jhoqo asked, not looking at her.

"Patriotism?" Adeenya said, sarcastically.

Jhoqo's grin widened as he looked at her and said, "Of the builders who come together to craft the wall? That's true. But I mean in a broader sense."

Jhoqo ran a finger along the gaps between the stones again and spoke softly, "If you stack these stones directly atop one another, no matter how many columns, they will begin to waver and eventually tumble after you pile six, maybe seven of them high, will they not?

"However, if you place several side by side and a similar row atop those, but shifted one way or the other from those below so that the gaps no longer line up, you achieve more balance, but no permanency, solidity, or strength.

"The strength—what keeps them together—is the weight of them. The pressure is spread amongst them, each taking its fair share and passing the rest down to its neighbor," Jhoqo said, kneeling on the floor near her. "Like soldiers working together, they take everything they can handle and trust in their fellow soldiers, their brothers and sisters, to do the same. Given enough stones, no height is unreachable, no weight too much, no pressure too great. The same is true of soldiers and patriots."

She frowned and ran her fingers over the stone. His words were surprisingly moving. Despite the situation, she longed to feel the connection between them, but she felt only cold rock, well placed by hundreds if not thousands of workers, and likely magically enhanced to be sturdy and durable.

"So how does killing and falsely accusing allies and comrades make them stronger?" Adeenya asked.

Still kneeling, Jhoqo shook his head and replied, "You live for that sense of camaraderie that only a soldier knows. You thrive on holding the trust of others, grasping it with every ounce of your strength. You love freely giving your trust to those same brothers and sisters, to see them cradle your life in their capable arms."

Adeenya offered no response. They both knew what he said was true. The truth he spoke was the same for all soldiers.

"It's the same for me, sister," Jhoqo said. "But my love of my comrades has grown beyond just my fellow soldiers. That sense of glorious obligation you feel to your brothers in arms, I feel to my fellow countrymen, in fact, all southerners as a whole. Their pain is my agony, their triumph my joy."

Adeenya did not attempt to hide her laughter, letting it echo in the room, hoping more than anything to watch it float to his ears and crush his head with its melodious force and wrathful earnestness.

Jhoqo frowned and shook his head. "I thought that, of anyone here, of anyone I've met in a long time, you would understand. He had hoped you would too."

Adeenya sprang to her feet, her face flushing red as she said, "Taennen thought I would understand your rhetoric?"

Jhoqo took a single step back, his hand going to the hilt of his sword at the woman's sudden movement. When it was clear she was not advancing, her words seemed to sink in, and the man shook his head. "Taennen? Gods, no. He doesn't understand, either," Jhoqo said.

"Then who?" Adeenya asked.

Without responding, Jhoqo moved toward the door.

"Wait. Who was hoping I would understand?" she asked.

"It does not matter. He was wrong, for the first time since I've known him," Jhoqo responded.

"Sometimes we don't know ourselves as well as others in our lives do," Adeenya said. She had gone too far, pushed too hard. She needed to keep him talking until the time was right if she wanted to escape.

Jhoqo stopped a few paces from the door, his eyes narrowing as he faced her and said, "Yes, that is so."

Adeenya started to speak, but no words came. She ran her hands through her ruddy hair and leaned against the windowed wall. "Maybe this person of whom you speak . . ." she said, hoping Jhoqo would finish the thought.

When no response came, Adeenya looked up to find him staring hard at her. "When I started this mission, I thought I knew what being in the military meant," she said.

"And now?" Jhoqo responded.

"I don't . . . you were right, you know, when you said that I live for the camaraderie of this life. More than anything, I long for that sense of community, of knowing that the man next to me on that battle line is living as much for me as for himself," she said. "I thought I had that. Maybe I did, even, but when I saw your men, I knew there was more," she said. "I'm not going to pretend that I agreed with all of your decisions as their leader, but they followed you without question, and they really seemed to enjoy working side by side. They know one another, and they care about one another."

"Your soldiers don't?" he asked.

"They do. We do," she said, sighing. "But part of me always wonders . . ."

"What?" he asked.

"They're mercenaries, more or less. Are they here solely for the coin?" she said, locking eyes with the man.

Jhoqo smiled and said, "And what's wrong with profiting from the work you do? A soldier works harder than any other person alive. My troops and I all benefit from our work."

She shook her head. "But you didn't join an outfit like the Maquar for that. You joined because you wanted to dedicate yourself to something bigger."

"But the two can go together," the Maquar said. "In fact, they must. That's what most people miss. That's what Taennen misses.

"Jeradeem Seltarir, father of the Adama, taught us that everything is part of everything else, no? That's why he was such a fine trader. He knew that the more business he did and the more coin he made, then the more he could spend to improve the lives of others, and the more he could pay the people in his own chaka," Jhoqo said, bending down to rest on his haunches. "Commerce is our lifeblood, and we must defend it."

"Taennen does not agree with you?" Adeenya asked.

Jhoqo sighed, settling on the floor, his legs crossing easily. If she wasn't careful and she ran, he would catch her with just as little effort. "It's not a matter of agreement, it is one of understanding. He has grown no closer to understanding during the past several years. I had hopes for him, but it appears Taennen will never be any more than he is now," Jhoqo said.

"And what is that?" she asked.

"Like most men, he is a tool, a device to carry out the commands of the craftsman who wields him."

"So he's a good soldier?" she asked.

"Excellent, I would say," Jhoqo replied.

"But?"

"A good soldier follows orders and even thinks creatively, but he is a tool. A good leader, on the other hand, needs to do more," Jhoqo said. "A good leader's orders can be mediocre, but he has the guts, the fortitude, and the assertiveness to give them and see them done."

"So Taennen is lacking confidence?" Adeenya asked, knowing the man's answer and finding herself grudgingly agreeing with him.

"Correct."

"What about his decision in the battle against the formians?" she asked.

"A costly one, to be sure," Jhoqo said. "However, if he had had the willpower to stand up to me when I addressed him about it, to stand by his decision and not even offer to defend it, then he would have shown more promise. As it was, he realized that he could not change things. Once he understood that, he did not mope on the subject further. A positive step, certainly."

"So your goal is to help your countrymen, not just your fellow Maquar?" Adeenya asked, eyes flicking to the door. The Chondathans' footsteps had not returned.

"To help all people of the Shining South, not just those from Estagund," Jhoqo said.

"How?"

"By opening new doors for them, by giving them new things to learn, new ideas to consider, and new trades to profit from," Jhoqo said.

Eyes squinted, Adeenya asked, "How do you manage that?"

Jhoqo smiled. "I'm afraid I can't share that with you."

"How does letting Marlke die achieve that?" she said, peeling the accusatory tone from her voice.

The man took a deep breath and said, "Like Taennen, Marlke was a device, and he had served his purpose. He was no longer capable of adapting to the situation, changing to be useful. In fact, it was only in death that he could serve our cause one final time."

"Tell me about the cause," she said.

Jhoqo merely shook his head.

"Then how am I to learn about this way of being that you've shared with me?" she asked. She was losing him, and fast.

"You're probably not going to, nor do you even want to. You've only been asking in order to distract me and purchase some much needed time to think for yourself," he replied.

"You've made me think," she said.

"Maybe. Maybe not. It doesn't matter," he said.

"Why not?"

"Because I cannot take the chance of setting you free and I cannot kill you," Jhoqo said with a shrug before turning onto his side to prop himself to his feet. "He would never allow it. I would jeopardize my place in the coming era if I acted to bring about your demise."

Adeenya saw her opportunity and took it. Dashing forward as Jhoqo came to one knee, Adeenya plowed her shoulder into the side of the man's face, bouncing herself off the wall but forcing him to take most of the impact. Scrambling to her feet, she dived into him again, this time sending her knee into his chest, letting it continue upward into his throat as her right hand snatched for the hilt of his sword.

Shuffling sounds outside the door told her the guards had returned and heard the ruckus inside. Without regard for stealth, she unsheathed the man's enormous falchion and kicked him in the jaw. The footsteps outside were just beyond the door. She had to move quickly.

Adeenya drew the sword high over her head. She felt something in her hands, a thrumming that urged her forward. The enchanted blade pulsed with power. She charged forward, the sword plunging ahead, biting into and through the wooden door with a loud report. Splinters flew outward, blasting the passageway beyond.

Adeenya barked in pain at the vibration running through her arms. With no time to see if her captor was still prone from the beating, Adeenya ran from the room, shoving past the surprised guards, and sprinted down the stairs. The hammering footsteps of the guards chasing her drove her on. She had no idea where she would go or what she would do, but freedom beckoned and she kept on running.

✝

chapter seventeen

Since he had arrived at the citadel, Taennen Tamoor had seen things he never would have believed possible and felt things he hoped never to feel again. He pushed open the door to the massive tower known as Neversfall and trudged up the stairs. A thousand shades of gray and black unwound before him as he climbed the steps. Lucha's light, filtered by the approaching clouds, aided the torches hung on the walls in guiding him. Upon reaching the top, he stepped into the tower room as delicately as if he were walking a tightrope. Khatib's face smiled at him in his mind as Taennen stood in front of one of the enormous viewing portals.

The Aerilpar forest looked closer and more real from that height than it had when he had been among its trees. The woods stretched before him as far as he could see, and somewhere beyond were the Giant's Belt Mountains. Nothing else was in sight, like being in the middle of the sea with only water around you. Each hillock of the plains was like a wave meandering on its way to a hidden shore. The only islands in the sea were Neversfall and the Aerilpar. Taennen scanned the forest for a long while.

Taennen had heard that when certain tracking animals were given a scent and ordered to chase it, they were overcome with a kind of frantic fever that forced them to chase the scent until they found its source, no matter the cost. He recalled one story in which a man's hunting dog had chased the smell of a wanted criminal—a young man who had raped the hunter's daughter—for nearly three days straight, leaving the hunter far behind halfway through the first day. The hunter had, so the story went, camped and rested, following the tracks of his companion until he came upon the loyal creature. Weakened from a lack of food, covered in cuts and sores from its long journey, the dog had died, literally running itself to death in pursuit of its quarry. The hunter was saddened but was filled with pride in and thankfulness for his friend, for the dog had insured that the man would have his vengeance. No more than two bowshots away from the poor animal lay the criminal in a pool of his own dried blood, his legs rendered useless by the dog's attacks.

Taennen felt as though he was beginning to understand the dog. Certain he had figured out something important, he ran through the citadel of Neversfall toward the only other potential source of information that might assist him. The night was warm, and sweat streamed down his face as he made his way toward the building that held the prisoners. Two of the Chondathan guards stood outside the structure, conversing quietly, their casual stance an insult to anyone who had ever served in a legitimate military unit. Taennen slowed his pace to model confidence without concern. He nodded to each guard in turn and reached for the door.

When the guards stepped together, shoulders touching in the middle to block his entry, Taennen said, "I'm to further interrogate the prisoners."

"No one's to see them," the shorter Chondathan said, his compatriot nodding his agreement.

Taennen allowed his anger to ride across his face. He would not be denied access to his own prisoners by a Chondathan. He placed his hand on the hilt of his khopesh and leaned in close to the man who had spoken. Before he could speak, both guards had drawn their weapons and were snapping at him in their native tongue. Seeing the shorter man's daggers and the other's long sword waving in his face, Taennen took two steps back, raising his empty hand into the air.

"No one sees them," the Chondathan repeated.

Taennen's eyes narrowed as he said, "We'll see."

The guards traded looks and a few foreign words before facing him again, the previous speaker saying, "Do as you will."

Taennen eyed each man and walked south of the building, turning past the next structure. He quickened his pace but tried to keep his step light as he went around the back of the quarters to come up behind the jail. Stretching his body, standing on the tips of his toes, Taennen tried to reach the narrow windows in the wall to no avail.

Summoning every lesson on stealth he had ever learned, Taennen lowered himself to the dirt and slid under the building, through the trench in the ground. He pushed on the stone floor above him, checking for loose slabs, but found none.

Slipping his khopesh from his belt, Taennen made his way toward the front of the jail. He reached the front corner of the building, took a deep breath, and began to move into view of the guards, ready to charge and catch them unaware. He felt certain he could get past the guards, although perhaps not without seriously harming them.

As he put his plan into motion, shouts emanated from the central courtyard in the strange Chondathan tongue.

The two guards, mere paces from him, acknowledged the calls and ran toward the source of the commotion. Taennen did not pause to wonder what the trouble was. A gift was a gift, his father had always said.

Taennen darted to the door. The fetid smell of the place had not improved since his last visit, and his nose burned with the acidic taint of waste. Some small corner in the back of his mind made note to reprimand the guards for not having followed his earlier orders to improve conditions for the formians.

"Guk!" Taennen whispered.

No response came and Taennen blinked, his eyes adjusting to dim light. Before him, standing in the very spot where he had last seen the creature, the large formian turned his head toward Taennen, his head cocked to one side. Taennen stepped in close and pulled off the creature's gag and blindfold, his nose a mere handspan from the formian's clattering mouth appendages, even though the bars separated them. The strange, hardened flesh that covered Guk's body glistened in the torchlight, seeming radiant when compared to its dull appearance in the open sunlight of the battlefield where they had originally met.

"It was the dwarf, Marlke, you saw go into the tower," Taennen said with no hint of a question in his tone.

"Yes," Guk said.

The formian's utter lack of an attempt to bluff, to strengthen his bargaining position, caused Taennen to step away from the creature. The otherworldly nature of the formian had never been so apparent, and Taennen suddenly felt ill-equipped to relate to Guk on even the most basic level. He stammered for a moment before gathering his wits and stepping forward again to stand face to face with the formian.

"The dwarf is dead," Taennen said. "Did you see anyone else go into the tower? Did you see anyone else talking with the dwarf?"

"No," Guk said. His antennae twitched as if considering a puzzle or some other curiosity.

"Your freedom . . . do you still want that?" Taennen asked.

Guk offered a simple nod, displaying no emotion.

Taennen felt a wave of relief, finally getting something positive from the strange captive. Though the thought of dangling freedom before a prisoner made his stomach roil, Taennen had no other bargaining chips.

"When we found you, where had you come from?"

"The trees," Guk said.

"The forest? Aerilpar?" Taennen asked.

Guk agreed and said, "The forest provided many workers."

"You were searching the forest for slaves before we encountered you?" the young durir asked.

"We retrieved many workers from there," Guk answered, and for the first time, Taennen thought he might have detected something in the formian's tone: irritation.

"How long were you there? How much of the forest did you see?" he asked.

Guk paused a moment, his mandibles clacking, before replying, "Almost two of your tendays we stayed there, keeping to the western edge and middle."

"In that time, did you see any other men—humans like us—anywhere? Any camps or signs of them? Any fires in the night?" Taennen asked, knowing that the beast clans who inhabited the forest would live much deeper in the woods than Guk would have traveled.

"No."

Taennen's pleasure at having been correct was quickly replaced by the void that comes from disproving the only available assumption. He had nothing to go on, no possibilities to investigate. His insight while staring at the forest from the tower had been correct. As he had scanned the trees he saw no smoke, no firelight. None of the patrols had reported even seeing a used firepit. That told him the bandits were not coming from the forest.

"In all the One . . . where are they coming from?" he said to himself.

"If you find these others, you will release us," Guk said.

Taennen's looked up at the formian's dark, empty eyes. "You know where they are," he stated, having no doubt about the assertion.

"Yes."

Only Adeenya's disciplined mind kept her pace slow and quiet. Making noise would attract the guards, and that could not happen. She slipped across the courtyard on the balls of her feet. Two Chondathan soldiers, their torches cutting through the dark, scanned the area. To the north, near a cluster of quarters, more soldiers scurried about. It would be the same all over the citadel, she knew.

Adeenya wondered what might have happened had she stayed in her prison and taken Jhoqo's words to heart. What were his plans for her? But mostly, she wondered if he could have convinced her. His words had begun to pierce her will—she had found some value in them, and that frightened her.

She tried to shake the doubt from her mind to focus on the task before her—staying alive and staying free. She needed to reach her own troops, to somehow communicate with them. She wondered if any of them had swallowed Jhoqo's rhetoric. She had no doubt the Chondathans were working with Jhoqo, but she was uncertain of the Maquar. While Jhoqo no longer fit into that organization's belief system, by her estimation, perhaps some of his soldiers still did.

Her first step would be to attempt contact with her own troops, so she turned toward their barracks on the far side of the citadel. She did not relish such a challenge and found great relief when she realized that some of her soldiers might be guarding the wall for the night duty. Only one more small building stood between her and the wall, and the shadows there were easier to hide in. Lucha was hidden by thick clouds, and Adeenya prayed that they would linger long enough to cover her.

The stairs leading to the walkway were less than half a bowshot away. Stealth was not her strength, but Adeenya had hope for the first time since her capture. Staying crouched, she prepared to make a dash for the stairs. Before she could overthink the plan, she darted across the courtyard to the stairs. Her heart pounded and her ears burned. She felt convinced that eyes were upon her. She reached the stairs and, staying as flat against the wall as possible, she slinked up the stairs.

Comforted by the shadows at the top, she proceeded toward the far end of the citadel. Lacking her armor, she was instilled with both a sense of dread and of freedom. The freedom and ease of movement without her stiff leather plate was pleasing, but she knew she would not survive long without it if she were forced into battle.

Several paces ahead, she saw the dim light of one of the watch posts, where guards remained stationed instead of pacing the perimeter. She crept forward, hoping the guard on duty would be one of her own soldiers. As she drew nearer she was disappointed to see instead the features of one of the Chondathans. Moving to the inside wall of the walkway, she inched toward the man. Adeenya was two steps from an ideal ambush position directly behind the man when he spoke.

Taennen clipped short the scream of frustration he had almost loosed. His face turned a light crimson as he trembled with impotent rage. The formian leader, in spite of the display before him, stood as silent and unmoving as ever. Taennen stepped back from the creature and calmed himself. He could hear more activity outside the building, soldiers answering some urgent call issued from the rear of the citadel.

"Where are they?" he demanded. "Where are the invaders?"

"We do not know," Guk replied.

"You just—" Taennen began.

"We do not know where they are at all times, but where they come from, into this place, that we know," the formian said.

"How? How do they get into the citadel?"

"Under," Guk said.

"Under? The ground?"

The formian said, "Tunnels."

It made sense. How else could the invaders have entered the citadel without discovery? It explained the lack of fires in the forest and how the patrols had found no trace of camps in the woods. His mind slammed the pieces into place, but he found one that did not fit. They had fought the enemy in the woods. If they moved and slept in the tunnels, how did the barbarians know to find them in the forest?

The answer came readily. The enemy knew where to find them because someone told the enemy where they would be. There *was* a traitor.

"You will free us now," Guk said, interrupting Taennen's thoughts.

The Maquar durir looked up at the formian and considered the words. He had implied the formian's freedom for cooperation, and he would not dishonor himself by failing to follow through on even a tenuous promise. Freeing them would mean his career, he did not doubt. Not freeing them might cost his life.

"Show me the tunnels and then leave by them," Taennen said.

Guk's head shifted from side to side for a moment, his antennae flickering, followed by the same motions from his cohorts. "Agreed," the formian leader said.

Taennen went to the door, opening it a crack to peer out. He saw no one in that part of the courtyard. He opened all the cells, untying the formians' bindings, and motioned for them to follow him. He stepped out of the building and looked both directions down the narrow paths between structures. He was turning to hurry the creatures when he found they were already behind him, moving so quietly that, even at a few paces, he could not hear them.

"Where?" Taennen asked.

Guk pointed to one of the outlying buildings, one of only a few not built on piers, and moved down the prison's steps toward it, his fellows following. The structure was one of the smallest, and it seemed an unlikely choice for an entrance to a secret tunnel. Perhaps, Taennen thought, that was the point. He fell into step beside Guk, keeping his movements as quiet as he could. His hand rested on the hilt of his khopesh, and his shield arm flexed in anticipation. They made the front door of the building, and Taennen ushered the formians through the door. Inside, Guk stood in the middle of the room, his antennae weaving back and forth.

"Where is it?" Taennen asked.

"I do not know," Guk said. Before Taennen could reply, he continued. "I know it is here but have not seen it from this side."

"What? You've been in the tunnels?" he said.

"No," Guk answered.

"Then how did you see it?"

"Others showed me."

"What others?" Taennen asked, clutching his weapon.

"My people."

Taennen looked around the room at the formians and said, "There are more out there? More who are not prisoners?"

"Yes. Small ones. Workers."

"How did they show you the tunnel?"

Guk's head jerked again, his mandibles clicking together. After a few moments, he stopped but said nothing. None of the creatures spoke or even moved. Taennen did not believe they wanted to be uncooperative or that they were trying to be secretive. Guk had proven himself honest to a fault, after all. Perhaps they could not explain it, he thought.

"That noise you were making, that humming . . . is that how they showed you?" Taennen asked.

"Yes," Guk said, and Taennen thought he saw something akin to relief on the creature's face.

"Well, this room is small, so it can't be hard to find."

Together, Taennen and the formians moved crates and barrels from one of the room's corners but found no trapdoor. The floor consisted of about twenty square blocks of stone. Taennen directed the formians to lift them. After only a few attempts, they found four adjacent stones that moved. Under the stones was a wooden door with iron hinges and handles. The door was opened and Guk ordered his people through it before Taennen could even offer to go first. All but one of the formians entered the tunnel. Taennen eyed the creature warily but slipped through the door to stand next to Guk. Soft light shone from a magical orb on the ceiling of the tunnel.

Taennen pointed up through the portal and asked, "Why isn't that one coming?"

"Our route of escape must remain hidden," Guk said.

Taennen felt ill when the truth became clear. Guk had ordered one of his people to stay behind to replace the stones over the door and lead anyone who might be searching for them away from the tunnel entrance. He had ordered men to make sacrifices before, but never like that. Above him, the door closed and he heard the scraping of the heavy tiles being moved into place.

"They'll kill him when he's found," Taennen said.

"Yes," Guk replied, and turned to move down the tunnel. "But the whole will benefit."

+ chapter Eighteen

Would you believe me if I told you that no harm will find you if you surrender?" the wall guard asked, turning to face Adeenya with a grin on his face.

Adeenya did not spare even the briefest moment to curse her luck. Instead she threw herself into the Chondathan before her. Though no stranger to physical confrontation, Adeenya had never tried such a maneuver in mortal combat without her armor on, and at that moment she understood why. Pain shocked her shoulder when she made contact. When she heard a cracking noise, she felt sure the bone was broken, but to her relief the terrible sound was the guard's ribs snapping, his leather armor having failed to absorb the force of her charge. Propelled by her momentum, the enemy lost his footing, and together they piled into the walkway's parapet.

With the man stunned by the impact of her attack, Adeenya managed to win the race to act first after the tumble. She sent a knee into the man's stomach and a forearm into his nose. Her opponent fell, huddled against the parapet, his face buried in his hands. Muted moans of pain streamed from his mouth, and blood ran down his wrists.

Before his groans could turn to shouts that might alert

his fellows, Adeenya jerked his hands from his face and lashed out with Jhoqo's falchion. She drew a wide, ugly line across his neck. The Chondathan thrashed for only a moment before stillness overtook him, his head lolling. Adeenya checked his body for anything of use to her. Pleased with Jhoqo's sword, she left the dead man's weapon behind but paused to strip some of the armor from his corpse and don it herself. It didn't quite fit, but it was better than nothing.

Without bothering to hide the evidence of her attack, Adeenya crept forward along the walkway toward the open end of the courtyard. It was there that most of the people in the citadel were converging. The black of night blended into the dark stone of the citadel so that the dim torchlight stood out in contrast. Adeenya had never minded the dark before, but as she skulked along the walkway, unsure of what might lay in wait for her, she hated it.

As she came within sight of the open courtyard, she saw the soldiers from all three organizations gathered there. A few crates were pushed together, indicating that someone— likely Jhoqo—meant to address the gathered audience. She was too far away to hear the oratory, so she crept forward.

Adeenya slowed her already deliberate pace as she approached the next source of torchlight on the wall and readied herself for another conflict with the guard who would be waiting there. Slinking along the outside wall, she came within site of the usual holding position—vacant. Pleased but disquieted by the lack of opposition, Adeenya continued forward to get a better view of the scene below her.

She blinked her eyes, sensing something ahead. The torch that normally lit the area had been doused, causing the darkness to swallow everything. Her feet found the stone beneath them, but not because she could see it well. Adeenya lowered herself to her hands and knees, crawling on all fours, hoping to quiet her movement even more. She stopped and saw someone crouched on the walkway several paces ahead of her. The dim light revealed a crossbow aimed into the courtyard. Whoever wielded it wore dark clothing that obscured his or her identity. Had one of her men discovered the truth and planned to assassinate the crazed Jhoqo?

Perhaps the bowman was not there to slay Jhoqo but Taennen. Had the younger man finally stood up to his commander, challenging the urir? Adeenya shook the thought from her mind. There was only one way to learn the shooter's intentions. If it were one of her men, she would apologize later.

She dashed forward on the balls of her feet, a dance blending speed with silence. The prone figure turned and began to stand much too late. Adeenya launched her booted foot into the bowman's face, knocking him off-balance and sending him tumbling into the walkway. She followed him quickly, leaping atop the rolling victim to bring the motion to an end. Finally able to see his face, Adeenya took satisfaction in her initial decision and punched the mouth of the Chondathan man she sat astride. Teeth buried themselves in her knuckles, but her fist dived in again, eliciting a spray of blood and a groan of pain. Though awkward from her kneeling position, Adeenya sliced the falchion's blade across the man's throat, ending his squirming.

As she caught her breath after the struggle, voices from the courtyard wafted to her ears. Indistinct sounds, like whispers in dreams, chattered away. Unable to distinguish much, Adeenya proceeded atop the walkway. Less surprised but still fearful of the meaning, Adeenya found another crossbowman crouched atop the wall, his weapon targeting the interior of the courtyard. Dressed in dark, drab clothing, this enemy scanned the area below as if looking for a target. She needed to strike as quickly and decisively as she had just moments ago. When her intended victim spun toward her and let loose a bolt, she hoped Taennen would figure out the truth in her stead.

Taennen followed the formians as they scurried through the tunnels. Utterly blind in the absolute darkness, he listened for their soft, almost soundless footfalls. They had run several hundred paces, but they had not yet seen another light like the one at the tunnel's entrance. Perhaps they were in an unused portion of the tunnels? The formians could be leading him anywhere. Taennen slowed his pace and came to a stop. Ahead, the formians halted as well.

"Come." Guk's voice floated out of the darkness.

"Where are we going?" Taennen asked.

"To the invaders."

"Why would you take me there?"

Silence reigned for several moments before the tell-tale clacking of the formians' mandibles echoed through the chamber, followed by Guk saying, "Because you freed us, as agreed."

"But you make slaves of my people."

Another long pause came before the formian spoke again. "We agreed. You free us, we show you the invaders. We gave you our word. Our word is law."

Taennen had little choice but to accept the given intentions at face value or wander lost in the tark tunnels, so he asked the formians to proceed and he fell in behind them. Extending both arms to let his fingers skim along the rocky walls to check his surroundings, Taennen felt safer, more grounded. He could smell fresh water even above the bitter scent of aged rock and the musty odor of the mildews and molds common underground.

The formians slowed down as the darkness began to break apart under the prying wisps of light ahead. Though not enough to distinguish any details, the dim magical light, like that near the tunnel entrance, allowed Taennen to make out shapes. He crept forward until he was looking past the formians into a large open area, a cave with a high ceiling and broad walls. Staying in the obscuring dark of the tunnel, Taennen squinted to make out details. Before he could focus, he felt a prodding at his back. He turned to face the creatures.

"Invaders are there. We are done," Guk said, turning to leave.

"Wait," Taennen said. "Where will you go?"

Guk turned back. The low light seemed to flee from the formian's face, which made addressing him difficult. "To join the others and look for more workers."

The absurdity of what he was doing crashed down upon Taennen, but he did not dwell on it. He paused before saying thank you. He had no other words.

Guk simply turned and left, leading his people back through the tunnel. Taennen turned once again to examine the open area ahead of him. Clinging to the darkness of the tunnel, Taennen crept forward and scanned the area ahead.

The walls expanded to forty paces across, and the ceiling was perhaps half that in height. Two exit tunnels, one at the far end of the cave and the other to his right, caught

Taennen's attention. The magical, smokeless torchlight was present though not plentiful, and no sounds came from the area. With little alternative, Taennen darted into the cave, coming to a stop against a wall in the nearest shadows.

He skirted the edge of the room sticking close to the wall, his feet shuffling on the ground. He followed the rounded perimeter to his right for several heartbeats. More than twenty crates over half a man long and as high as his knees were spread out before him, stacked in piles of two.

Watching both entrances, Taennen crouched and pried a lid off one of the boxes, cursing its squeaks. Swords of fine manufacture lay in the box, instruments of death waiting to fulfill their purpose. The slender blades were indicative of Durpari style.

Taennen moved to another box and found six score daggers, dull and ordinary, not for mercantile use. He glanced back at the swords and noted the same quality. No jewels shone in their hilts, no ornate filigree decorated the handles. The weapons were not intended to serve as display pieces in markets or on the walls of the wealthy. They were designed to display the blood of other men and women on a field of battle.

As he stepped toward another crate, Taennen heard voices from the other end of the cavern. He dashed to the shadows, not sparing the time to close the boxes of weapons. From the tunnel straight ahead, two figures entered the cavern.

At first it seemed as though the pair were speaking some other tongue, but as they came closer, Taennen realized they were speaking Common but at an amazing rate. One could not even finish a sentence before the other started speaking, and then the reverse became true. Though he could not follow the conversation entirely, it seemed they were bickering over prices, for he heard almost as many numbers as words.

Stepping into the light of a torch in the wall, the two figures—dwarves, he determined—stopped and argued as they pointed to various crates. After several moments, one of the short folk tossed his hands into the air and nodded, causing the other to pump his fist in victory and pat his companion on the back. Together they stacked three of the crates and hefted the load between them, trudging back the way they had come, chatting and laughing as they did.

What in the All and the One were dwarves doing there? He remained in the comfortable shadows and made his way to the eastern tunnel. The passage was well lit, the magical light burning away the darkness and the security it afforded him. Slipping his khopesh from its sheath and lifting his shield to his chest, Taennen crept forward. The air was warm and moist. His skin was sticky and clammy, from both the air and the nervous sweat he shed.

Thirty paces in, the passage opened into another cavern, this one many times the size of the first and crowded with much more than crates. Taennen's eyes went wide at the sight before him as he stepped into the massive space before realizing he was out in the open. He quickly stepped back to lean against the passage wall.

At least two dozen large tents and semi-permanent structures filled the cavern. Dwarves and humans swarmed about, moving from tent to tent, some carrying crates, some barking orders to others constructing more of the shacks, and a few tables of dwarves drinking and gambling at a game Taennen did not recognize.

With better visibility from many magical torches, Taennen could see the markings on the armor of some of the dwarves and recognized the symbol as the same one Marlke had worn, the mark of the Gemstone Chaka. Some of the humans wore the familiar clothing of the barbarians who had plagued Neversfall with their attacks and wiped out so many of Taennen's comrades. Two humans exited the largest tent in the cavern, and Taennen restrained himself from shouting out when he saw they wore Chondathan uniforms.

He stood there watching for several breaths. The Chondathans were allied with the attackers who had killed so many of his friends. His body began to tremble with rage. Taennen's breath caught when he asked himself if Jhoqo knew about the Chondathans. Taennen was driven from his baffled reverie when he heard the scraping of steel behind him.

The twang of the crossbow string found Adeenya's ears at the same time the pain in her thigh pulsed. When she next stepped on her newly injured leg, Adeenya stifled a scream but continued forward, arcing her blade toward the shooter. Eyes wide, he rolled clear of the strike. She redirected the huge falchion before it struck the stone where her target had just been. She swung the weapon around, and it struck the crossbow the man had tossed aside as he was drawing his sword.

Adeenya grunted through her pain and thrust into the man, who slid aside trying for a chop of his own across her midsection. Adeenya threw her weight to her right, avoiding the attack, and then overextended herself attempting to send her blade into the guard. No inexperienced fool, he hopped backward. In doing so, he granted Adeenya the time she needed to recover from her risky move. Facing one another, they stepped around each other, neither one attacking. Down below, a new wave of sound erupted from the gathered crowd. With a glance, Adeenya saw that the middle of the crowd parted from the back to the front allowing Jhoqo through, escorted by two Chondathans.

Adeenya's opponent grinned and lowered his sword, though not all the way. "It's too late. You cannot stop all of us. Let's just walk down there together and see him."

"All of us?" Adeenya asked.

The man's grin widened for a moment before Adeenya lunged forward, her falchion entering the soft spot under his chin. Warm blood splashed her face as she turned away, eyes closed. She heard tiny gurgling noises as she withdrew her blade from the body before it slumped to the ground.

Adeenya turned to face the courtyard where Jhoqo was stepping onto the crates, waving for the crowd's attention. She needed a plan and needed it quickly.

Below, Adeenya could then hear Jhoqo speaking to the gathered crowd. "My brothers and sisters, I come to you with more grievous news and a choice that I, unfortunately, must ask you to make. The traitor, Adeenya, has escaped."

Adeenya watched from her perch on the wall as the Chondathans in the crowd roared their displeasure, the Maquar murmured among themselves, and the Durpari stood silent.

"Fear not, for she will be found before she can kill again!" Jhoqo said to the cheering Chondathans who outnumbered the Maquar and Durpari combined.

Jhoqo waved for quiet before continuing, "These are difficult times, friends, when one of our own might turn her back on everything we fight and die for. And what is that? What drew each of us to this life?"

Jhoqo paced across the crates looking at the crowd. "We love the South. We love its people. Though we hail from different countries, we are the same people! We love the same things, believe in the same principles. Everything is connected—the Adama has taught us that. Every bit of life you give to the South helps someone else. But the opposite is true too. If you spend your time and energy fighting against the South and her children, then we all feel that! It hurts us all!" More cheers, as well as the mixed reactions of the original forces, greeted him.

Adeenya continued skulking across the wall even as a Chondathan rushed into the courtyard below, running directly to Jhoqo's side. The Maquar urir bent low and listened to the man before nodding and motioning for four of the Chondathan to follow the messenger. Adeenya stopped and listened as Jhoqo stood tall again.

"Friends, I am sorry to say that I have just learned that there was a third traitor working with Marlke and Adeenya, another who wanted to harm us," Jhoqo said, causing the crowd to go silent quickly. "This news both saddens and shames me as the conspirator is none other than the man I've raised as my own son for many years."

The gathered throng erupted with noise and motion. The Chondathan howled, the Durpari began to shove their way out of the crowd, and the Maquar shouted their protests. Jhoqo bellowed for some semblance of order, and the Chondathan soldiers began corralling the Durpari, keeping them from leaving the gathering.

"Maquar, silence!" Jhoqo shouted, this time achieving the desired effect. The soldiers quieted, but the tension was still palpable, even to Adeenya from her place on the wall.

"My friends, I know how you must feel," Jhoqo said,

his head hung low. "We trusted Taennen. We loved him as brother and son. We fought with him, saved his life, and were saved by him in turn. I loved him as my own, but I have been offered damning proof."

Adeenya could not guess what proof Jhoqo might have. She knew that for the man to take such extreme action, Taennen must have discovered something important. She hoped the younger man was not in custody as she had been. She had no clues as to what Jhoqo's plan might be, but she felt both hope and fear that Taennen might have stumbled upon it. She needed to find him quickly. Amid protests, Jhoqo spoke again.

"Brothers and sisters, can't you see how fragile we are here? We are besieged by an enemy we cannot even find, while they slowly eat away at us, deep in this hostile environment. We have only one another to depend upon. For one another we must live, for the South we must work! This place, this Neversfall, will be a shining beacon to the Southern ways—to fairness, to connectedness, and to commerce. To everything that makes us who we are. But to do that, friends, I need your help! I need to know who my family is, who my fellow patriots are."

Quiet fell over the crowd again, though Adeenya thought they were stunned by Jhoqo's words as much as they were interested in what the man had said. The Chondathans were surveying the other two groups. Jhoqo was pacing his stage like the best showmen in the Durpari carnivals. His gestures were large and flowing, his arms emoting along with his words.

"I ask you here and now to help me, to prove your loyalty. Search this citadel, search for Taennen and Adeenya," Jhoqo said. The reactions to his request ranged from cheers to nods to silence and scowls. He finished by saying, "They are betrayers desperate to escape. They may do things you find unthinkable. You are hereby authorized to bring them to me by any means necessary."

Jhoqo's last four words washed over the crowd like blasphemy in a holy congregation. Several of the Maquar and Durpari tried to push to their way out of the crowd, while a few of each group shouted at the rest. Division was an effective tactic, and Adeenya had to admit that Jhoqo was using it well. Perhaps he could not sway all the troops, but those who wouldn't come to his side only made his claim of betrayal more convincing in the eyes of those who did.

The Chondathans fanned the flames of anger, pushing both Maquar and Durpari alike, shoving them back to the center of the crowd. The shouts grew primal, the soldiers became wild animals grunting and butting heads. The volume rose well beyond Jhoqo's shouts. Nothing comprehensible could be heard until one undeniable sound rose above the others: the ringing scrape of swords being drawn from their scabbards simultaneously in the warm night air, as crisp and clear as a bell.

chapter ninteen

Taennen ducked into a roll that brought him back up facing the opposite direction. He came to his feet, blade in hand, and saw Bascou, holding his sword before him, a smile on his face.

"Hello, my friend," the man said. "You should not be here, I think."

"Traitor!" Taennen said, glancing behind himself to see if anyone else was approaching.

"Traitor? No, no. I am doing my job, my duty. I am no traitor," Bascou said. "I was hired for this."

"Hired to secret away a hoard of weaponry under the citadel? Hired to kill Marlke?" Taennen said.

Bascou laughed for a moment, holding his palm out toward Taennen. "The dwarf? No, I did not kill that one. He was good, very useful. He gave us these dwarves. Very good in the caves, those little men. And those," he said, pointing to some nearby crates, "they are not staying here. Not hoarding, no."

Taennen felt strangely relieved that Marlke hadn't died an innocent. Adeenya's trap had worked, at least in part. It had caught the traitor. One traitor, Taennen realized. But if they weren't stockpiling the weapons, then what was going on? Taennen's mind suddenly flashed to the map he had seen with Neversfall marked on it. He could see the proposed trade route from the southern lands to the north.

"You're running weapons to the Mulhorandi for their war," Taennen said.

Bascou smiled the smile of a teacher whose pupil has finally grasped something difficult.

Taennen looked around at the tunnels, the dark walls, and the cramped space. "Why here? Why underground? Neversfall is meant to be part of the trade route."

Bascou nodded and said, "Oh, yes, the citadel will help many merchants take rugs, food, jars, and pretty little things women sew to the Mulhorandi."

"But not weapons," Taennen finished for him, remembering the trade laws of the southern nations. "It's illegal to interfere in the Mulhorandi action. When the Estagundian and Durpari governments find out about this, you and your troops will spend many, many years in servitude, if you're lucky."

Bascou laughed. "I think not. You think, maybe, I organized all of this by myself?" he said, motioning to the encampment in the cavern.

Taennen stood stunned a moment before answering, "Who? Who hired you? One of the rajah's opponents?"

Bascou smiled again but only shrugged.

"The Durpari leaders?"

Again, Bascou smiled.

Taennen's mind struggled with the man's words. His weapon hand dropped to his waist. The scraping of boots on stone returned his focus. Taennen's khopesh rose in time to block a stabbing blow from Bascou's sword, the two metals resonating in a single note of discord. Taennen hopped backward, assuming a defensive posture low to the ground.

He held his shield before him and readied his blade.

"Who killed Loraica? And Marlke? Who else is with you?" Taennen said.

"Other than my men?" Bascou asked, with his customary smirk.

"Who are they? Who are you?" Taennen asked.

"We are mercenaries," Bascou replied as he began circling. "Men of commerce." He held his sword before him, but Taennen did not miss the dagger in his offhand, though the man tried to hide it.

"The intruders, they're your men," Taennen said.

Bascou swung his sword in a feint Taennen easily recognized and sidestepped to allow himself to block the dagger thrust that followed the swipe. They stepped apart, circling one another again.

"Why? Why kill us like that? Why do that and then come into our midst as allies?" Taennen asked.

"I suggested that we kill you all, but I do not give the orders," Bascou responded, stepping in with another clumsy blow that Taennen easily dodged. "I was no more pleased by the tactics we were forced to employ than anyone else."

Taennen glanced past his opponent to the cavern camp and began stepping backwards. He wanted to lead the Chondathan man toward the smaller cavern away from the ears of the others.

"But you couldn't attack us directly, not without a larger force. So you invented these barbarians and picked us off a few at a time in the damned forest," Taennen said, launching his own unsuccessful feint.

Bascou answered with his own blows, no longer bothering with feints. His sword arced toward Taennen from the right. The Chondathan man spun with the attack, reversing the grip on the dagger in his left hand. Taennen ducked the sword strike and parried the dagger. The small blade hurtled down the passage to land on the stone floor. Bascou offered a slight bow, drawing a short sword from his belt.

"Who is giving the orders? Who killed Loraica?" Taennen asked, still back-stepping toward the first cavern.

Bascou's only answer was a growl as he leaped forward with his short sword, aiming for his opponent's gut. Taennen was faster and he sliced at Bascou's stomach, biting into the man's armor but causing no serious injury.

"To the citadel! Go!" Bascou shouted past Taennen.

"Who?" Taennen shouted as he barreled into the Chondathan man, his shield slamming into Bascou's chest with a dull thud.

Taennen knew he would soon be surrounded by others from the cavern and he let his desperation lead him. Bascou twisted to his left after the initial impact, clearing himself of the tangle with the shield. As Taennen continued past him, Bascou sent his short sword slicing across the younger man's back, finding flesh. Taennen stifled his cry of pain but recovered his feet and spun to face Bascou. Voices shouted out rallying cries from the tents. Bascou grinned as Taennen charged him again.

Taennen's khopesh sliced only air as Bascou twisted and danced away on the balls of his feet. The Chondathan recovered and dived back into the fray only to be rebuffed by Taennen's shield. They circled one another again. Bascou grinned as the sound of footsteps on stone thundered from behind him.

Taennen batted Bascou's larger sword to the left with his shield and stepped closer to his opponent. Bascou fell for the trick, letting his sword go wide, stepping in with his shorter blade driving for Taennen's chest. Taennen held the long sword at bay with his shield but twisted the opposite direction. As he spun, his back facing his lunging foe, Taennen drove the khopesh into Bascou's hip, eliciting a foul scream from the man.

Bascou drew his short sword in as Taennen continued to spin away. The Chondathan's blade found purchase in the Maquar's side but caused only a small wound before the two men separated. Taennen sidestepped through the dim tunnel as the cries of alarm from the larger cavern grew in intensity. Bascou's forces would be upon them any moment.

Ten paces from the northern tunnel where the two dwarves had gone, Bascou swept in with his long sword in a feint that Taennen easily knocked aside. Taennen raised his shield in anticipation of the short sword strike only to be fooled when Bascou threw the smaller blade. It sank into Taennen's left leg, provoking a grunt of pain, before slipping out and clattering to the floor.

Bascou shouted in victory as he swung his sword back toward his target. Taennen jumped over the man's blade, pushing off the wall with his injured leg. The pain blurred his vision as he drove the steel deep into Bascou's shoulder. Taennen plucked his blade from the bloody wound and landed hard, but kept his feet.

As Bascou growled in pain, he slashed at Taennen with his sword. Taennen knocked it aside and dodged the Chondathan's counterattack.

Taennen turned and ran as hard as he could into the unlit northern tunnel. Behind him, Bascou called him a coward and gave chase. Taennen blundered through the dark passage until his feet found a puddle of water and he slipped, crashing to the ground in a heap. His cheek opened wide on a jagged edge of the stone floor as he landed. Breathing heavily, he scrambled to his feet and ran again.

He could hear Bascou behind him, the footfalls echoing in the tunnel. Taennen had felt fear in battles before, even been convinced he would die, but he felt something new in that moment. Terror seized him, but it wasn't death that struck such great fear in him. It was not living long enough to see Bascou and anyone else responsible for the atrocities at the citadel get what they deserved.

Taennen slowed to a stop in the dark tunnel. He lowered himself, shield braced and blade ready, to meet Bascou's charge. The Chondathan man crashed into his shield, not expecting his prey to have stopped in the middle of the tunnel. Taennen landed hard on his back but rolled, launching Bascou over his head.

Bascou's momentum tossed the Chondathan farther down the passage to land on his face. Taennen was on his foe in a blink, straddling him with his shield brought to bear on the Chondathan's back. Bascou's breath sped from his lungs under the weight of the Maquar. Taennen laid his blade across the man's throat but did not apply the necessary pressure to break skin.

"Tell me who! Who sent you? Who is responsible for all this?" Taennen screamed, spraying angry spittle into the prone man's eyes. "Who killed Loraica?"

Behind them, footfalls echoed through the tunnel, getting closer with every heartbeat. Bascou's face was turning red from the weight atop him, but he managed a strangled chuckle at the sound. Taennen listened over his shoulder and heard the figures bearing down. His anger bubbled over at the hated Chondathan leader and, for a moment, Taennen considered letting himself be captured if he would find the answers to his questions. He heard another laugh escape Bascou's lips and made his decision, pulling his khopesh across the man's throat. Bascou's laughter faded as his blood flowed over the stone and his eyes closed. Taennen jumped to his feet, dashing into the darkness.

✚

chapter twenty

Adeenya's heart crowded her throat as a handful of the remaining Durpari soldiers drew their blades amidst the gathered troops. Instead of attacking, they clustered together in the space granted to them by the rest of the throng. A dozen Maquar did the same and joined their fellows in the center of the crowd. More Durpari fell into place as did more Maquar until almost thirty soldiers stood back to back, a circle inside the crowd. Only a handful of Maquar and Durpari remained on the outside, shouting their disbelief at their fellow soldiers for their apparent betrayal.

Jhoqo called for quiet once again and hopped down from his crates, walking toward the gathering. "Brothers, sisters . . . please, do not do this."

"Let us leave, and we will cause no harm," shouted one of the rebel Durpari.

Jhoqo stepped closer saying, "I cannot allow that. If you drop your weapons right now, I will not need to report this. You can still save yourselves from the charge of treason. Please, friends."

Despite herself, Adeenya believed the man was telling the truth. Even from her height atop the wall she could see that Jhoqo was troubled. His shoulders sagged and his face all but drooped, but his jaw remained resolute. He wanted peace with his soldiers, that much was clear. But she also had no doubt that he would wade through their blood if he needed to, and he would sleep fine after offering a few prayers for their departed souls.

Suddenly, her last opponent's words made sense. Jhoqo knew there would be resistance to his call for absolute loyalty, and he had planned ahead. He could not allow anyone to leave Neversfall, not with so many strange happenings. Crossbow assassins in lofty positions were the perfect solution, even if the potential rebels on the ground got the upper hand. No one could get to all of the crossbowmen to stop an inevitable massacre from raining down. Cursing herself for having wasted time, Adeenya raced along the wall, hoping to stop as many of the crossbowmen as she could.

In the courtyard below, Jhoqo continued to move closer to the dissidents. "Please. I cannot beg, though I wish I could. I love each of you and do not wish you harm. Do not do this."

"Urir, something is very wrong here!" a tall Maquar in the middle shouted. "Taennen is not capable of what you say. You know this even better than I!"

"I thought so, too, brother, but even now he is sowing the seeds to undo all the work we've done here. He stands as an impediment to free trade and the Southern ways, son. You don't want to do that, too, do you?" Jhoqo said, his hands held away from the borrowed sword that hung on his belt.

"The Maquar have never killed one of our own, but you just told us to do that very thing!" the tall man said.

"No!" Jhoqo snapped. "I want him alive, but you know him. He will not allow himself to be captured."

"No, sir! I will not kill him," the tall man replied, and a chorus of agreement joined his voice from those around him. "You should not be asking us to do that!"

Jhoqo waited for the noise to subside before saying, "Don't make me do this, friends. I want everyone here to remain alive to see the glorious future of our lands. Some of you have been with me longer even than Taennen. You've always trusted me. I ask you for that again."

Waving their weapons to keep the loyalists at bay, the inner circle of Maquar and Durpari soldiers pushed as one to move toward the main gate of the citadel. Their shuffling feet sounded like cattle skittering from the brand. A trio of Chondathans along the edge of the conflict drew their swords and stood together, a bladed barrier against the shifting mass of dissenters, who ceased their progress at the gesture. The Chondathans yelled for their surrender, the Maquar and Durpari shouted their refusal, and Jhoqo tried impotently to wade into the growing scuffle.

Adeenya wanted to join them, to help them rail against Jhoqo and the Chondathans. But she knew that one more body would do little good in the courtyard. The best thing she could do at that moment was to take out the crossbowmen.

She ran toward her next target—the bowman in the dark patch ahead of her. She entered the dim space, Jhoqo's falchion drawn back for a wild swing. She took some small comfort that the noise in the courtyard likely masked her brash approach. The assassin lay flat atop the wall, half a dozen paces before her, taking aim on the crowd.

Below, one of the Durpari soldiers squeezed past the Chondathans and dashed across the courtyard toward the gate. The bowman fired a breath before Adeenya's feet left the ground in her leap toward him. The bolt flew true, piercing the young Durpari in the leg. He stumbled and fell but quickly came to his feet and resumed his escape. He made another three paces before a second arrow from the opposite side of the courtyard found his throat, dropping him.

Adeenya's blade sliced into the archer with all her anger, strength and weight, burying itself into his hipbone. The Chondathan man screamed for only a moment before Adeenya whirled about, sinking the blade into the top of his skull. She yanked the weapon free with a splash of sanguine fluid. The orir ran along the wall toward the corner, seeking her next target.

The bowman's scream had brought a temporary quiet to the courtyard, which she took advantage of, yelling to her comrades. "Do not leave the crowd! Hold your places! Let the crowd be your shield. Archers are on the walls! They will shoot down any who run!"

Though they could not see her in the dark, the rebels in the courtyard knew her voice and accepted the truth of her words. No more evidence than their fallen fellow and the arrows protruding from his corpse was needed. The Durpari cheered to hear her voice and tightened their formation, batting away anyone who attempted to get too close. The Maquar seemed to take heart as well, sending up cheers of their own. The tense, celebratory sounds were short-lived, cut off by a Durpari soldier's shout of pain as he slumped to the ground, his blood dripping from the blades of one of the Chondathans.

"No!" Jhoqo shouted in vain. The jumble of people in the courtyard roiled out of control into a chorus of steel on steel as every man and woman fought for their lives.

Adeenya's steps froze for a moment when the fighting began, but she quickly recovered and hurried along the outer wall. The bulk of the Maquar and Durpari forces were squaring off against the Chondathans and a few of their former comrades in the courtyard. Other Maquar and Durpari stood doing nothing, not sure which side to choose.

Already at least four dead lay on the ground, never to rise again. Crossbow bolts winged their way into the battle from unseen sources in the dark. If as many crossbowmen lay in wait along the northern and western wall as there had been on the eastern, the soldiers in the courtyard would not last long. For the sake of her comrades, Adeenya pressed on.

Jhoqo waded into the clashing soldiers, launching the pommel of his sword into the head of a nearby rebel Maquar. The soldier fell in a slump as consciousness fled him.

"Please!" he shouted. "Stop this now. We can still recover," he said.

The Maquar commander swung again, stealing the breath from another confrontational Maquar when the pommel of his blade connected with the man's gut.

Adeenya ran the entire length of the northern wall without finding any crossbowmen, but her luck did not hold as she turned onto the the western wall. In the darkness she could barely see him, but her eye caught a deadly shaft soaring into the back of a soldier in the courtyard.

Adeenya launched herself into the man who was already standing and ready for her. Their swords met, and both fighters gave way, steel grating on steel. Her opponent was Chondathan, an older man with wrinkles and scars covering his face and neck. She drove the falchion toward his chest with a blow he easily parried. She prepared herself for a counterattack that never came. The Chondathan paced side to side, awaiting her next strike. She feinted right at waist level before whipping her blade around high from his left. Again, the man deflected the blow and resumed his defensive posture. She lunged again, leading with her blade and attempted a punch with her off hand, leaving herself exposed for an attack.

Her foe made no move for her exposed belly, and she knew she had been fooled. She figured out his ploy a heartbeat too late as four Chondathans ran toward them from the south, grim-faced, with weapons drawn. Her lack of stealth on the northern wall had cost her, but she had no regrets. Her people in the courtyard needed her, and for them she had to do what she could, as long as she could. At least the Chondathans coming toward her were not firing into the crowd any longer.

Below, the resistance was not faring well. Three more had dropped to Chondathan blades while only two of the northerners had fallen.

Adeenya's opponent smiled as his comrades came closer. He still refused to attack her. She glanced between the on-rushers and the gate and back again. The choice was easy. Striking out with a feint, Adeenya withdrew her attack. She turned to run back to the northwest corner of the citadel, to the stairs. Her opponent shouted to his approaching fellows to give chase, and he did the same.

Adeenya reached the stairs and vaulted down them in five leaping steps. She sprinted across the courtyard toward the fray, bearing Jhoqo's sword poised to strike. She charged for the Maquar urir, whose back was facing her.

The guilt of running through an unprepared man from behind tried to tangle her legs, to squeeze her lungs, but failed. She pushed past her emotions and charged ahead. If Jhoqo were dead, the insanity before her would end, the Chondathans would crumble without their wrangler. Pity struck her next—pity for Taennen for the father he was about to lose, and even pity for Jhoqo, who was only doing what he thought right. She batted aside the feelings and focused on her strike. Six steps away, Adeenya gripped the hilt of the falchion with both hands and steadied the blade before her, aiming for the small of Jhoqo's back.

The dank tunnel air was thick, like water in his lungs, as Taennen ran. His feet threatened to slip with every step. The many wounds on Taennen's body throbbed and ached, but his hands hurt the most. Those hands had taken the life of a fellow officer, even if that officer were from another nation and a traitor besides. He knew Bascou was a criminal, but what did it mean that he had orders from higher up? Were his actions still a crime, if those in charge had ordered him to do so? Taennen had killed a man who followed orders, just as he himself always had.

His hands ached with each thought, but the pleasure, the thrill he took in ending Bascou's life made him want to howl in distress. He had wanted to do it, had enjoyed it. What concerned him was the thrill he got from it. He had seen bloodlust in the eyes of foes before but never thought he would feel it himself.

But in the end Bascou had needed to die. Taennen found comfort in that thought and found himself comfortable with it. There was nothing evil in understanding that an enemy was too dangerous to live. For the greater good of all southerners, Bascou's part in this scheme had needed to end. The shiver of freedom he felt from it, the itch of happiness—that bothered him. That was not fine and well. Maybe it never would be.

As the thrill settled, he hoped he never would feel such

bloodlust again. The scraping of boots on stone drew closer and he decided he would have to reconcile those feelings later, if he survived.

He had turned left at two different intersections of the tunnels and hoped he was headed south again. There had to be an alternate route back to the spot where he had entered the passages. The dark walls rushed by as he ran, his ears marking the distance better than his eyes in the darkness. He might have smashed face-first into a wall at any moment, but still he moved as fast as his legs would carry him. Taennen felt more than saw the tunnel curve left ahead and changed course without falling.

Not more than thirty strides after the turn, the light from a magical torch glowed dimly at the next intersection. The direction the light came from was indistinct, keeping its origin a secret amid the dark rock. Taennen went right, his left foot pushing off the opposite wall as he made the sharp turn. The darkness soon swallowed him up, evidence that the light had been to the left. The hunters still behind him, he continued south with no time to lament his choice. His only hope was that the tunnel would let out somewhere outside the citadel.

Though his stride was longer than the dwarves', Taennen's lungs and legs were burning with effort, and he slipped occasionally. His pursuers were accustomed to the tunnel, and the dwarves could see where they were going in the dark. The ground sloped up suddenly before him, promising entry to the surface world. Taennen scrambled the slanted wall of stone, his hands finding purchase at its top. He nearly sang out in joy as his fingers felt the the cool grass of the world above. Taennen pulled himself from the hole in the ground, emerging in the woods.

Trickles of light from Lucha filtered down through the

dense canopy, but compared to the tunnels, Taennen felt as though he stood next to a campfire merrily lighting the whole woods. The muscles in his legs felt refreshed as his jog became a sprint in the open, more familiar terrain. Though he dodged trees and the grasping tendrils of plants with every step, Taennen raced through the Aerilpar, confident he could outpace his pursuers. His mind turned to his next task, returning to Neversfall.

Jhoqo needed to be warned—or did he? The thought troubled Taennen. Bascou had made it clear that others above him had ordered the illegal operation. Jhoqo had kept many things from Taennen in their time at Neversfall: the magic of the tower and Khatib's part in the plan, the location of Adeenya's holding cell, the call for the Chondathans, and who knew what else. Taennen's mind drifted to Jhoqo's speeches about free trade and loyalty to the Southern ways. Jhoqo's ideals were furthered by all of this. But killing his own men? Taennen wanted to deny it, to bury the thought and never see it again. But it stayed in his mind, outshining any other thoughts.

Jhoqo was involved. There was little room for doubt. Those thoughts were obliterated as screams of terror from behind him drifted to his ears on the night wind.

Taennen stood on the edge of a patch of Lucha's pale light as it caressed the forest floor. He remained still, listening for the direction of the wailing in the dark. The monsters of Veldorn, maybe? He could not waste time wondering. Neversfall would not be far, and he needed to get back there.

To find what? he wondered. Adeenya would still be imprisoned. Jhoqo would still treat Taennen like a child, hiding away secrets he thought his son couldn't handle. Bascou would not be there, at least. The thought gave

Taennen pause, and he quickly wiped away the tiny smile that came unbidden to his lips.

The wailing had stopped, but the rustling of underbrush could be heard. Aerilpar came alive with sound at night, hunters stalking their prey, foragers gathering their stores, and close by, something killing something else whose screams caused gooseflesh to rise. The coppery smell of blood was detectable in the air. It was not an unfamiliar smell and not always an unwelcome one.

Taennen ducked under a low branch and peered around the trunk of a massive, ancient tree. Twenty strides ahead, a clearing on the forest floor was a jumbled mess of sticks, leaves, and blood. Even in Lucha's pale light, the vivid red stood out against the green background of leaves and grasses. A night bird flapped its wings and departed from a nearby tree, but Taennen did not move, did not make a sound. Something or someone—likely several someones judging from the amount of blood—had died in that place not more than a few heart-beats earlier, yet there was no sign of anyone.

Taennen skirted the clearing, sticking to the dense foli-age where Lucha could not wrap him in so tight an embrace. The scene showed no trace of the victim or perpetrator of the incident, as though the forest had dined, and chewed before swallowing, leaving its slop everywhere. A black patch, no larger than a fist, marked a spot on the ground toward the center of the clearing showing that a torch had been dropped. Taennen slipped into the open area and knelt to examine the scorched dirt. He leaped to his feet as a familiar voice warbled into the night.

"They are no longer a threat," Guk said, emerging from the darkness. Lucha's light shone on his carapace causing it to gleam unlike the torchlight ever had, shining points instead of waves.

Weapon in hand, Taennen asked, "Who?"

"Those who chased you," the formian replied.

"You killed them? How many were there?"

"Four dead, two escaped, one lives," Guk said, his mandibles chattering.

"Why?" Taennen asked, returning his khopesh to his hip.

"You would be dead otherwise."

"But why save me?"

"For your help," Guk said. "This is how you do things, we have seen."

Taennen spoke, already guessing the forthcoming response, "I helped you, so you helped me. That was your payment. We were even."

"Yes, we were," Guk said. "Now we are not."

Guk stood unmoving, awaiting Taennen's response, statuesque as was his custom. The thought of further obligation to the formians caused a roiling ripple to pass through Taennen's stomach. Before Taennen could speak, the other formians slinked out of the dark woods, one of the larger ones was carrying the unconscious victim of their attack. Guk motioned to the prisoner, and Taennen held his tongue, stepping over to inspect the man. His face was bloodied, but he was alive.

"I have to get back to the citadel," Taennen said, stepping around Guk as he turned north. "I can't deal with him right now."

"He will give you answers," Guk said. "He will tell you how to save your people in the stone building."

Taennen took four steps and stopped. The Chondathans in the caverns would have notified their compatriots in the citadel that Taennen had discovered their plans. Walking into Neversfall would bring his death or imprisonment. The enemy held all the advantages. They occupied Neversfall, they had superior numbers, and, Taennen admitted again, it seemed as though they had Jhoqo on their side.

Taennen closed his eyes and took a deep breath. Feelings about his father's betrayal from many years prior bubbled up inside him, but he did his best to put them aside.

A groan stirred Taennen from his thoughts. The Chondathan man wriggled in the arms of the formian, who set him on the ground. Taennen approached the man and knelt. The injured soldier lifted his head and blinked before bringing his hand to his eyes to wipe away the drying blood there. He groaned again and hissed as sweat from his hand found its way into the open wounds. He squinted, his focus finding Taennen, but said nothing.

"Rhalov. That's your name, isn't it?" Taennen said, bending low to look the man in the eyes.

The Chondathan nodded. Gashes lined his left cheek and he bled from several wounds on his back and legs. He was a sturdy man, but the many cuts and scratches had taken their toll and he was weak.

"Your leader is dead, Rhalov. You know that, don't you?"

The man gave a slight nod as his lips pursed.

"I killed him, and I'll do the same to you if you lie to me," Taennen said.

The Chondathan coughed trying to laugh, blood-colored spittle gathering on his lips. Taennen growled and struck the man, bringing his humor to an end.

"I need answers to questions. Make no mistake, I will do what it takes to get them," Taennen said.

"You would not. You cannot fool me, Maquar," Rhalov said, rising to a seated position. He turned from Taennen and prodded his injuries.

Taennen drew his arm back to strike the man again. He tried to bring to mind all the hard men he had known in his life, men of resolve who were not afraid to do whatever it took to get a job done. Taennen had always believed that, while those men had not been bad people, they'd had lower expectations of themselves than he had of himself. In that moment, he realized the limitations of such thinking. Doing what was necessary did not make one a bad person. The enjoyment he took from the death of Bascou—perhaps that made him a bad person. But could that single feeling, that one bit of pleasure, really unravel him as a person? Could it undo all the good he had accomplished in his life? Maybe good and evil weren't such clear-cut concepts. Perhaps they could not conform to such rigid definitions.

None of that mattered. Taennen stood and stepped back from the Chondathan, who sneered at him. "You're right. I can't bring myself to murder or even hurt a helpless prisoner," Taennen said.

"But I think I can see my way clear to letting them at you," Taennen said, motioning to the formians still gathered in a circle around them.

The cacophony of screams and weapons on weapons did not distract Adeenya in her charge. She was five steps away from stopping the actions of a madman, and she wondered how long she would live after ending Jhoqo's life. Surely an archer would cut her down or the Chondathans would swarm her. Four steps, and she thought about how her troops might escape this trap. Three steps, and Taennen entered her mind, his conjured smile lightening her grim mood even in what would likely be her last moments. Two steps before running her stolen blade through its rightful owner, Adeenya shifted her weight and fell to her right as Jhoqo spun to face her with a punch aimed at her face. She dodged the blow, hit the ground rolling, and found her feet fast.

"I will have my sword back now," Jhoqo said, striding toward her as he drew the smaller sword at his belt. The sweat on his brow shone in the torchlight, causing the lines on his furrowed brow to give off sickly light.

Adeenya batted aside the man's first sword strike but could not dodge the kick that followed the blow, causing her knee to buckle under his boot. Jhoqo reversed his hand, the butt of his hilt careening toward Adeenya's head. She let the momentum of her fall carry her to the ground so that Jhoqo's second blow passed overhead.

Adeenya spun onto her side, her legs kicking up the dry dirt, and kicked Jhoqo's shin. The man kept his feet but jumped backward to avoid becoming tangled in her legs. She came to her feet poised and on the defensive. The battle beside her raged with nearly a dozen bodies littering the courtyard, mostly rebel Durpari and Maquar who were still trapped in the middle of the mass of writhing fighters.

"His faith in your determination was deserved, but coming back here was mad," Jhoqo said, wading into her with a flurry of blows from his long sword. "I think he would be disappointed in your tactical choice."

Deflecting each attack with a turn of the man's wide blade, Adeenya said, "My father does not know me as well as he thinks."

For the first time since she had met the man, Jhoqo's face showed surprise at her revelation about the unnamed agent to whom Jhoqo had alluded. To her dismay, though, it did not stop him. Jhoqo's sword dived toward her belly, slipping past her defenses. She pulled her waist back to let the blade slide past and cursed as Jhoqo changed his sword's direction, sending the hilt into her face. She stumbled backward, blood trickling from the fresh cut on her cheek. Adeenya stepped back from the engagement wondering why her opponent had not finished her while she was stunned.

"You cannot harm me, can you?" she shouted at the man. "My father would have your hide!"

"I do not kill you out of respect for the man. That is all," Jhoqo replied.

Adeenya laughed. "You have no power. You have no command! You're a tool, just like you said Taennen was. My father wields you no differently than you claim to have wielded Taennen."

Jhoqo did not leap for the bait, remaining calm and watching her every move.

"What's he paying you? Is it as least as much as my allowance growing up?" she said with a sharp laugh.

Again, Jhoqo did nothing and moved with her as she tried to find an advantage. The man was disciplined and Adeenya knew her barbs would find no purchase on his slippery ego.

Adeenya slid her right foot forward in the feint of a thrust. Jhoqo turned sideways, minimizing her target, and brought his blade up to defend just as she had hoped. She shifted her weight to her right foot and twisted to her right in a leap. Her left leg went backward in an arc until that foot found the ground, her back momentarily to Jhoqo. Completing the spin she faced him again, their positions parallel to the battle beside them. She evaded his retaliatory strike. His furrowed brow brought a grin to her lips.

Jhoqo sent his blade toward Adeenya in a wide arc.

When she blocked with his falchion, the urir twisted his blade under the larger weapon and pulled back hard. Adeenya hissed as the sword flew from her hand to land in Jhoqo's empty one. He tossed the smaller blade he had been using to her, shifting the falchion to his proper hand. She did not try to hide her surprise that he had rearmed her. Jhoqo gripped his returned blade and smiled, welcoming back a lost limb. His men in the courtyard were holding the rebellious faction at bay, though more of the Chondathans had died.

"Help me stop them," he said to Adeenya, pointing past her to the roiling mass of fighters.

"Stop your own people so that the Chondathans can slaughter them?" she spat.

"All of them! Help me stop all of them. No one needs to be dying," he said.

Adeenya squinted, her sword hand lowering for a moment before resuming its guarded position. Maybe she could see the sense of it. With her help, Jhoqo could put an end to all of this madness and help his soldiers and even the Durpari to see the truth of things, to help him build the future. He smiled at her and drew his arms out wide. Adeenya stared for a few moments before lunging forward in an obvious feint, and then turning to dash into the warring crowd before Jhoqo could recover from his dodge and stop her.

"No!" he shouted, chasing her into the mass of bodies, both living and dead.

Adeenya was slim and nimble and easily made her way through the crowd, while behind her Jhoqo was forced to crash through, shoving aside Chondathan, Maquar, and Durpari alike.

"To me!" Adeenya shouted. "For the Shining South!"

The orir gutted a Chondathan before cuffing another on

the head, sending both men to the ground. She was shouting for the rebels to rally around her, and they came. Soldier by soldier they made their way toward her, tightening their circle of solidarity in the writhing mass of battle.

✠

chapter twenty-one

Pulling her blade from the thigh of one of the Chondathan soldiers, Adeenya looked past the clash in which she had become embroiled, at the front gate of Neversfall. The dark night could not hide that the portal had been opened. The remaining loyal Durpari and Maquar soldiers rallied behind her. Many had fallen in the skirmish, but, functioning as a cohesive unit, they were fending off the Chondathans and evening the numbers. Adeenya kept several of her compatriots close as she slashed through the opposition, trying to wound her foes enough to remove them as obstacles.

Her newly formed army was nearly free of the swarm of Chondathans and nearing the gate when she spotted those who had opened it. Two of the Chondathan soldiers ran across the courtyard toward the battle, though they already bore many wounds. Leaves and grass stuck out of their armor at their joints. Their presence did not change her plan, so she pressed on, running her blade lengthwise down the exposed arm of another enemy soldier, who leaped out of her way after the cut. She continued to shout, encouraging those behind her to keep in step, to move in unison and march toward the gate to freedom.

Shouts from behind told of a break in the Chondathan mob, and Adeenya ordered speed in the evacuation. Her orders rippled through the crowd as others repeated her shouted commands. As a group, the rebel Maquar and Durpari turned their tactical maneuver into a running retreat. The surprised Chondathans waited a heartbeat too long, and most of Adeenya's followers escaped their reach. A handful stayed behind to serve as human dams against the onslaught, sacrificing their own lives to cover the exit of their comrades.

At the head of the fleeing force, Adeenya sprinted toward the gate that was already being closed by unseen hands. The two Chondathans who had just entered turned and ran out of the path of the stampede. Dust floated into the night air as the soldiers ran as hard as they could, fleeing the fortress they had come to defend. No one understood what had happened, but everyone knew that something was wrong. Their experience at the citadel had been strange and ill-fated, so much so that seasoned veterans who would never have imagined fleeing from a fight did so with abandon simply to escape a situation they did not understand.

Chondathan soldiers were closing the gate, standing on both sides. Adeenya barked the order to cut them down, and ordered the nearest soldier to her, a Maquar man, to keep the troops moving. She broke off from the pack and steered herself toward one of the small buildings nearby. A handful of the Maquar and Durpari saw her intention and left ranks to assist, covering her from their pursuers. Adeenya ran to the door, slamming into it with her unbreakable momentum. The door burst open, revealing the prisoners within.

Several Chondathans veered from the hunt of the larger force and approached fast. A dozen former captives, all anxious for their freedom and perhaps a taste of revenge, bolstered the rebel defenders. Corbrinn, at the lead, quickly disarmed the nearest enemy and used the Chondathan's own dagger against the man. Former prisoners, Maquar, and Durpari all fled out the gate into the flatlands beyond, only a few steps behind the larger portion of their group. By the time the last of them passed through, the first were already invisible, swallowed up by the pitch black of night.

Adeenya was the last to leave, her long legs easily catching her up to the bulk of the pack and quickly to the fore. The soldiers ran for several breaths until even their conditioned and honed bodies ached, and the undernourished prisoners begged for a halt. Slowing their pace, Adeenya steered them toward the Aerilpar against the objections of several of the soldiers. She insisted they would need the cover and secrecy the forest could provide. Those who were still not convinced did not argue further as arrows from the chasing enemy began to fall.

The formian who had carried the wounded soldier moved out of the darkness toward the sitting Chondathan man. The mercenary gaped at the creature, his eyes wide.

"What in all the hells?" the man said, pushing himself away.

A storm destroys a home not because it chooses to, but because it simply exists. The large formian gave much the same impression as he lifted the Chondathan man into the air with strange, double-clawed hands and began to apply pressure.

The formian squeezed the Chondathan's shoulders

with force great enough to elicit a scream from the man. Guk's antennae flicked, but he did not speak. Taennen had learned that the smaller formians did nothing without Guk's permission, if not instruction, so he knew Guk was somehow commanding his underling.

The formian dropped the Chondathan, who crumpled on the ground. Blood trickled out from under the man's arms as he lay on the grass with tears welling in his eyes. The Chondathan grew pale and weak. Sitting there in the dirt, he looked like a little boy roughed up by street urchins looking for coin, trying to stifle the tears and not be thought a coward.

The mercenary tried to stand in defiance only to be knocked down when the formian skittered forward and swept his feet out from under him. Guk's slim appendages jerked wildly again, and his cohort bent to grab the Chondathan once more.

"Stop," Taennen said.

"You will ask questions now," Guk said.

"Yes," Taennen replied.

Guk's underling grasped the Chondathan and began to lift him.

"Stop, I said!" Taennen shouted and moved to wrest the man from the creature's grip.

The formian dropped the Chondathan and stepped back, once again concealing itself in the shadows.

"He will answer to stop the pain," Guk said.

"Yes, he will. But that does not make it right," Taennen replied.

"He stands against order," Guk said, as though the words were explanation and justification enough.

"It doesn't matter. Besides, if you torture him enough, he'll tell you he's a troll and can grant your greatest wish,"

Taennen said, kneeling next to the Chondathan.

"He defies order. If he does not serve the purpose of answering your questions, we will end his life. We have suffered him to live this long only because we thought he might help you. He does not respect order and should die," Guk said. The unsettling timbre in Guk's voice settled into a rhythm that Taennen found even more alien than usual.

"No," Taennen said, standing and turning to face the larger creature. He stepped closer to Guk, moving out of Lucha's light filtering down through the tree tops. Though dark, they could see one another, and their gazes locked, neither of them flinching nor blinking. Taennen held his ground, hand on his weapon.

"I can't let you murder him," Taennen whispered. "Maybe we can trick him somehow."

"Lie," Guk said. Formian voices did not lilt when inquisitive and so Taennen did not respond for the span of several heartbeats, finally identifying the words as a question.

"Yes. Fool him into telling us how many more of them there are, whether there are any secret tunnels we can use, and anything else we need to know," Taennen said.

"We will not lie," Guk said as he moved toward the Chondathan, who gasped when he saw the largest formian. Guk stared hard at the man, his head twitching slightly. "Ask him your questions."

Taennen eyed the big formian but stood over the Chondathan, lowering his voice and scowling as best he could. "How many more of you are underground?"

"To the hells with you, Maquar," Rhalov said.

"Approximately forty," Guk said. Rhalov's eyes went wide staring at the formian.

Uncertain what was happening, Taennen continued. "Why are you here?"

Rhalov said nothing, but Guk spoke. "For coin."

The Chondathan stared at Guk, his lips pursed, his brow furrowed.

"Why are the Chondathans here?" Taennen asked.

Again, Guk spoke when the human would not, saying, "For coin."

Taennen growled at the answer, upset with himself for being so vague, and angry at the stubborn prisoner.

"Is there a way to use the tunnels to enter Neversfall?" Taennen asked, turning to face Guk in anticipation of the response.

"Yes," Guk said, eliciting a moan from Rhalov.

"Where? How?" Taennen said.

Before Guk could respond, Rhalov did. "I'll speak! Just get it out of my head!"

"Speak," Guk said, though Taennen was uncertain whether he had stopped his magical reading.

"Enter the tunnel where you just exited. Take the second tunnel left, the first right and the second left again. You'll see a ladder built into the rock," Rhalov said.

"Is it guarded?" Taennen asked.

Rhalov nodded. Taennen paced, running his fingers through his dark hair.

"Who is in charge? Bascou?" Taennen asked.

The Chondathan grinned and shook his head. "You know who."

Taennen lashed out and slapped the man's face. He already knew the answer but could not bear to hear the name aloud. His suspicions confirmed, he turned from the prisoner and stared at the ground.

"You are finished with him," Guk said.

"Yes. We'll tie him up and come back later. . ." Taennen started to say but was cut short as a glow caught his attention.

He turned to see what looked like the bars on a prison cell, horizontal lines crossing verticals, beams of blue light floating before Rhalov. The strange, lighted lattice floated forward, pressing slowly into the Chondathan, who loosed a high-pitched scream as his torso was seared by the strange force. A sound like meat sizzling on a skillet and the rough scraping of a shovel filled his ears. Rhalov's scream was cut off as the bars faded from existence on the far side of his body and he slumped to the ground.

"For all the One," Taennen said, turning from the sight of the man's chest splayed open and the smell of burnt flesh.

"You did that?" Taennen said, facing Guk.

"He defied order. Be careful that you do not," Guk said with no hint of threat in his voice.

Taennen wanted to scream, to denounce what the formian had done, but he knew it would do little good. While he objected to the deed, he was not in a position to argue. His mind turned to his next task, and there was a pressing matter still to attend. He wondered what part of himself he had lost that might have objected more strongly. Could he get it back?

"You helped me get the information I needed. Now what? We were even, and now I am in your debt again," Taennen said.

"You will need help at the fortress," Guk said.

Taennen squinted but agreed.

"His answers, and our help in taking the keep. That we offer," the formian replied.

"And what price do I pay?"

"We lost many of our kind and all of our workers. We need workers. We cannot return with fewer than we had when we left," Guk said.

ed Gentry

"I can't give you back your prisoners. They're not slaves. They'll be freed," Taennen said, taking a step backward.

"Not them," Guk said.

Taennen cocked his head and raised an eyebrow. After a few moments he understood what the formian was suggesting. The idea made him sick at first. But the idea of not seeing justice done broke his heart. He wanted an end to all the wrongdoing at Neversfall.

"Fine. Any of the invaders we capture . . ." he said, unable to finish the sentence. Part of Taennen was disgusted with himself, another part proud for making a hard decision that he knew was the right one. The decision had not been as hard as he imagined. That bothered him.

"There are others near," Guk said.

"Chondathans? Where, in the woods?" Taennen asked.

"Not the invaders," Guk replied.

"Who?" Taennen asked.

"Many like you and the others," Guk said.

"Maquar and Durpari?" Taennen said.

Guk affirmed, and the formian ranks began to move forward again. Taennen restrained himself from dashing ahead to see the others, to find out what had happened. Lucha's light had become brighter, and though the formians moved quietly, even they could not avoid rustling through the underbrush. He wondered how they had ever surprised the Chondathans who had been chasing him. So it came as no surprise when he heard human voices shout in warning from the west, closer to the edge of the forest.

"Peace," Taennen said.

The formians stopped their shuffling, and the woods soaked up every bit of sound. Silence reigned for several moments before a single voice called out.

"Taennen?"

282

It was Adeenya. Taennen smiled and pushed past the formians to step into a less crowded patch of the forest. Gasps from the darkness greeted him a mere moment before several Maquar ran to him, cheering in low voices. Joy was in the air, but the seasoned warriors knew quiet was a necessary tool. Taennen greeted his friends with hugs and claps on shoulders.

After exchanging greetings, the formians stepped out of the trees just enough to be seen by the humans. The Maquar and Durpari gasped and cursed, lifting their weapons.

"No!" Taennen said, his arms high. "They want to help."

"Help what?" a Durpari woman asked.

"Help us retake Neversfall," Taennen said in a low voice.

Before the gathered humans could respond, Adeenya stepped out of the crowd. Taennen smiled to see her again. Her smile was no smaller than his, though it fled her face as she turned to face her makeshift army.

"He is right. We will retake Neversfall. We must. Go, rest," she said, pointing to a nearby clearing.

As the soldiers grumbled and walked away, Taennen nodded to Guk, whose people followed him in the opposite direction several paces away. The two officers stood in silence a few moments before Adeenya recounted her escape, never mentioning who had captured her. Taennen shared his own, and Adeenya fumed at the news of the weapons smuggling.

"Taennen," she said, "I didn't murder Marlke. I tried to stop him. I stabbed him after he attacked me, but he could have been healed—*would* have been healed. Jhoqo let him die. He's mad, Taennen. He—"

"I know. I should have seen it," Taennen said.

Adeenya nodded but said nothing further on the matter. "So how are we going to take Neversfall?"

"I know the way in," he replied.

"That will help," she said, "but our men are disillusioned, wounded, and hungry."

"It's amazing what a lack of choice can do, and we don't have one," he said.

She nodded and glanced toward the formians. "Are they really helping?"

He followed her gaze to the creatures and said, "Yes."

She said nothing for a few heartbeats, but then asked, "Why would they help, and why would we trust them?"

"We trust them for the same reason we take the fortress," he said. "We have no choice."

She ceded the point but asked again, "But why are they going to help?"

"For payment. The same reason anyone does anything," he said.

She glanced back at the formians again and said, "They wanted coin?"

"Payment doesn't always mean gold or silver," Taennen replied.

Before Adeenya could respond, Taennen walked toward the soldiers in the clearing. Jhoqo had always said that a good soldier knows when a command is a poor one, be it unjust or simply mad. Taennen was about to give an insane command, and he could only hope that his soldiers were good and that things weren't as simple as he had always believed them to be. The world had come to look quite different in the last couple of days. Maybe he was seeing things that Jhoqo could not.

"Please, everyone, listen to me," Taennen said, waving for the displaced people to gather around him. Blood spattered his flesh and his armor, his face was worn and haggard.

"Maquar, we have been betrayed," Taennen started. "No, not just us. Everyone who hails from the South. Sadly, that betrayal came from within our ranks."

The Maquar and Durpari stood silent, though the former prisoners began to shout at Taennen, having picked him out as the person in charge they hoped would help them.

"Listen, please, all of you," Taennen said. "I know you want to go home. I know you are beside yourselves wondering why your former slavers are standing only paces away," he said, indicating the formians still gathered nearby.

"My fellow soldiers, I know your minds are spinning right now. Mine is too. Though I was not with you in your battle against the Chondathans, the full weight of Jhoqo's betrayal sits on my heart as well," he said.

The Maquar lowered their heads in unison, a sign of respect to the relationship between Jhoqo and Taennen.

Taennen spoke again, an orator emerging from him out there in the wilderness. "Beneath Neversfall are forces that would break the laws we hold dear, and that some of us have sworn to defend. Weapons are being smuggled to feed the war machine that is Mulhorand. This citadel will make more coin in a month than most chakas make in a year. Illegal coin! Blood coin! Coin pried from the hands of the dead citizens of the next country that the vicious Mulhorandi target. This must be stopped."

The former captives seemed unmoved, standing huddled together away from the soldiers, separating themselves as though some caste system were in place. Who could blame them for not wanting to get involved? This was not their affair. They had sworn no oaths, they were not being paid. Their faces showed only the desire to remain free, to return to their homes and the lives they had known before being taken by the formians.

Taennen noticed the disinterest from the citizens as well and turned to address them. "I am sorry you have suffered. Some of you have been away from your homes for a long, long time. Little would please me more than to take each of you to your homes right now and know that you would never have to return to this place," he said, pausing before continuing.

"But I can't do that. The truth is that the people in that fortress must be stopped. Many, many more people will die if they are not. The Adama tells us that we are all connected, that our goal should be the good of all things because all things are part of us and we are part of them.

"Good trade benefits everyone, but what the warmongers behind this are doing here does not. The victims of the Mulhorandi will not benefit, the citizens of the South who devote themselves to the laws we live by will not benefit."

The former captives murmured among themselves but seemed largely unmoved. Taennen moved closer to them. "And you and those you love will not benefit. You may be harmed by this action," Taennen said.

"How? The Mulhorandi don't attack my homeland," said a short man in shabby clothes.

"Not yet," Taennen said. "But these weapons will allow them to expand their borders farther, to extend their reach into lands that may not have interested them previously. Perhaps they will come after your home next. When they conquer those around them, what will stop their appetite for more war and more land?"

The former captives muttered amongst themselves. After a few moments, one of them stepped forward and spoke.

"We're not fighters, sir. What are we supposed to do? We

just want to go home to our families. For some of us, it's been a very long time."

Taennen nodded. "I know, my friends. If I saw a choice, I would latch onto it, but I do not," he said. "Friends, please trust me. You do not want to be alone here in the wilds of Aerilpar," Taennen said. "There are far worse things in these woods than you have encountered before."

✠
chapter twenty-nine

Jhoqo stared at the corpse of Bascou laid before him in his command building. He dismissed the Chondathan soldiers who had brought the body to him, and then crumpled into a chair. Bascou's thick cheeks hung from his face like sacks of emptied wheat. His wounds still dribbled, sprinkling the floor with red. Jhoqo had barely known the man and would not miss him.

He was a cursed darkblade. Damn all the Chondathans to the Hells, he thought. He would trade the whole lot of them for ten Maquar or even Durpari. He sighed and let his muscles relax, slumping in the chair.

The Chondathans were unimportant, but the people they represented were not. The men and women who had hired the mercenaries knew what needed to be done, and they gave Jhoqo the means to do it. So why couldn't his own soldiers understand? Couldn't they see the degradation of Southern ways all around them?

Fair and open trade was being stifled by petty laws and politics. The very idea of declaring trade with another country to be illegal was absurd, even offensive, to anyone who loved the South and the ways of the Adama. The citizens he was working with understood that, and he knew that he would have to walk away from his entire career. For the South, he would do that.

Jhoqo stood and took a deep breath. So be it, he thought and walked out the door, leaving the lifeless Bascou behind him. He called out to the Chondathan guard who was his shadow, "Go and fetch me your second in command."

The guard, with his downy beard, was one of the youngest the Chondathans had brought. He did not move, though his eyes went straight to the ground.

"Go!" Jhoqo barked.

"He's dead, sir," the boy said, twitching.

"Then the third, and if he's dead, then the fourth. Just get me somebody, boy!" Jhoqo yelled, and he started toward the central tower, namesake to the citadel.

Before he reached the door, an older man, a bit thick through the belly, came to a stop in front of him and saluted.

"You have a wizard in the mines, yes?" Jhoqo said.

The man nodded.

"Go and get him right away. Tell him I have a challenge for him," Jhoqo said, craning his neck to look up at the top of the tower.

Of all the feelings that swirled through him, Taennen dwelled the longest on foolishness. He was afraid, intimidated, uncertain . . . but mostly, he felt foolish. The torchlight held by the man behind him guided his steps through the tunnels. Taennen glanced back once to see the ragged squad behind him, stumbling through the stone corridors. Foolishness.

Here he was, hoping to lead a score of soldiers and ten

utterly untrained farmers and craftsman against a fortified citadel held by veteran soldiers who weren't as worn and weary, and who outnumbered them besides. The only advantage they had, by his reckoning, was that the Chondathans and their dwarf cohorts would be unlikely to expect an attack by the very forces they had just routed.

"How many can we expect?" asked one of the former captives—a farmer by trade—and not for the first time.

"We should be ready for at least twice our numbers," Taennen replied.

The soldiers nodded and traded words of encouragement and reassuring claps on backs. The few citizens all seemed to pale at the same moment. They would be the first to die, Taennen knew. Unable to skillfully wield the weapons they had been given and facing trained foes, they would fall quickly. They would serve the cause best if they could live long enough to distract an enemy, allowing a Maquar or Durpari soldier to end the attacker's life swiftly. It was a matter of stretching their numbers. Taennen stopped, the people behind him stumbling into him.

"Sir?" someone said.

But Taennen barely heard the question. He turned to look at the former captives, their eyes wide and knuckles white on weapons that would likely not help them. A soldier knew that his life might be forfeit at any time, but these men and women—farmers, brewers, herders—they had sworn no such oaths. Taennen needed their numbers and their swords, but guilt tugged at him. Surely many of them would die.

Looking at the former prisoners, their thin faces reflecting a lack of proper nutrition, he spoke. "Go back. Turn around and await us at the edge of the woods. If we don't return, head straight south. You'll come across an expedition sooner or later, likely some halflings who will take you in."

The soldiers stayed quiet though a few exchanged glances. The former captives, frail and tiny compared to those around them, stood stunned.

"You said you needed us," one of them said

Taennen nodded. "I do, but people are going to die. The soldiers among us have all sworn oaths to fight for our lands and have training. You owe no one anything and have lived your lives away from conflict. If you go with us, you will die and quickly."

"We know that," the same man responded to the reluctant nods of several of the others.

"Then why come?" asked one of the Maquar before Taennen could respond.

Another man, shorter and rounder in the belly, shrugged and said, "Like you said before. They have to be stopped before they come to my front door. Besides, lots of innocent folk will die by these weapons they're selling. I won't have that on my soul while I sleep in my comfortable bed."

Taennen shook his head. "Innocents die all the time. We can't save them all. We can't stop it all. You aren't responsible."

The man nodded and said, "True enough. But I'm here. Maybe I can save some. I have to try."

"Very well. Thank you. Thank you all," Taennen said.

A few of the civilians looked less eager.

"The offer is still open to anyone. Anyone who wants to leave, should. We will find you when this is over. Feel no shame in leaving," Taennen said.

A bearded man in tattered brown robes and a woman in a filthy silk dress both pushed their way back through the line toward the forest exit. A few breaths later, two more men joined them. Some of the other civilians tried to stop them, to talk them out of leaving, but Taennen insisted that they be allowed to go.

No one else chose to leave, so Taennen led his troops toward the large cavern where he had encountered Bascou. He hoped the man was truly dead and hadn't been saved by the other brigands. How many would there be? Would they be waiting in ambush? Could they retake Neversfall?

Taennen did not know, but he was there and he had to try.

Adeenya directed a group of four soldiers to her left, then another group to her right. The remaining few under her command fell in behind her, all of them trying to slip through the woods as quietly as they could. The southeast corner of Neversfall peeked through the woods. This was as close as they'd get under the forest's cover. She gave the signal.

Her squad of roughly fifteen soldiers dashed out of the obscuring cover of the Aerilpar forest and into the flat plains beyond. Speed was their priority. The less time they spent in the open, the less time archers had to target them on their approach to the citadel's gates.

Sprinting across the field, Adeenya listened as best she could over the thumping boots and the swishing grass for the telltale whisk of an arrow whirring past. She was certain Jhoqo's forces would send them flying soon.

Adeenya made her way to the front of her runners, less than a bowshot from the main gate of the citadel. She was waving a soldier on faster when an emerald ray of light lanced through him from her right. His body flaked into ash and scattered in the warm breeze.

"Gods damn it! The tower! Get close to the wall now!" Adeenya ordered. Jhoqo had found an arcanist potent enough to wield the powers of Neversfall tower itself. Her mind raced, wondering what might come next. The damned thing might stand up on huge stone legs and come after them for all she knew.

The scent hit her as she sucked in breath after screaming. The man's charred remains, meat on a fire, mixed with a scent that reminded her of cleaning agents used by maids in her father's house. The green ray had cut a swath of grass from its path before it had sliced through the man, leaving behind black marks and the smell of cleanliness.

The soldiers around her held their speed through the discipline of their training. No one wavered from their goal of reaching the front gate, their pounding legs drawing them closer every moment. One soldier near the rear of the pack spat a curse, drawing everyone's attention to the tower just in time to watch as a small bead of red and orange light coalesced into an enormous ball of fire barreling toward them.

The ball continued to grow in size as it sizzled through the air. Adeenya, and those around her, leaped to the ground and fell flat. Most of the licking flames passed over their prone forms, though several, including Adeenya, did not escape unscathed. Taking no time to look at the fresh burns, Adeenya jumped to her feet and resumed her charge. Her flesh cried out against the pulls and tugs as she ran, but she grunted the pain to the background of her mind and pushed on.

The scent of burnt flesh filled her nostrils and dared her stomach to keep its place. Light flashed in the corner of her eye, followed by a scream from behind her, but Adeenya did not slow, did not turn her head to look.

She reached the front gate, slowing just in time to avoid slamming into it due to her momentum. She stood in the archway of the door, relatively safe from missiles or spells from above. Two Durpari soldiers joined her, and the three began hammering at the center of the doors with the butts of their weapons and hard kicks.

"Out of the way!" Corbrinn shouted behind them. His chest heaving from the run, the halfling closed his eyes and murmured as he laid his hand on the door. Its thick wooden beams began to bend and curve, writhing as though in pain. The wood creaked and groaned, the sound like nothing less than the death knell of some wild animal.

A gap four handspans wide opened in the door. More of Adeenya's forces arrived, levering their weapons in the new opening, and in moments, the door splintered open wide enough for them to pour through a few at a time. The snarling faces and shouts of the Chondathans within greeted the invaders as they followed Adeenya. She loosed a battle cry and charged at the oncoming line of enemies.

✚

chapter twenty-four

The torchlight shimmered off the curved tunnel walls like sunlight on water. The drumming of running feet announced the arrival of the intruders. Taennen rushed toward the cavern where he had found the crates of weapons. He hoped his squad would not get trapped in the confining tunnels before engaging the enemy. As he rounded the final bend in the corridor, his hope was dashed. Twenty paces from the entrance to the cavern, the tunnel walls still hemming them in, two dwarves were running toward him.

They stood shoulder to shoulder, their bulk occupying the width of the corridor with little room to spare. The taller one readied his halberd while the other drew up his shield and axe. Behind them, half a dozen more dwarf and human mercenaries gathered.

The eyes of the dwarf pair went wide when Taennen did not slow his charge, even though the men behind him had stopped. Five steps away, Taennen shouted for his troops to fight hard and punch through the defensive pair quickly. Three steps away, the muscles in his legs, hips, and back tensed before releasing and sending him into a dive through midair. He sailed over the dwarves' weapons and tucked himself into a roll as he landed. He found his feet quickly, groaning from the impact, but he did not look back.

Taennen swiped at another of the dwarves in the cavern even as the clash of metal on metal began ringing behind him as his troops engaged the duo in the tunnel. His target ducked the blow, tripping in surprise. Taennen disregarded him and rushed at one of the Chondathans. The foreigner was ready for Taennen's charge and sent a racing thrust toward him. Taennen turned the blade aside with a snap of his shield and sent his own weapon toward the man's shoulder. The Chondathan parried the blow but too late saw it for the feint it was. Taennen planted a foot in his chest and kicked out. The darkblade stumbled backward, his arms flailing. He had no chance of defending himself as Taennen sprang into him with two cuts that severed his throat.

By the time his troops had felled the taller dwarf behind him, Taennen had killed two men, harried a dwarf to distraction, and started a fight with another. The dwarf, wearing a gleaming suit of armor ornamented with a holy symbol, slammed his hammer into the ground where Taennen had stood a moment before and cried out in rage at the miss. Trying to end the fight quickly, Taennen risked exposing his side, leaning in for a quick slice across the dwarf's throat. The warrior's gorget saved him as the khopesh glanced off the steel.

Taennen paid for his boldness as he felt at least two ribs give way under the impact of the hammer's head. The Maquar leaped back to catch the breath that had been stolen. The dwarf gave him no respite and charged with a battle cry. Taennen sidestepped the dwarf's trajectory only to stumble into another human darkblade who had been trying to work his way into the fray. The Chondathan tripped in the collision, but Taennen kept his feet and delivered a hard kick to the man's jaw before readying himself for another charge from the dwarf paladin.

The dwarf stepped around the prone darkblade and into Taennen's reach. As the warrior drew his hammer back, Taennen fell forward, aiming his shoulder at the ground. The heavy bludgeon sailed over him as Taennen lashed out, his khopesh digging into the dwarf's face. Taennen hit the ground and rolled to his feet in time to dodge another blow. The gash in the dwarf's face bled, a river of red on his ruddy face, but if it slowed or pained him much, he did not show it.

Taennen feinted again, and the dwarf obliged with a thrust of his hammer. Taennen easily avoided the blow and sent his blade across the forearm of the dwarf's weapon hand. His enemy roared in pain, clasping the wounded wrist with his other hand. Taennen did not hesitate, and in two strokes the dwarf fell to the ground, his face unrecognizable through the blood and exposed bone.

Two of Taennen's soldiers were down—one dead, the other screaming in pain as blood pumped from his stomach. All of the former captives were alive and faring well against their opponents. They worked together, covering one another with dedication. The shorter dwarf with the axe had been dispatched, and Taennen's troops now engaged other opponents in the cavern.

"Finish them and join our brothers above when you can!" Taennen shouted.

Three soldiers fell in behind him as he ran to where the Chondathan captured by the formians had said he would find an entrance to the citadel. Taennen spied a ladder carved into the stone wall. He raced up the rungs and shoved himself through a trap door to find himself standing in one of the outlying buildings in the courtyard of Neversfall. Without waiting for the men accompanying him, Taennen ran out the door and into the open space of the citadel beyond.

Adeenya shoved the corpse of her first opponent off her sword and twisted her body just in time to deflect the attack of another. The Chondathan held her block and tried to slip his second sword into her abdomen. She skirted out of his reach and stabbed toward him. He parried the blow with one weapon while slicing low at her legs with the other.

The sounds of battle erupted all around as her troops engaged the Chondathans. Her burnt flesh ached for relief, and pain cried out against the constant motion flexing and stretching the skin painfully. Suddenly her opponent dropped, a shortsword in his back. Corbrinn nodded at her and leaped to his next quarry after plucking his sword from the man.

Her next opponent landed a painful thrust on her hip. She stifled a cry and twisted to remove the blade from her body. As she spun, she saw that only seven of her troops had breached the gate, the rest likely dead or severely injured by the magic of the tower. Much of her force was gone, and those who remained were utterly surrounded by the enemy, outnumbered at least four to one. Adeenya growled as her opponent sliced her upper arm with another strike. She returned the attack blow for blow, giving better than she got, but her troops were not faring as well.

Adeenya fought on, convinced the battle was lost, hoping only to soften the enemy for Taennen's invasion from below. She hoped he was having better luck, but she pushed the thought away as she finished off her opponent with a vicious stroke across his chest.

She faced off against two more before the previous one had even settled on the ground. Adeenya's arms were made of stone, her muscles fatigued from exertion and blood loss. She felt faint and questioned her eyes when both of her opponents were suddenly yanked backward away from her.

The big formian, Guk, appeared out of nowhere, sending four of the larger formians into the fighting. Two of them ripped and clawed at the Chondathans she had been fighting, the humans already bleeding from fresh wounds. Guk disappeared, leaving his soldiers behind to fight. Where he had gone, Adeenya did not know, nor did she care. The possibility of surviving until Taennen's forces arrived to meet them in the middle of the battle suddenly seemed real.

Adeenya stumbled forward, strength returning to her limbs as though her newly regained hope was healing her. She stayed on the fringe of the formians, stabbing their opponents where she found openings. The Chondathan body count quickly rose, and the foreign mercenaries came together, tightening their formation to protect themselves.

Guk appeared again, the last two formians beside him. They leapt into the battle alongside their leader. Guk picked up a long axe from the nearby corpse of a fallen Chondathan and drove the weapon into an enemy. The big formian edged around the fighting, picking his attacks carefully.

Adeenya swore aloud when half a dozen more Chondathans came sprinting across the courtyard to join their pressed comrades. Her curse was followed quickly by a shout of elation as Taennen came into view, ahead of the new Chondathan force. Behind him were some of his soldiers. Instead of following him, they turned to face the threat of the oncoming Chondathans, thus segmenting the courtyard into two battles. Adeenya thrilled to see Taennen again, but she kept her focus on the fight before her. She became concerned when Taennen stopped, still some distance away.

Adeenya's forces had been badly reduced, but she was alive. Guk's warriors were handling the Chondathans well, rendering the darkblades unconscious when possible instead of killing them. Dead slaves made poor slaves, after all.

Taennen's legs burned with fatigue, but the battle raged and nothing would stop him. Nothing—except the voice he heard from behind him. Taennen turned at the sound, two words uttered in a booming voice that carried over the din of clashing steel between them.

"My son," Jhoqo said, standing on the far side of the skirmish.

Taennen glanced over his shoulder at Adeenya before facing the man who had raised him. He sprinted in that direction, a snarl on his face. Jhoqo walked toward Taennen, his steps even and steady. The Maquar urir parted the combatants before him like herd animals, pushing through them with no regard for their quibbling or their blades. His gaze never left Taennen just as Taennen's never left him. Jhoqo stopped, standing his ground on the near side of the engagement.

Taennen charged at him, recalling the tactics Jhoqo had taught him to guess his opponent's defense and determine how to penetrate it for a quick kill. If he did not kill the man quickly, he would lose the battle. The image of Jhoqo's blood spilling onto the brown, dry earth in the early morning haze of rising heat and cresting sun came into his mind. He felt no thrill at the notion, but neither did it disgust him as it once would have. It was necessary to ensure what Taennen believed in—a duty to himself and the others.

The first strike of his khopesh rang off Jhoqo's armor with a metallic screech, but for the first time Taennen heard only his own voice in his mind with no interference from his father, Jhoqo, Loraica or even Adeenya.

Jhoqo spread his arms out wide and stepped back from Taennen. "Please, don't do this. You have to know that I love you. You are my son," the urir said. "I do what's best for you."

"Like you loved the men and women who have fallen here? Like you did what was best for Loraica? You killed her, didn't you?" Taennen asked.

Jhoqo frowned. "No, of course not. She was my daughter."

Taennen stepped back, wary of the man's blade. "Your love cost Loraica her life."

Jhoqo said nothing.

"Who killed her? Whose blade?"

"Marlke. Marlke did it."

"Then at least Loraica is avenged," Taennen said. "And your Bascou is dead."

"I wish I could have seen you fight him. I've no doubt I would have been heartbright of your prowess," Jhoqo said.

Taennen roared and charged the man, lashing out with his weapon, again to no avail. Jhoqo stepped to the side but did not return the attack.

"I love you. You are my son."

Taennen kept his weapon ready but nodded and said, "I do not doubt that you do, and I am grateful for the man you helped me become. The man who misses his murdered friend. The man who knows that what you've done is wrong."

Jhoqo cocked his head to the side and asked, "Then you intend to kill me yourself? Would Loraica want that?"

"I do not wish your death, but I understand its necessity now," Taennen said.

A Chondathan man harried by two Maquar stumbled between Taennen and Jhoqo as they spoke. In a flash of brilliant green light, one of the Maquar turned to ash, his sword dropping to the ground with a rattle. The tower glowed and pulsed with the power that it poured down upon its enemies.

Jhoqo's eyes narrowed, ignorant of the interruption. "Tell me why it must be that way."

"Tell me why your former friends and soldiers are dying right now! Tell me why that cursed tower is slaughtering them!" Taennen said.

"It shouldn't be happening this way. They shouldn't be dying. But you have given me no choice, so I ask you the same question," Jhoqo said.

Taennen scowled and said, "We've been dying since we came here!"

Jhoqo nodded. "A few deaths, to bring the rest together. Unity has always been my goal," he said

"More than a few died!" Taennen said.

"It became clear to me that I could not sway as many of you as I had hoped. When Bascou's men came, I saw in the faces of our own soldiers that they would never see the light and truth. I knew then that more had to be done," Jhoqo said. "Fear inspires where loyalty cannot. Things needed to escalate."

"Escalate? Listen to yourself! You sound so . . . practical about it all," Taennen said.

"It is for the glory and benefit of Estagund that I do what I do now! I had hoped you would understand too."

"So you shut me out of your plans? You kept me in the dark to your true motivations? You killed my best friend? A soldier whom you loved?" Taennen asked. "That does not sound hopeful to me. But now that I see your plan, I owe you thanks. Before we came here, I probably would have followed you blindly down whatever path you chose. But now I can see your depravity and save myself from your fate."

Jhoqo stiffened his posture and said, "You must choose your way as everyone must. The South does not seek unseeing dolts and, as its defender, neither do I. We abound in mindless followers as it is. I wanted you to choose. I wanted to tell you everything. I wanted your help in righting the wrongs. But you are making the wrong choice."

"Then you've not presented me with one at all," Taennen said as he began to circle his opponent.

Jhoqo answered the maneuver by moving as well, his head hanging low. "No. You still have a choice and have had all along."

"Did you give Loraica a choice?" Taennen asked.

"You see the injustices every day, but you choose to do nothing! I am a freedom fighter. I see the inequities and work to right them," Jhoqo said, ignoring the question.

"Freedom fighter? Fighting for the wealthy merchants who pay you to make them more coin illegally?" Taennen said. "For the chakas who can't see past their own purses?"

"For everyone!" Jhoqo shouted. "For everyone, son. Philosophies are murky, messy things, impossible to interpret, but the Adama is very clear on one thing: All is one. Everything is connected. You believe that, I know you do."

Taennen did not respond but lowered his khopesh, even as the screams of dying soldiers rolled in waves through the courtyard. More scorching rays from the tower rained down.

"That's all I'm fighting for. If our people are allowed to trade with Mulhorand, then they make more coin. They spend that coin at home where more of our people benefit from that spending. It comes full circle, elevating the wealth of the lesser merchants as they sell to the wealthier, thereby spreading the wealth. All around it, our people will be better for it," Jhoqo said.

"Until they are crushed by the Mulhorandi's endless war," Taennen replied. He lifted his khopesh and advanced. "When you became a Maquar you swore to uphold the rajah's laws. What about those? You're breaking a law."

Jhoqo retreated a little way. "An unjust law. A law that limits the freedoms of our people, a law that benefits no one other than those countries who are selling Mulhorand their goods without competition from us!" Jhoqo said.

"Sell to them. Sell them the shirt off your back, but not weapons with which they will spill more innocent blood," Taennen said.

"For a man leading a rebellion against his commanding officer, you are clinging strongly to laws," Jhoqo said.

Taennen paused a moment before responding, "I don't care about the law anymore. I care about what's right. Profiting from blood and war is wrong. Stopping you from making that happen is right."

"War is business, and it will happen with or without us. We should benefit from it!" Jhoqo said.

"You see benefit for our people measured by the coin in their pockets. I see the benefit of a clear conscience, a clean spirit, and bloodless hands, the benefit of other countries expanding their trade with us because of our morals and beliefs, the benefit of trusting our leaders."

Jhoqo's face twisted, and he lunged forward. Taennen avoided his blade and stumbled back. He gained his feet in time to block another attack with his shield. His slash at Jhoqo's lower arm was likewise thwarted.

Taennen moved faster than he had ever moved before, but it was not enough. Jhoqo's blade sank into a gap in his armor near the bottom of his stomach. Taennen hopped back from the man's reach but ignored the wound.

"This place, this citadel, represents everything the South should be. It is strong, promotes community, and offers opportunity for both trade and security," Jhoqo said.

"It was built on laws and trust and charged with maintaining them both. It does all those things you said, but it does them openly, not in the dark, behind closed doors, and not by the murder of innocents," Taennen said.

The noise of battle around them was dwindling. The Maquar, Durpari, and formians outnumbered the Chondathans, and the two separate clashes had become one as the Chondathans converged near the front gate. They formed a tight defensive circle and held their enemies at bay. The dazzling lights from the tower stopped, and a cry of the mage manning the post was heard below as the man fell to his death in the courtyard.

"The tower is ours," Taennen said.

Jhoqo growled and ran for Neversfall. Taennen's eyes locked with Adeenya's as she was finishing off an opponent. His eyes lingered a moment before he turned and gave chase to Jhoqo. He followed the man through the door and up the stairs, both of them leaping several steps at a time. His body ached and his muscles quivered with fatigue.

Taennen closed the gap between them to only a few steps as they were halfway up the staircase. He reached out with his curved khopesh, entangling Jhoqo's ankle. The older man fell forward, his face slamming into the edge of a step. Jhoqo rolled over quickly, his sword held aloft in defense. Taennen winced to see his mentor's face covered in blood, his nose askew. His stomach did not ache with remorse, but his heart filled with pity.

"Kill me, then," Jhoqo said, blood dribbling from his mouth when he spoke.

"Not unless I must," Taennen shook his head.

Jhoqo smirked. "You speak of what is right, yet you're simply a coward, too afraid to do the right thing. Too afraid to see our homeland attain the glory that is its right. Like everyone else, you're not troubled by your conscience, you're scared. That's why the others had to die, that's why I sacrificed them on those patrols. They would not allow the future of the South to emerge from destiny. I thought better of you, but I was wrong. The right thing isn't always easy, son. I tried to teach you that. I can see I failed." He swung the falchion at Taennen's ankles, only to be blocked once more. Taennen shoved the blade away, breaking Jhoqo's grip. The falchion clattered down the steps.

Taennen stared at the man for a long moment before driving forward, his blade sinking into Jhoqo's gut. He twisted the weapon, eliciting a groan from the man. "You did not fail. I learned the lesson well."

+
chapter twenty-five

Adeenya limped toward Taennen as he emerged from the tower. Strips of cloth applied by one of her men stemmed the blood flowing from several wounds. The sword in her hand was dull, covered in gore that hid its sheen. She motioned toward the tower but did not ask the question.

Taennen nodded and scanned the courtyard. The fight was over. Weapons, shields, and armor littered the ground. Many Chondathans were dead, their bodies scattered across the stained courtyard. Those who had surrendered or been knocked out were being corralled by the formians at the front gate. The monstrous prisoners, goblins and others, were also dragged from the prison building and lined up at the gate in chains. Many of them screeched in protest but were quickly quieted by the formians.

"How many of ours did we lose?" Taennen asked.

Adeenya grimaced and said, "More than half. There are barely a dozen of us left now."

Taennen nodded and stared at the rain-laden clouds, wishing they would drop their burden on his face to cool and soothe him.

"Why did he do it?" Adeenya asked, staring at the sky.

"For the good of the South," Taennen said. "He felt he had to."

Adeenya dropped her eyes to face him but said nothing.

"What now?" she asked. When Taennen did not answer, she continued, nodding toward Guk. "They can take us easily now."

"They could," Taennen said.

"So we win the citadel just to become worker slaves?" she asked.

"No," Taennen said.

"So they'll leave, having helped us out of kindness?" she said, incredulity obvious in her tone.

"No. They received their compensation," he said, pointing to the shackled monsters and unconscious Chondathans the formians were dragging away.

Adeenya's face wrinkled before her eyes went wide. "No! You didn't . . ."

Taennen said nothing, only stared at Guk, who returned the gaze. Adeenya looked away.

"We needed them," Taennen said, not looking at her.

"You're a slaver. You realize that, don't you?" she said.

"We needed their help. Without the formians, we'd be dead by now and Jhoqo—" Taennen swallowed. "The Mulhorandi would have their goods."

"Giving those men to him makes you no better than a slave trader."

Taennen nodded. "Maybe that's true . . . I don't think I know what a crime is anymore. Is it worse to cheat, or to kill? And who decides that?"

"The laws decide," Adeenya said.

"They follow laws too," he said, pointing to the formians. "Their laws are just different from ours . . ."

"They're wrong," she said.

"Not to them," he replied.

"Laws can't be subjective like that," Adeenya said. "Their meaning, their purpose, must be agreed upon for them to work."

Taennen shrugged. "And when does that happen?"

Adeenya did not respond but furrowed her brow.

"So everybody should just break the laws they don't agree with, like Jhoqo did?" she said after a few moments.

"No," he said. "But they should have the courage to stand against the ones they feel are wrong."

"I don't see the difference," she said.

Several breaths passed in silence. Then Guk approached them, stopping a few steps away. He seemed no worse for the battle, showing no injuries at all.

"You'll leave now?" Taennen asked.

"My other people will come soon to help us move the new workers," Guk said.

"And then?" Taennen asked.

"We will gather our strength," Guk said. "Some workers will stay. Others will join the main hive. More from there will come here."

"And then you'll come back for more workers," Taennen said.

"Yes," Guk said.

"Until then," the Maquar said. The formian's honesty, while brutal in impact and intent, was refreshing to Taennen. He'd had his fill of deception.

"Yes," Guk said, before turning back to his followers.

"They'll come back and take anyone in the citadel, won't they?" she asked.

"They'll come back for everyone in the South, eventually," Taennen said.

Adeenya failed to breathe for a moment before nodding, her eyes finding Taennen's.

"We could try to kill them now, stop them," she said.

Taennen's mouth formed a tiny, tight grin. "With what army? They would slaughter us with little effort," he said.

Adeenya nodded. "So we just let them go?"

"Yes. They were out there before. Nothing's really changed," he said. "Besides, they kept their word, and now I'll keep mine."

Adeenya frowned but said nothing.

"Both the men I've called father in my life taught me the importance of keeping my word. They couldn't have both been wrong," he said.

"They were both criminals, Taennen," Adeenya said.

Taennen agreed and said, "One broke laws he thought unjust for what he believed was the good of everyone. He, at least, died trying to do what he believed in. The other broke laws he did believe in to feed himself and his child. He lost his freedom, betrayed by someone he loved."

Adeenya raised an eyebrow. "The Taennen I met when all of this started wouldn't have condoned either crime," she said.

"He's in that tower if you want to go ask him," Taennen said, turning to face Neversfall. He craned his neck to take in the full height of the structure and thought about why it had been built. Some said to protect the South. Others said to fill the pockets of Southerners. Looking at the smooth stones that climbed toward the heavens, Taennen knew both were right. He also knew that it did not matter. Intention meant nothing, motives were pointless. Declarations and dedications never made anything happen. The tower had been built because someone saw the need to take action. The tower stood because accomplishments meant more than plans.

"I'm not sure, even after all of this, if I would condone either," Adeenya said.

When Taennen did not respond, she continued. "Maybe the reason for breaking the law is more important than the law itself."

"Sometimes, I think, you have to do the wrong thing for the right reasons."

"Sounds like justification to me. A criminal might say the same thing about stealing," Adeenya said.

"A criminal does the wrong things for the wrong reasons," Taennen countered. "It's a fine distinction."

"What do we do about the people behind the operation that Jhoqo worked for?" Adeenya asked. She paused a moment and added, "My father is one of them."

"I'm sorry he is involved, Adeenya."

Adeenya nodded. "I probably shouldn't feel so surprised. When Jhoqo talked of patriotism, he reminded me of my father. It was almost as though the two were of the same mind. My father has always taken the path of profit for profit's sake. But there have to be others. What do we do about them?"

"We find them."

"Taennen, how do we do that? Anyone could have been involved. The rajah himself might be behind it, for all the One!"

"They'll come to us," he said.

"Why would anyone reveal themselves by coming here?"

Taennen kicked a sword from the hand of a nearby Chondathan corpse.

"The weapons," he said. "They need weapons. There's a

fortune down there. They'll have to come for them. How we stop them is the better question."

Adeenya patted him on the shoulder and said, "We collapse the tunnels."

Taennen looked at her, beautiful even through the pain, sweat, blood, and fatigue on her face. "We stay, then?"

"The citadel needs to be defended," she said.

"Reinforcements?"

"With any luck, we'll find among these bodies a pendant that was stolen from me. With it, we can contact someone back home for help," she said.

"Whom do we trust?" he asked.

"We contact those we've always trusted and hope we're right to do so."

"What if the leaders of Durpar and Estagund are behind it all?" he asked.

Adeenya looked back to the sky and said, "Then we stop them. All of them."

"Of course," Taennen said, casting his eyes up to the tower again. "Of course we do."

RICHARD A. KNAAK

THE OGRE TITANS

The Grand Lord Golgren has been savagely crushing
all opposition to his control of the harsh ogre lands of
Kern and Blöde, first sweeping away rival chieftains, then
rebuilding the capital in his image. For this he has had to
deal with the ogre titans, dark, sorcerous giants who have
contempt for his leadership.

VOLUME ONE
THE BLACK TALON

Among the ogres, where every ritual demands blood and every ally can
become a deadly foe, Golgren seeks whatever advantage he can obtain,
even if it means a possible alliance with the Knights of Solamnia, a
questionable pact with a mysterious wizard, and trusting an elven slave
who might wish him dead.

December 2007

VOLUME TWO
THE FIRE ROSE

With his other enemies beginning to converge on him from all sides,
Golgren, now Grand Khan of all his kind, must battle with the
Ogre Titans for mastery of a mysterious artifact capable of ultimate
transformation and power.

December 2008

VOLUME THREE
THE GARGOYLE KING

Forced from the throne he has so long coveted, Golgren makes a final
stand for control of the ogre lands against the Titans . . . against an
enemy as ancient and powerful as a god.

December 2009

Land of intrigue.
Towering cities where murder is business.
Dark forests where hunters are hunted.
Ground where the dead never rest.

To find the truth takes a special breed of hero.

THE INQUISITIVES

BOUND BY IRON
Edward Bolme
Torn by oaths to king and country, one man must
unravel a tapestry of murder and slavery.

NIGHT OF THE LONG SHADOWS
Paul Crilley
During the longest nights of the year, worshipers of the
dark rise from the depths of the City of Towers
to murder . . . and worse.

LEGACY OF WOLVES
Marsheila Rockwell
In the streets of Aruldusk, a series of grisly murders has rocked
the small city. The gruesome nature of the murders spawns
rumors of a lycanthrope in a land where the shapeshifters were
thought to have been hunted to extinction.

THE DARKWOOD MASK
Jeff LaSala
A beautiful Inquisitive teams up with a wanted vigilante to take
down a crimelord who hides behind a mask of deceit, savage
cunning, and sorcery.
November 2008